D1235813

COLD
DREAM
DAWNING

ALSO BY
A.R. KAHLER

The Pale Queen

Pale Queen Rising
Cold Dream Dawning
Black Ice Burning (forthcoming)

Cirque des Immortels

The Immortal Circus
The Immortal Circus: Act Two
The Immortal Circus: Final Act

The Vampire Diaries

The Tristram Cycle
The Initiation (A Short Story)
With Blood on His Hands (A Short Story)

Other Titles

Shades of Darkness (Ravenborn: Book One)
A Child of Wight (A Short Story)
Love Is in the Air

COLD
DREAM
DAWNING

The Pale Queen: Book 2

A. R. KAHLER

47NORTH

Text copyright © 2016 A. R. Kahler

Published by 47North, Seattle

www.apub.com

Amazon, the Amazon logo, and 47North are trademarks of Amazon.com, Inc., or its affiliates.

ISBN-13: 9781503953567
ISBN-10: 1503953564

Cover photo by Kindra Nikole Photography
Cover design by Jason Blackburn

Printed in the United States of America

One

There is a very strict no-assassination rule within the kingdom of Winter. Being Queen Mab's right-hand assassin, I'm not allowed to kill within her walls unless she herself bids it—cases of political intrigue, long-standing grudges, slander, that sort of thing. Seeing as she's the Faerie Queen, such instances are rare; no one wants to cross her. She made it very clear that if I ever killed one of her subjects without explicit permission, my neck would be on the non-proverbial chopping block. As much as I might be one of the few who *do* want to cross her, the risk outweighs the benefits.

Because tonight, I don't just *want* to spill blood. I *need* to spill it. Lots of it. And that's why I'm in the mortal world.

Mab's words still thunder in my ears as I stalk down the crowded street, pushing past pedestrians without the slightest hint of apology. A few of them try to start shit, but they don't get much further than an aggravated shout. I don't linger long enough, not that anyone would cross me if I did. These jerks might be clueless mortals, but no one wants to fight a girl in bloodstained leather, especially when it's clear she's barely keeping the rage in check. I am a fired bullet, a loosed arrow. I won't stop until I hit a target, and no one really wants to get in my way.

My name is Claire Melody Warfield. I kill people for a living.

Tonight, I'm killing because it's my preferred coping mechanism.

I force Mab's curses down to a dull roar and turn a corner. My destination is just off of Bourbon Street in New Orleans, and the city is alive with magic and alcohol and sin. On any other night, that alone would be enough to make me feel at home. Tonight, it just reminds me that home is a broken concept. Mab ensured it.

Halfway down the adjacent alley is a metal gate stuck in the wall, seemingly out of place against the brick and mortar surrounding it. It leads nowhere, but there it is, locked tight to the wall and revealing nothing but grey brick. The metal isn't iron, but a heavily tarnished silver so enchanted it's no doubt stronger than titanium. Magic meant to keep mortals like me out. Impenetrable by any weapon.

I grab a piece of chalk from my leather coat and scrawl a series of symbols on the wall between the bars, crossing thick lines over the padlock. The symbols probably appear innocuous to anyone passing by—not that there *is* anyone passing by. Triangles and concentric circles and words that haven't been spoken on this side of the Faerie/Mortal divide in centuries. I complete an Eye of Horus over the padlock, then open myself to the small amount of magic I can access and send a pulse through the symbols.

A second later, the gate vanishes in a whirl of dust.

No bang, no flash of light, just a silent disintegration that floats off into the night. My symbols still stain the brick wall. I glance down the empty alley, the sounds of human revelry almost as potent as the Dream cloying my nostrils like whiskey fumes. Then I press a hand to the seven-pointed star and step through the wall.

I'm not the life of most parties. Kind of goes with the territory. Which means that when I step into the dim speakeasy-style bar, I'm not at all surprised that the room goes silent. It's actually a little comical. If not tiresome.

"Your highness," someone whispers, and for a moment I go cold, worried that Mab somehow came here with me. Then I realize that the stranger is talking to—*about*—me. Someone wants to save their own skin by being all honorary.

This place has been on Mab's (and thus, *my*) radar for years. But a small den selling untaxed Dream in a city teeming with the resource was barely more than a prick in her side. Just thinking of Mab makes her words creep back in, but I force myself to stay in the present. Where the fun is. Or will be. The Fey in the room watch me, still as statues and tense as piano wire; some are glamoured to look like humans, but most are in their true forms—winged harpies or balls of light, thorny dryads or oil-slick shadows. Creatures to fear, all of them. And all of them currently terrified of me.

Normally I'd feel a hint of pride at that. Now I just feel numb.

"You're all in violation of faerie law," I say, my voice carrying to every corner of the room. Not that I'm talking loudly; it's just *that quiet.* And no, there is no written faerie law, no "Section 3A" or whatever. But New Orleans is claimed for Winter, which means any buying or selling of Dream in this city has to go through Mab. I glance to the vials and decanters of multicolored distilled Dream stockpiled behind the bar. Enough to condemn them, and that's only the Dream out in the open. I have no doubt there are piles of powdered or tar-like Dream under the bar. "As such, your lives are forfeit." For the first time that night, I smile. "I suggest you start running now."

No, it's not the ideal statement, but I'm not interested in eloquence. The rage inside me craves blood, and knowing that every creature within this room is guilty of a crime punishable by death makes the hunger almost painful.

I tell myself it's the anger. And nothing else.

There's maybe a half second between my final word and the first spark of movement. It comes from a floating ball of light in the back corner, a Wisp the color of blue cotton candy that beelines for the curtain behind the bar. My smile cracks wider as I stand there, silently watching the Wisp try to flee. The moment it hits the curtain, it explodes in a shower of sparks.

"I should have mentioned," I say, reaching into one of my coat pockets and pulling out a deck of Tarot cards. They are worn and earth-toned and humming with power. "The place is enchanted against escape. No one comes or goes. So perhaps telling you to run was a bit misleading. Sorry about that." I fan the deck in my hand and snap my fingers. Two cards slide out a little farther, and I pull out the bottom one and study it. "There's another way, of course. You kill me, and the magic vanishes." My smile turns wicked as I flip the card around to face the room. *The Wheel of Fate.* "Who's ready to test their luck?"

I don't just want to fight; fighting is easy, something I've been conditioned to do, like breathing. I want a challenge. Something to prove I'm alive for a reason, alive because I've earned it. Alive because I'm worth more alive than I am dead—worth more than the people I'm about to kill.

As expected, no one moves. Not at first.

"Come on, guys. I need a pick-me-up after what I've been through today. Don't leave me hanging."

Again, silence.

"Fine. I didn't want to have to do this."

That's a lie. I *did* want to have to do this. I wanted to very much. That's the biggest perk of being a mortal, one the rest of them take for granted. We can lie through our teeth. We can make it an art. Roxie was proof enough of that.

I pull out the second card and push down the traitor's image in my mind. *Five of Wands.* On it, five men are caught in a struggle, battling each other with great wooden staves. Definitely not a happy card. Anger, frustration, violence.

Time to get this party started.

I pulse a small amount of power into each of the cards and toss them to the center of the room.

The Wheel of Fate's power is subtle, but I can taste it spreading through the bar, can hear it like the rattle of dice in a cup as it fucks with the luck of everyone in here. Even mine. With that card in play, this is anyone's game. Any of us could slip on a banana peel and stab ourselves or throw a dart through our opponent's skull. Tonight, luck is fluid. Devious. Which means, if I come out of this alive, I'm riding on more than luck. I'm pulling out skill. Precisely the ego boost I need.

The *Five*'s power is potent. It coats my lungs like cayenne. I feel it in my veins, pumping through my blood as delicious poison. I wanted to kill before I set foot in here. But now, with the card of conflict overriding my emotions, unnecessary violence is all I can think about. Clearly, I'm not the only one.

Before the cards even hit the floor, the nearest Fey attacks.

It's the harpy chick, her beaklike mouth open and emitting a strange cross between a caw and a scream. She flaps her wings and lifts her vicious clawed feet, aiming right for my head, but a second after she's airborne a dagger is flying from my hand. It thuds straight into her chest with enough force to thrust her backward. She falls to the floor, and two dryads covered in thorns and vines race over her body as it collapses into oil.

You wanted to know about your mother. And now, it is time for you to meet her. Mab's words come back unhindered as I lose myself in the frenzy of battle. I leap toward the dryads, two more daggers in hand. The first dryad falls with a blade across the throat. The other one I miss. I skid on what's left of the harpy as my luck momentarily turns south and a lash of thorns whips my back. The thorns don't pierce my enchanted jacket, but the pressure of them still stings. I barely feel it. All I feel is the rage from Mab telling me that tomorrow morning, I would seek out my mother. My real mother, who was apparently one of the most powerful figures in history.

My mother, whom I have never truly known.

Something screams behind me, and I turn in time to catch the lucky dryad getting impaled on a sword held by a figure that's nothing but bones and shadow. The two topple over, the dryad's whip twining around the wraith's neck and severing it clean in two. Maybe not so lucky after all.

My rage takes over, everything cast in a haze of red as I duck and stab and move through the crowd. I don't see my victims. I don't hear them. I don't even feel their flesh giving way under my blades. All I see is Mab. All I hear are her words. All I feel is the hot emptiness of battle, the void within the curl of a wave, right before it crashes down.

No. That's a lie.

As I disembowel a humanoid Fey with dark skin and darker hair, I see Roxie, right before she betrayed me. I see her kneeling before that damned summoning circle and bringing something back into this world. Something that should have been locked away for eternity. Something that had fled to the Wildness beyond Mab's kingdom, where it could build an army and march.

A pang pierces through me, the hint of an emotion I thought I'd burned hours ago.

A second later, a different pain stabs my side, and I look down to see a twisted rod of rebar sticking out above my hip.

My body goes numb, and whatever bloodlust I felt before pales in comparison to the rage that takes over, transforms pain and weakness into strength and fury. I drop my blades and grab the bar in both hands and yank. It slides out of my flesh like a sword from a bloody sheath, scraping against my pelvis as it goes, the grating a vibration I feel in my toes but don't even register as painful. Already, the runes along my spine are hot, coursing magic through my tissues, spells for healing and reflexes and endurance. The Fey that stabbed me has no such runes. The moment I yank the bar from my body, I twist and stab him right through the eye. He screams, just for a second, before dissolving into ash.

I slide my fingers over the freshly knit wound in my side as the other hand goes for a knife. But there's no one else to kill.

My breath is barely a pant, and my heart races no faster than if I'd run a block. Even with *The Wheel* in play, this was too easy. The blood not enough. It still hurts, the wound Roxie left me with. Mab's promise of finding my mother—an act that surely comes at great cost—still burns.

Then something clinks behind the bar. I tense, ready for another throat to slit, another potential release from the hell I know I'll never be free from. But the bartender isn't readying a weapon. The suave Fey with flowers in his hipster beard barely seems to notice the bodies littering his bar as he grabs a bottle of bourbon from the well and pours it into a large tumbler. Save for those flowers, he looks like your average dude.

"Rough night?" he asks as he pours.

"Poison?" I reply.

"And kill the queen's daughter? Please. These assholes aren't worth *that* much to me."

"I'm not her daughter," I respond. "And you're still breaking the law."

He shrugs and slides the tumbler toward me. I eye it. I don't take it.

"Suit yourself," he says, and takes a swig from the bottle before setting it on the bar. Fey don't normally drink regular alcohol—does nothing for them—but I recognize the gesture. *It's safe.* I still don't grab the glass, though.

"It's getting worse, you know," he says conversationally as he pushes the mossy entrails of a dryad I don't remember killing off the bar. "Times are hard for everyone—have been for years. But it's getting worse."

"What are you talking about?" I walk closer to him, careful not to slip on any blood. I can still feel the lingering effects of *The Wheel*. I'm not about to take any chances.

He gives me a level stare.

"You know precisely what I'm talking about."

"Enlighten me."

He reaches into his pocket and pulls something out, tossing the slip of paper toward me. I catch it, or try to—it slips from my fingers and flutters to the floor, landing in a pile of orange goo. I suddenly regret using that damned card. Still, I lean down and extract it and wipe off the slime the selkie left behind. The moment my fingers touch the card stock, I feel the familiar tingle of latent magic.

"Where did you get this?" I ask. I twirl the small ticket in front of my face. *Cirque des Immortels* is on one side, the generic *Admit One* on the other. Perfectly innocent, if not for the magic underneath it all. The Immortal Circus is Mab's gig, but this ticket isn't from her. This is from the Pale Queen—the figure I unwittingly released from her astral prison hours ago.

"We all got one," he says. "Summer or Winter or unclaimed—every Fey out there has gotten the invite. The smart ones have already taken up the offer."

I flick the ticket to the counter and grab the tumbler of bourbon. I sniff it. It doesn't smell like poison, but when I raise it to my lips, I don't actually take a drink. I wasn't born yesterday. There are plenty of toxins out there that do nothing to the Fey and would kill a mortal in a heartbeat. I can practically feel the bartender relax when I fake it, though, which means it either *is* poison or he's hoping it loosens me up.

"What does that make you?" I ask.

"An entrepreneur." He gives me a sly wink. The smoothness of it makes me want to gag. "There's always a profit in war. But you know all about that, don't you?"

I raise my glass in a mock toast. I want to strangle this guy. Slowly. But bartenders are great at amassing information. Especially from an unhappy populace.

"What do you know about her?" I ask. "This *Pale Queen*."

He starts idly wiping down the bar as he talks. "Just that she's set up shop in the Wildness and is looking for willing subjects. Promises freedom from Mab and Oberon and their games. All the Dream you could ask for. Et cetera, et cetera."

I glance to the ticket on the table. I need to find this Pale Queen. Have to kill her before she can destroy Mab's kingdom. And for that, I need to find my mother, the Oracle. Because apparently, she has the power to find someone in a place where no one can be found.

"And yet here you are, selling untaxed Dream to riffraff right under Mab's nose."

"It's a living," he says. "Which, speaking of, you shouldn't be doing anymore."

I laugh.

"You really thought I'd fall for poison?"

"I'd hoped." He looks completely nonchalant about it, as if he's discussing a shipment of beer and not my botched murder. Not that I blame him in the slightest. I *did* just kill his entire clientele.

I push myself from the bar.

"Clean up your act," I say as I head to the exit.

"It won't matter," he says. "The Pale Queen's coming. And when she rises to power, Mab will have much bigger things to worry about than a few rogue Dream Traders."

"You're right," I say, my hand on the door. "It won't matter." Then I step forward, through the magical portal, and out into the hot Louisiana night.

I glance to my handiwork, the intricate web of chalk and symbols laced out like some arcane cosmology. Then I drag one finger from the top right to the bottom left, smudging a handful of lines.

And just like that, fire explodes from the basement windows. So loud, I can't even hear the bartender scream.

"Bad luck, pal," I say.

Then I turn and walk down the alley, fondling the handful of chalk in my pocket.

I'm not going to lie to myself and pretend I feel better—it's going to take more than a few meaningless Fey for that to happen. But I *did* make a dozen or so people feel worse, right before I killed them.

Tonight, that will just have to do.

Two

I don't linger on Bourbon Street long. I'd considered going out to a club, but the pleasant thought of getting obliterated and playing tonsil hockey with a group of bro-dudes is quickly replaced by the gnawing need to sleep. A yawn escapes my lips, and suddenly, I want nothing more than to be back in my tub with a bottle of unpoisoned bourbon and maybe . . . yes, maybe some Enya.

Desperate times.

So, after putting enough distance between myself and the burning building (to be fair, it's only the *basement* that will burn, leaving everything above it magically unscathed—I'm not a total monster), I grab another piece of chalk and head into an overcrowded bar. The place reeks of sweat and booze, and on any other night, that would be enough to make me want to stay. Not tonight. I head straight to the bathroom and start screaming gibberish as loudly as I can, smashing my fists on the stalls.

Instantly, the handful of girls in the room leave. Works every damn time.

The moment they're gone I lock the door with a simple chalk charm. I don't like creating portals home in public, and for as many dark alleys as New Orleans has, there isn't much secrecy. This is a city that thrives in darkness and shadowed, dangerous streets. Ironic that the only place I can get a little privacy is here. At least until the bouncer comes by.

I start scribbling in all the necessary symbols to get me home on a stall door—equations and coordinates, Vedic chants and Celtic Ogham. The whole process is routine, and my eyes keep drifting over to the mirror before darting back to my work. I don't want to see myself, not in this fluorescent light. Not when I'm smeared in who-knows-whose blood and the shadows under my eyes could swallow sunlight. I used to think of myself as a bombshell, but tonight, I just feel like a bomb. My platinum hair is singed and coated with ash, my coat ripped, and my skin covered in fresh—albeit healed—scars. Definitely more like a bomb. One with a lot of shrapnel.

Someone is pounding on the bathroom door. I don't even look over. Unless the bouncer's a witch, there's no getting in, not so long as I'm here. I sigh. I've gotten quite good at locking people out.

Then, with a mental slap to the face, I pull myself together before I can get all self-deprecating. There's nothing more unattractive. I push open the stall door, but it's not some gross toilet staring back at me. Instead, it's a door to a dim room filled with bookshelves and hurricane lamps and perpetually lit candles. Something in me cracks at the sight, and I actually whimper as the weight of the day makes itself known. I step through, into my study, and let the magic holding the bathroom door shut wink out. I hear the bouncer burst in just as the stall door begins to close. I look to him and grin, then flip him off right as the door slams shut and the link between the worlds of Mortal and Faerie is severed. Back in the bathroom, I know, my chalk work dissolves into vague, inflammatory graffiti—just for kicks.

It takes all my self-control not to collapse right there in my study, fully clothed and filthy. But I don't. The promise of a full tub and a full bottle spurs me on. I shuffle toward the bathroom, peeling off my clothes as I go and tossing them into the open fireplaces dotting the walls. Being in the heart of the Winter Kingdom—which is exactly as warm and welcoming as it sounds—the fireplaces are always burning. I give my jacket one last lovelorn look before tossing it into the flames, which instantly turn purple with flaring magic as the room fills with the scent of charred leather. My shirt and bra are next, tossed into the fireplace in my living room. I kick my shoes into the fireplace opposite, then peel off my jeans and trudge into the bathroom, where I throw both denim and underwear under the large golden lintel and into the waiting flames.

The bathroom is my architectural coup de grâce, all polished gold and smoked glass and mirrored candlelight. I snap my fingers, and a stream of water pours from a dragon's maw on the stucco ceiling into a tub the size of a small pool inset into the tiled floor. Instantly, the room is filled with steam and the scent of lavender and sandalwood. Another snap of my fingers, and music floods the room, a string quartet I reserve for nights my nerves are a millimeter away from snapping. Enya can wait.

I walk over to a vanity in the corner and open the mirrored medicine cabinet. Bottles of high-end alcohol glint in the light like jewels, amber and quartz and aquamarine. I grab a bottle of Scotch and pull out the cork. Tonight's not a night for glasses. I'm pretty certain this bottle cost a few hundred dollars. I'm also pretty certain half of it will be gone before I leave this room.

When I turn back to the tub, it's already filled and brimming with bubbles.

I take a swig of the Scotch and sink into the hot water, let it lap up to my neck. Perfect temperature. Perfect ambience. Perfect booze. Honestly, it feels like the first thing to have gone right in weeks. I take another long drink and settle back, rest my head on the cool tile, and close my eyes.

Then I see her again. Roxie. Smiling and poised while she admitted to leading me on, to working for the Pale Queen. Roxie, when my blade buried itself in her chest. And then, for some reason, I see the girl I'd been shown in my visions—the blonde with the bloody jeans. The girl Mab took in to the Immortal Circus. The girl who was to become my true mother. Before Mab stole me away and forced me to a life of murder.

A dozen emotions war within me. I want to cry, a realization that startles me with its foreignness. I want to scream. I want to make the whole world burn.

I decide I will only do one of those things. So, in silence, and with dry eyes, I take another drink and let the heat melt my weaknesses away.

***

It takes more time than it should to realize I'm dreaming.

I'm walking down the halls of Mab's castle, and for the first time since I was a little girl, I feel afraid. Something is behind me. Chasing me. Shadows slip up from the floor like hands as I walk. As I force myself not to run. *Never run from danger. Never be the victim.*

I take another step, and a great shudder runs through the hall. Not like an earthquake. Like the whole castle is shifting over—like a beast, rising from its haunches. I slam against a wall, and when my hand comes away, it's covered in blood. Black blood, like glittering oil. Faerie blood.

And I realize, in that moment, I am dreaming. I have to be dreaming. Because I know, somehow, that this is Mab's blood. Splattered over the walls of the castle like a Pollock painting. Mab, who can't bleed. Who can't be dead.

That's when I start to run.

The hall twists and turns in front of me, a labyrinth shifting with my terror as shadows ooze blood and light inks out. Panic grips my chest, and I can't force the tears from my eyes. My fragmented heartbeat is a mantra: *Mab is dead. Mab is dead. Mab is dead.*

Behind me, always two steps behind me, running through the shadows, is Roxie. Her laughter and lips always right behind my ear. And it's not just my heart whispering those words, but her. The traitor who broke my heart and broke apart the barriers between worlds to summon . . . something. A Pale Queen. A new matriarch.

The moment the name crosses my mind, the hall bursts open. Walls crumble around me, and I am no longer in a hall, but in a room swept with rubble and snow. Mab's towering throne of ice and shadow stretches up from the center, but the Winter Queen doesn't sit there. No. Mab's small body lies broken at the foot. And sitting atop, nearly two stories up, is a different figure. A woman robed in the palest white, her shining crown blinding so I cannot see her face.

I run to Mab. To the unstoppable Winter Queen, the fiercest force of nature. She looks small now. Her usual seductive dress is smeared with black, a crown of black ice shattered around her head in a halo. Her lips are pallid, her white skin hollow. She looks like a doll—so small I could cradle her, so broken the merest touch would shatter her. I want her to be a doll, an illusion. But I place a hand on her forehead and I know. This is the feared Winter Queen, the woman who ruled over nature and shadow, who inspired the greatest minds with fear and desire.

And she is dead.

"This is a dream," I whisper repeatedly.

"Of course it is a dream, little girl," comes a voice. I look up to the peak of the throne, where the Pale Queen's dress drips like blood. "It is *my* dream. And thanks to you, it shall soon become a reality."

She descends from the throne then. Gliding down like a snowflake. No. Mab is the queen of snow. This woman floats down like a spiderweb spun from the rafters. A curse.

I back away. My hands reach for weapons that are not there. "I'm not helping you." My words sound like coins in a bucket. Am I voicing them aloud, in the waking world? And if so, why am I not waking up?

"But you have, and you will continue to do so." The woman reaches out and strokes my cheek, sending flame across my skin. Still, I lean into that touch. In the land of eternal cold, it feels seductively inviting.

Then I am reminded of the body at my feet. Mab's body. My queen. And, for all intents, my mother.

I step back.

"Who are you?"

The woman moves her head, causing more light to shine off her crown, and I still can't see her face through the glare. Somehow, though, I know she is smiling.

"That is the trouble with names," she says. Her voice is smooth, oceanic. Mab's words might have dripped shadow, but this woman is a melody of sea breezes and undertows. "If you were to know me, you would have power over me. And I prefer we keep it the other way around. Do you not agree, Claire Melody Warfield? Or should I say . . ."

I don't hear her next words. Because the moment she utters my true name, I am struck to my knees, the breath knocked out of me and a great ringing in my ears. When the haze clears, I find I can't move. I can only kneel before her like a servant, staring at the overlapping folds of her dress.

"How?" I manage to ask. *How can you control me so completely?*

"You learn much, when you live where I have." Then she kneels before me and places her hand under my chin. Once more, I'm filled with that warm fire. Once more, I can't see her face through the glare of her crown. "Hell teaches us so much about ourselves, and about those around us. As you well know."

I expect her grip to tighten, for her nails to dig into my skin and pull forth blood. Or for her to slap me. If she were Mab, either of those would be the case. Instead, she pats my cheek gently.

"Do not worry," she says. "Unlike your Winter Queen, I do not wish to rule through coercion."

I feel the bonds around me relax as she speaks. I actually gasp in relief, and immediately hate myself for it.

"You will serve me because you wish it," she says, standing. "You will see. When the chains of Winter and Summer are broken, you will be free to live and serve as you desire. And I think you will find, Claire, that I am a much kinder mistress than the Winter Queen. Especially to you, whom I owe for bringing me back. You have helped me rise to power. I will never forget that, Claire. And, unlike your old queen, I reward those who serve me well. Remember that, when the time comes. Remember my promise when you see how Mab treats those who lose everything so she may rise in power."

The castle shudders again, large chunks of ice and stone crashing to the floor. Like waves. Like muffled howls.

"A new age beckons," the Pale Queen says. "And you, my dear. You will be its harbinger."

Stones collapse. The throne topples. The last thing I see before the dream winks out is Mab's face—her green eyes wide and dull. But not terrified. Demanding.

As though even in death, she expects my full devotion.

***

Morning dawns as it always does in the land of eternal winter darkness—to the illusion of sunrise behind my drawn curtains and the promise of blood.

Today, however, it's not alcohol poisoning keeping me in bed. I roll over on my side and pull my covers tight and try to convince myself that what I know to be true is an illusion.

I dreamed last night.

I never dream. Not in Winter, especially, where my nighttime musings are immediately siphoned for Mab's personal gain. I don't want to know what this means, to remember my dreams. I just know it can't be good.

I don't remember much. Every time I squeeze my eyes shut and try to grasp an image, it filters through my fingers like opium smoke. All I know is the feeling lodged in my chest. Fear. Fear, and the Pale Queen's hazy image.

"It's just stress," I say aloud, trying to convince myself. Probably not a dream at all. Just some hallucination brought on by deep anxiety and mental trauma. Funny, that that's what I have to make myself feel better.

When I do finally force myself from bed, I push the fear down. Down to where I lock everything else that doesn't serve me. I'm not saying I feel immediately better. But at least I feel a little less awful.

I slip on a bathrobe and pad out into the kitchen, flicking my hands at the fireplaces as I go, their embers bursting into fresh flames. The curtains over the windows in the living room and study slide back, revealing a sunrise over snowcapped mountains that I think are the Himalayas. Not sure. I'm also not sure what time it actually is. Time is a tricky thing in Faerie, and that enchanted sunrise could be some stock footage for all I know—after all, it's always sunrise *somewhere* in the mortal world.

I stand in my tiny kitchen and turn on the stove to boil water for coffee (all of these things being complete anachronisms in the world of Faerie, where the denizens live almost entirely off of Dream). As I go through the routine, I can't shake the ghost of Roxie's presence—she'd been there, standing in the doorway to my kitchen, looking all innocent, barely a week ago.

"Snap out of it, Claire," I mutter as I grab some eggs from the icebox (no, not a fridge, a legit metal box with a chunk of enchanted ice) and start making breakfast. "Roxie betrayed you. Roxie is dead. Focus on the present."

Ah, yes, because the present is so much better than my past. Just the thought of what I'm prepping to do makes my stomach roll over. Breakfast is no longer appealing, but damn it, I'm going to eat anyway.

"Today's the day you meet your mother," I say as I scramble the eggs. "The day you've been waiting for."

Only now that the day is here, I dread it more than I desire it. This is the day I meet the woman I've been denied seeing my entire life. And if I've learned one thing about being an assassin, it's that meeting your role models is never a good thing. Mainly because I usually have to kill them.

You're not killing your own mother, I hiss, not willing to voice the words aloud.

Well then, another internal voice whispers, *why is Mab having you meet her after all this time? And only after you signed your own contract, binding your life to her whims?*

Mab had said my mother was the Oracle, and that the Oracle's powers had vanished after the war that nearly brought Faerie and Mortal to their knees. But apparently there is still a spark, albeit a small one, that Mab needs me to coax out of her.

Of course she wouldn't say how. I refuse to believe she *couldn't* say, because I refuse to believe there is anything she doesn't know. I wouldn't go so far as to call her omnipotent, but she is pretty damn close.

"What am I going to say to her?" I whisper, putting thoughts of work and destiny aside. I'm not exactly "heartfelt reunion" material. I kill for a living—who besides Mab would be proud of that? There is literally a lifetime to make up for, and I . . . am burning my eggs.

I focus on cooking and try to salvage the food before it becomes charcoal. I mostly manage, and after breakfast and some really shitty coffee (it's something in the water or maybe the fabric of Faerie itself— this place refuses to let me enjoy a satisfying espresso), I change into my normal attire: tight black jeans and a leather bomber. Then I head to my living room for the most important accessory a girl can own.

The weapons rack is impressive at first glance. It's even more impressive when you realize that what you see isn't even close to what you actually get. The wood and glass cabinet is about twelve feet high and stocked with weapons mostly from the Dark Ages—halberds and bastard swords and pikes—but that's just what's on display. I run my finger down a metal plate on the cabinet door, and a line of violet runes flare into light. There's a whir of clockwork and click of latches, and then the cabinet doors swing outward to reveal not the weapons on display but nearly two dozen obsidian shelves, a faint purple light peeking between the cracks. I slide one out and am greeted with a sight that makes me smile.

An array of daggers is fanned out on the black silk, in all different shapes and sizes. There are leaf-shaped throwing knives and austere dirks, wavelike kriss blades and an array of folded butterfly knives. My fingers hover over them as I select which ones to pack. It's not just an act of reverence. All of these blades are enchanted in some way—to kill Fey, to poison mortals, et cetera—and some days, in the strange way of magic, some blades just don't want to be used.

I select a few butterfly knives and shove them in the various pockets of my coat, then grab a kriss blade and slide it into my boot. I skip the Tarot cards and grenades and magicked whips waiting in the other drawers; this should be a fairly low-bloodshed mission, but I'm not about to take any chances. Then, before I can stop myself, I head into the bathroom and look at myself in the mirror.

I don't exactly look put together, but at least I'm no longer as sleep deprived and bloody as I was last night. I actually roll my eyes as I consider all this, but today, I want to impress. I'm meeting my estranged mother. I have to look good. Or, at least, presentable. Like a daughter she'd *want* to have. A daughter worth missing. I don't own any makeup. Don't need it. Mainly because, again, I kill people for a living, and it doesn't matter what they think of my appearance—they're going to hate me showing up no matter what. And also because there's a reason faerie magic is called *glamour*. I pick up the small golden canister on the vanity and pop it open. No salve or glitter inside, just a ruby that glows faintly. I press a finger to it, and warmth floods across my hand; I bring my finger to my face, and the energy flows off, running across my cheeks and over my forehead and through my lips, enchanting me. Changing me.

The effects aren't drastic—I don't immediately look like some air-brushed model after a Botox binge. But the glamour does clear away the bags under my eyes and smooth out the scars scratched across my cheeks. My pale skin gets a little more lush, my lips a little plumper. When the magic is done, I look . . . well, I look like I have a perfectly respectable job and lifestyle, one that involves a lot of smoothies and something called *beauty rest* and probably yoga. It kind of looks out of place with the leather bomber bulging with its odd pockets of weapons and chalk, but I'm not about to change *all* my habits. Especially not the ones that keep me alive.

"Is that how you plan on leaving the house?" comes a voice from behind me.

Instantly, my skin goes cold.

"I thought I asked you to knock," I say, not looking from the mirror. I don't need to; frost is already starting to rime the edges of the glass. There's only one person in this kingdom with that sort of entrance.

"My palace, my rules," she replies. Her voice is smooth as velvet and deep as night.

"What do you want, Mab?" I make it a point not to call her *Mother* or any derivation thereof. Not anymore. I also make it a point to keep my mind clear—no thoughts of dreams or the Pale Queen. Mab knows everything that happens under her roof. And she knows everything that passes through my mind.

"To check in on you," she says. My heart gives a small sigh of relief when she says nothing about dreams or sleeping. She glides forward—actually floats, I think—and comes into the mirror's reflection. Save for pallid skin tone, she is my complete opposite: short where I am tall, long black hair where mine is shoulder length and ashen, lush lips and green eyes where I honestly look a little faded out. As if when I'm around her, I don't exist in the same capacity. Even the sheer black dress she wears appears more vibrant compared to my dusty leather. I am the pale shadow to her moonlight.

When I blink, I can't help but see her coated with blood.

"You might not be able to lie," I force myself to say, "but that's a real shitty half-truth and you know it."

She smiles, her lips full and painted a color that's probably called "Bad Girl" or "Baby's Blood."

"I've heard you made a house call last night."

I turn from the mirror and lean back against the vanity. I almost expect her to vanish when I meet her gaze, but I'm not that lucky—she's definitely not all in my head.

"Why are you here?" I ask again. I try to keep my voice level and fail miserably. "Yes, I killed some wayward Fey; I know you don't give two shits about that. What are you here to rub in my face?"

The smile slips.

"You think so poorly of me, Daughter," she says. Her voice is as smooth as her expression—if she's actually hurt by any of my anger, she'll never let it show.

"I'm not your daughter. Or did you already forget my mission?"

And there it is, that small crack in her demeanor that lets me know I've hit my mark. It's the slightest narrowing of her eyes, but after spending my entire life trying to glean the slightest bit of any sort of emotion from her face, I know her tells well. Faeries don't feel much beyond lust or hatred, and they reveal even less.

"I have not forgotten. And that is precisely why I am here."

"What?"

Faeries also have never been good at getting to the point, and Mab—being their Queen—is the worst of the bunch.

"While you were . . . away . . . last night," she says, glancing to a corner of the room, which lets me know just how much it pains her to deliver whatever it is she's about to say, "there was an exodus."

"Exodus? How surprising. You keep this kingdom so cozy."

I know it's a step too far, but Mab doesn't react. Not the way she should. On any other occasion there'd be a handprint across my face or, at the very least, a trip to the dungeons. Instead, she looks to the floor and takes a deep, unsettling breath.

"The Pale Queen has been in Faerie for less than a day," Mab whispers, "but she has already taken in over half of my subjects. Last night, when she was released, I lost thousands. My kingdom is dying, Claire. Soon, I will have no one left to govern. We will have no one left to protect. As the Pale Queen grows in power, mine wanes. And a world without Winter is thrown terribly out of balance."

I raise an eyebrow in an attempt to play this off. In reality, her fear makes me want to collapse to the tiles. Mab is never afraid. Mab is never uncertain. Mab is the icy Queen of Winter; she is as soft and insecure as a glacier.

"Why are you telling me this?" I ask. One of us has to play calm and collected in this scenario. I'm surprised it's me.

"Because you must know the burden you bear. When you find the Oracle, you *must* do whatever it takes to learn the whereabouts of the Pale Queen. Only the Oracle will be able to trace her exact location, and only her insight will show you how to kill her. You know how the Wildness functions—in there, those who wander are indeed lost."

Oh, I know about the Wildness, that fathomless expanse of forest that separates the kingdoms of Winter and Summer. There are no paths, no clear ways in or out. And, like a living thing, it changes by the moment, providing haven for those seeking refuge within and deterring any from without. Finding the Pale Queen in there would be impossible—those seeking her out for sanctuary would find her easily, but me? The Wildness would know my purpose, and it would see to it that I never reached her. Unless, apparently, the Oracle could tell me exactly where to go.

"You haven't even told me where she is," I say, brushing past Mab. I don't have anything left to *do*, but being active while talking to her keeps me from feeling trapped. "My true mother, I mean. Since you obviously don't know where or who this Pale Queen chick is."

Again, Mab lets the slight slide off. I'm impressed. With this new change of heart, I could literally get away with murder.

Mab follows me into the living room.

"You will find her in her home," she says. "With her husband—your father—and the changeling looking after them both. I trust you won't cause trouble with the changeling; I needed someone who could look after your mother. Protect her. You were just a little girl, and I couldn't watch over Vivienne from afar forever. This was for her own safety."

Yeah, right. Like you've ever thought of anyone else's best interest.

Her lips thin, and I wonder if my thoughts went too far. *That's what you get for reading my mind.*

"Where is it?" I say.

"Hidden," she replies. She steps forward and places a hand on my arm. I feel the magic snake through my limbs. It is cold and burning like frostbite, and as it slithers up to my brain I hold back a gasp from the ache of it. When she steps away, I know how to find my mother. The coordinates are seared into my mind like a brand. A very cold brand.

It pisses me off to think that she could have done this at any time. And that the location was probably hidden not only for the sake of Vivienne, but also to keep me away. *Why would she need to be kept safe, though?*

Mab doesn't answer my unspoken question.

"I have something for you," she says instead. I honestly feel a little giddy in spite of everything. Mab gives me only two things in this world: orders and weapons. And since she's already given me the first . . .

Shadows and pale lightning curl in her palm, and when they congeal, I expect her to be holding a dagger of ice or something equally cool. Instead, she holds a small black box. The sort you'd give your wife on a particularly boring anniversary.

"Whatever's in there better be poisoned or alive," I say.

"It is neither. It belonged to your mother."

My heart thuds.

"How long?" I ask.

"I do not know how long she wore—"

"No. How long have you had it?" *How long have you been hiding another piece of my mother from me? How long have you been hiding away another piece of her life from* her?

Mab doesn't answer. Instead, she holds out the gift. Despite myself, I shake as I reach for it. Gifts from faeries are dangerous things—never without a catch or promise. But if this is my mother's, I'll take whatever curse goes with it. It's not like I have another choice.

Inside is a piece of grey silk, a necklace coiled on top. The pendant is smooth and black, simple obsidian, the chain just as unremarkable. It doesn't look like something my mother would wear, at least not the version of my mother I'd been harboring for so long. This looks like something a Goth princess would covet.

When I pick it up, however, my fingertips buzz with power.

"What is it?" I ask.

"The stone is hewn from my castle," she says. "How your mother got her hands on it, I cannot say. But it is mine by right, and now, I bequeath it to you."

Only Mab would say something as ridiculous as *bequeath* and pull it off.

"What does it do?" I glance from the necklace to her. Anything from Mab's kingdom has a trace of magic, and I have no doubt this thing packs more than even I can pick up on.

"It stores memories," she says. "Sadly, your mother was unable to do so in her later years, so I'm afraid it is now merely a necklace. What it *does* contain are fragments of her energy. Perhaps, in uniting owner and owned, her powers will manifest."

"And what if they don't? You still haven't told me how I'm supposed to get her to, I dunno, *awaken* to her inner Oracle nature or whatever." I feel like an idiot saying that—it sounds like something from a talk show about reclaiming your inner goddess.

"The magic that binds her memories is beyond my realm of control," she says. "It was the work of the magician."

I nearly laugh out loud, but the stake to my heart prevents it. I should have known.

Of course Kingston had something to do with it. He seemed to have a finger in everything. Pun intended.

"So I bring her back to the circus to get him to undo it?"

She nods.

"Why couldn't you bring her there yourself?" I ask. "Or have him make a house call? I'm an assassin—shouldn't I be using my expertise for something other than human trafficking?"

She raises an eyebrow, the curve of her expression drawing up like a nocked bow.

"I am needed here. If you hadn't heard, we have a terrible enemy on the loose, thanks to you. One with her sights set on my throne. I believe your strengths will be perfectly fitted to this task. And you would do well not to question my motives. You'll quickly find your contract looks poorly upon such thinking."

Just that phrase, *your contract*, feels like a noose drawing across my windpipe. I don't even want to know what else is forbidden.

If she outlawed sex with her subjects . . .

It's then I realize she made no response about Kingston.

I sigh and slide the pendant around my neck, then toss the box into the flames of a nearby fireplace. My stomach is suddenly in knots—*I'm wearing something of my mother's. I'm connected to her. I'm about to see her*—but I don't let it show. I can't let Mab see how much this gets under my skin. I can't let her see just how badly I want this reunion. Which is funny, since a month ago I couldn't have cared less about my mother. I guess that's just the way of things—when you live your life thinking something's a myth, you don't give it much thought. But when you're about to face a dragon . . .

I grab a piece of chalk from my coat and head toward the study, where I normally create my portals.

"Claire," she says, and I can't tell if it's a question or statement.

I halt. It's answer enough.

"You'll need to go through the front gate."

"What do you mean?" I ask. Not that it's a big deal; I just don't like being told what to do. Not when the rest of my life is micromanaged by her.

"In light of recent events, I have made it impossible to enter or leave the kingdom via magic."

Another big sigh.

"Fine," I reply. "Anything else, *your highness?*"

Mab bites her lip, a movement so small and fast I should have missed it.

"Your mother has sacrificed a great many things for the good of my kingdom," she says. "But do not, for one second, believe I would not do anything to save us from destruction. Your mother holds the answers we seek. You will recover them. No matter the cost."

"I'm not killing my own mother," I reply.

In response, she turns and strides away.

"You will do what must be done," she says. "Or have you already forgotten? Your new contract demands it."

When the door closes behind her, I chuck my piece of chalk at the space her head just occupied.

"Bitch," I whisper. Then I head after her, the hallway already deserted.

Three

The moment I step from my room I'm ensconced in cold. The air in the hallway beyond is subzero, and ice cracks in thin panes over the onyx walls like the graffiti of a frost sprite. Though I've learned all the Fey curse words in their native script, and the fractals along the wall don't make the cut.

Mab is pissed.

The castle is like her mood ring, and I know the moment the first wave of goose bumps races across my skin that she's in the worst mood I've ever seen her in. Even if she was hiding it well.

The hall stretches before me and fades off into shadows, the floor covered in a fine coating of snow that glows faintly. Which is good, because the torches that usually give trace amounts of warmth and light along the wall have all gone out. More snow falls, tiny glowing pieces of dust, and a part of me thinks it's beautiful. Magical. The rest of me thinks it's a sign of the end.

Mab's palace always feels empty. It's part of its charm, I guess. But today, it feels like a vacuum, like being void of bodies is an active thing. As if at any moment it could just suck me out into the ether and I'd never be heard from again. Not that that would be a bad thing.

I walk quickly, my footsteps not making a sound, and honestly, it feels as if I'm being chased. Shadows congeal behind me, covering up the door to my room. With every step, I expect them to lash forward and swallow me up. Maybe it's just my imagination, or fragments from my dream. I highly doubt it. The castle is like Mab, out for blood and not picky about who pays the price.

Normally, I'd be out the front door in a matter of seconds. Being enchanted, the castle has always been good at granting a quick exit. But as I walk, I realize today's just not going to be that day. My hand doesn't leave the pendant around my neck; the other stays close to a knife. I keep walking, turning down corridors I've never seen before as a sense of weight settles on my shoulders, as though I'm going deep, deep underground. And yet the halls don't get darker. They get lighter, whiter, more filled with ice and snow and an azure light that filters through it all. I've seen a hall like this once before, but it was a fleeting thing. Now, every corridor is the same icy blue and white. *What the serious fuck?*

And then the hall opens.

The snowy corridor ends in two stalagmites of ice that jut toward the ceiling like inverted walrus tusks.

"Seriously?" I whisper as I walk into the room.

Because it *is* a room. Cavern, really. Filled with mounds of ice that rise from the ground like waves on a torrid sea. More drip from the ceiling. I edge around a rather large ice chunk and stare. I've never been here before. And I've scoured every edge of Mab's castle—sometimes inadvertently. Whatever this place is, it wanted to stay hidden until now.

A low hum wavers in the air, the sound of a distant river, or like the stones themselves are vibrating. It makes more goose bumps ripple over my skin. Something about this place seethes with power, but it's not vibrant Dream or even the wild Fey magic. This is something older. Something dormant. And, I think, something outside of even Mab's control.

"Where the hell am I?" I ask the ice shards that mirror my reflection in paler hues.

Smoke or fog curls at my feet, and as I walk through the maze of ice, I can't help but feel the first pang of fear. If I'm stuck in Mab's castle with no magic to get me out, I'm screwed. And I really, really don't want to have to eat a limb. I need all of them.

Then I round the corner, and there, in a small clearing, is a slab of ice. I don't know why I'm drawn to it—it's no different than any other chunk of ice in here, though this one is mostly horizontal—but there's a gravity I can't escape, a hum in my bones that drags me forward. The pendant around my neck is heavy. Pulsing. And in a far-off corner of my mind, I know that the necklace is what dragged me here. My hand curls tighter around the stone at my chest. I expect it to be hot, but it's colder than ice, and the energy coursing off it is like needles.

I pause when I near the slab. Something about this feels momentous, but I can't place why. Still clutching the necklace in one hand, I reach out and touch the ice.

A shock ricochets through me, dropping me to my knees in a heartbeat, and when I glance up to the slab, I nearly gasp. It's no longer empty.

Kingston lies across it like some rugged Sleeping Beauty. His lank black hair is frozen to the ice, and he is clothed in flowing black linen like some medieval royalty. He isn't moving. He looks very much not alive. The slash across his neck doesn't help matters. Suddenly I'm reminded of him showing up in my room, jokingly wondering what it was about his neck that begged to be cut.

Before I can get too lost to the vision, Mab steps up beside me. But it's not Mab, not really—I can see the ice through her, as though she's some terrible, twitchy hologram.

"I know I should not ask this of you, old friend," she says to his corpse. "But we must do that which we fear we cannot. Her life is important to us. To you. But she must sacrifice it so we may live. As you sacrificed your life. As you will many times. You must convince her."

She steps forward and lays a hand on his neck, slides a finger slowly across the clean cut. It seals itself up in her finger's wake, a zipper closing on silent teeth.

"Convince her your love is strong enough to die for," she says. "Otherwise, I fear our world will falter."

Something cracks, a gunshot of broken ice, and then the slab is empty and Mab is gone, and my heart is racing while the stone burns like frostbite against my chest. Who was Mab talking about? Me? Was Mab responsible for sending Kingston to my room, for getting him to sleep with me? But that didn't make sense.

No, you idiot. She meant your mother.

My hand goes to the necklace while the other pushes me to standing. This couldn't be my mother's memory, could it? Because no, that wouldn't make sense—Vivienne wasn't in the cave when this happened; I could tell that much. Mab never would have spoken so openly if my mother had been watching. So was it the castle, reaching out to me? Showing me Mab's secret plans?

Mab had never told me much about my mother, or the Oracle. I knew the Oracle had saved all of Faerie. And now I knew that the Oracle was a force within my mother, one that Kingston had magicked away after whatever she had done to save everyone. But that was it. So why this room? Why this memory?

Why does even the castle want me to know the lengths to which Mab went to betray my mother?

My stomach is in knots. I stare at the slab, feeling colder than the ice. I've always known Mab was a treacherous bitch. I've known my life was built on half-truths and deception and blood. And I was okay with that. I never knew anything else. But seeing this, knowing that Mab had Kingston manipulate my mother . . . The ice within turns red with rage. Maybe it's just the tie of blood, but the very idea of someone screwing with my mother, lying to her, hurting her, makes me want to make Mab pay. More than I've ever desired that before.

And lately, I've desired it very much.

You were lied to, I think to my mother's shadow. *You were sacrificed why? Just so Mab could continue ruling?*

I turn and walk away from the ice, toward an archway in the walls that I know wasn't there moments ago. Then I halt.

Soon, Mab's imagined voice whispers in my skull, *you, too, will have to lie to her. Just as I have done. And you will hurt her deeper than I ever could.*

***

Ten minutes and countless more frustrating hallways later, I'm finally released from the castle's hold. Not from the front door, but from one of the many hidden entrances along the palace's exterior.

I make my way down a dark alley, the buzzing faerie lights above (real faeries: captured Summer Fey doing penance) casting a soft-blue glow over everything, making the flakes drifting down glimmer. Even out here, the emptiness is palpable. Snow drifts higher at the edges, and the breeze that blows through the alley carries a heaviness, a weight of loss. I fully expect to see fragments of the exodus Mab spoke of— discarded dolls and furniture, broken mirrors or bits of food—but the alley is clean. The only sign is the deepening snow and the cold that clutches my bones.

I eventually make it onto the main boulevard leading to the front gate. Normally, there would be at least a few people walking back and forth along here, coming to the castle to air a grievance or something like that. I don't actually know why anyone would want to come and talk to Mab—it's never a pleasant interaction. But the path is now completely empty. The wide cobblestones are covered in snow, and the only figures dotting the white-and-black landscape are the statues that line the boulevard like sentinels. Honestly, it wouldn't surprise me if they *were* sentinels, out here as a sort of last defense against anyone stupid enough to attack.

My gut is churning, and it's not just because of the emptiness of this place; it's also because of the statue nearest Mab's castle, the one my feet walk toward with a mind of their own. A statue of a girl, poised as though floating with one toe on the ground, her ebony skin covered in live blue flames. I place my hand on the plaque on the pedestal and look to the only physical manifestation of my mother I've ever seen. At least in my memory.

The girl's features are smoothed down, barely discernible through the flames, and it's impossible to tell if her chin is lifted in anguish or ecstasy. "The Oracle's Sacrifice" is engraved on the plaque, and that really doesn't bode well.

Convince her your love is strong enough to die for. Those had been Mab's words to Kingston, and suddenly my blood boils. Kingston, the bastard who now runs the Immortal Circus. The sex god who'd slept with me and then called me my mother's name. The guy I still can't get out of my head, not fully. When I see him again, I will do more than slap him in the face like some vengeful ex. I will see if he can be killed and brought back a second time. And a third. And however many times it takes for me to feel like my mother was avenged.

Speaking of . . . I can't delay this homecoming any longer.

I shove my frigid hands back into my pockets and send a small course of magic through one of the sigils inked down my spine; my skin immediately flushes warm. A minor magic, but damn if it isn't necessary in this place. Then, before I can get too sentimental, I turn and head down the boulevard.

I know there's more than one reason Mab sent me out this way. She made the magic keeping everyone from magically leaving, which means she could have easily removed it for me. She wanted this: wanted me to walk down the empty lane and see just how dire it was. And she was smart to do it, really. Had I not just watched her tell Kingston to lie to my mother, I might have felt a kernel of responsibility for helping get her kingdom back after seeing this. This place is absolutely devoid of life, no Fey wandering or laughing or tempting mortals in their eternal dance. No music lingering in the alleys like a bad dream. And when I turn down one of the more, shall we say, *rowdy* streets, it, too, is empty as an open grave.

I walk down the row of buildings, staring into hookah bars and saloons and brothels, and everything is silent. Empty. Barren. When I pass by my haunt, the Lewd Unicorn, I fight the urge to go inside and see if my main friend in this wasteland is still here. But I don't want Celeste to see me right now—she's the one faerie who can get into my head, literally and figuratively, and I'm in no state to pretend that everything is fine.

And Mab would definitely not appreciate it if I blew the morning on alcohol and Dream highs.

It's funny. I should be running toward the front gate. I should want to see my true mother and father more than anything else. But I don't. I really, really don't. I mean, I'm okay with a reunion with my dad, but there's something about the bond I always thought I'd have with my mom that makes this painful. It's not just the fact that she's never been a figure in my life; it's the fact that . . . well, I can't really deal with any more emotional turmoil. I was raised to be cold and unflinching. Heart of ice, touch of steel sort of thing. But that facade is proving to be more and more difficult to keep up. I have no doubt that seeing my mother, seeing the human who bore me into the world and gave me up, will shatter that illusion of strength completely.

What if she doesn't live up to my expectations? What if I don't live up to hers? And I want to punch myself in the face for even wondering that, because that's not who I am. That's not what I care about. And yet here I am, strolling through the abandoned streets of Winter, pissing time away because I can't face the music.

It's not just the fear of meeting my mom. On any other day, I'd be okay with that. There's something about Winter, though, something in the endless dance of darkness that lets you convince yourself that you are insular, that here, nothing changes. Human things like emotions and death don't hold sway. Here, I'm safe. From myself. From the world outside.

From the ache Roxie left me with.

I've barely let myself think on it, not in the wake of everything that's happened since Roxie summoned the Pale Queen from the great beyond. But I know that when I step into the mortal world, I'll feel it. See her laughter in the people I cross or her voice in the music from car windows. Hell, I'll probably be lucky enough to hear her music played on the radio, seeing as her band had gotten so successful. It would be my luck.

I can't tell what it is I feel. Well, beyond hurt and betrayed. Was I falling for her? Or was I just yearning for mortal friendship? Some connection to a life that didn't involve blood, but instead entailed nights of movies and pizza and good wine and not worrying about who you had to kill the next morning. Love isn't a notion I've let myself entertain—it's not something faeries understand, so it's not something I was raised to know. Just desire and lust and passion. But what I feel—no, *felt*—toward Roxie wasn't any of that. It was softer. Quieter.

And it hurt a hell of a lot more.

She betrayed you. Anything you felt toward her is a lie. And now, she is dead. You got your revenge by taking her life. You don't live in the past. You live here, now, and this is the last thought you will give her.

"You've grown soft," I whisper to myself. "And now you're talking to yourself. Pull your shit together. You were worth nothing to her, and she is worth nothing to you."

The rune on my back might make me warm, but I pull a heat from somewhere far deeper, a rage I've cultivated for years, the need to be worth something in *someone's* eyes. The hatred for never being good enough to keep. Unless I was useful. I will be useful. I am worth more than they know, and I will prove it even if I have to make the whole world kneel.

I turn down a side alley and beeline for the front gate.

When I reach it, I barely give the great thing a cursory glance. It's a few stories tall and thin as glass, made of some opaque smoky crystal that's harder than steel. Trust me, I've tried making a crack in it many a drunken night. The moment I near, a shiver of power runs through me as another set of runes along my spine blazes into life, their mirrored counterparts slashing a blue line from the top to the bottom of the sharp-angled gate. It opens slowly, silently, snow bursting through the crack the moment it shifts. I press through, into the gale, and am out before it stops opening.

It's clear from the packed snow that the exodus was recent. Even with a blizzard raging around me, the path from the gate into the barren woods beyond is clear. It's a razor's line, leading right into the Wildness that looms in the blizzard like an ink stain on parchment. It's frustrating, knowing that I can't just follow it into the woods and find where this Pale Queen is raising her army. The magic within would just divert the path. It's a magic Mab and Oberon can never tame, let alone control. It's the chaos between balance. The disorder before creation. And it doesn't like being toyed with.

So I flick my hand and send a small wave of magic around me, a very simple shield that keeps the worst of the snow from blowing into my eyes and ears and prevents the cold from shearing off my lips. I follow a different path, a side trail that leads up a snow-swept mountain to a long stone wall that stands maybe ten feet high. It's a waystone of sorts, a fixed point in a world of change. And it's where I begin to make my portal.

Despite the snow whipping around the castle, the air surrounding the wall is clear, calm. Snow drifts against my ankles and a light breeze flurries my coat, but there's nothing to disturb me as I pull a piece of green chalk from my pocket and sketch the outline of a door. The process is so familiar by now, I nearly fall into a trance doing it, or maybe it's just the magic at work: the vibration in my fingers as chalk drags over stone, the power that flows through my arm and chest as sigils and runes and equations blossom under my fingertips around the door's perimeter. Not all of the marks are arcane, and some are pretty ridiculous from an outsider's point of view—hearts or stars or GPS coordinates—but the magic is still there. Sometimes it's not the words but the intent behind them, the angle of the letters or arc of the shapes. Magic flows through everything, and as I draw, I craft a channel for it.

Finally done, I grind up the nub of chalk, raise my hand to my lips, and blow toward the sketch. Tendrils of dust snake out from my hand, swirling over the door like serpents seeking warmth; equations are completed, shapes fill in, and then, without flash or lightning, the magic's done. The wall still looks solid; the symbols still look ridiculous. But I can feel the rip between the worlds, the power that will drag me through.

As I step forward, into the stone, I can't figure out if I'm entering home, or leaving it.

***

I land in the middle of suburbia.

It's early morning, light just spilling over the horizon, turning all the identical whitewashed houses the same shade of pastel pink. Before me is a two-story house with the same lawn and same flaccid décor as every other house stretching along this block. One manicured tree in the front yard. Shuttered windows. Small porch with two chairs and a side table. It's the picture-perfect cookie-cutter home, and I cannot for the life of me believe that this is where my mother—the woman who toured with an otherworldly circus and saved all of mankind and Fey—now spends her days.

In truth, I'd been hoping for something grand, a better parting gift from Mab. Maybe a mansion overlooking Hollywood, or at least a Tudor in the foothills of New England. But this . . . this just fuels the rage inside me, the anger I can do nothing about. My mother definitely got the short end of the stick. And there's no way in hell I can avenge that.

Worse, I feel no stirring inside when I look down the sidewalk leading to the front door. No memories of home. No whispers of a forgotten childhood. I feel empty, cold. And even though I'm no longer surrounded by whirling white, I feel as if I'm staring down a storm.

I actually gulp. My throat is dry and my hands are clammy and *what the serious fuck is wrong with me?* I've hunted down the meanest creatures the worlds of Faerie and Mortal had to offer, and I'm freaking out over knocking on a goddamned door. I take a deep breath. Square my shoulders. And then I remember this is supposed to be a family reunion—albeit one tinged with business—and try to slouch. Try to look a little more like a twenty-five-year-old human girl.

And then, before I can psych myself out anymore, I walk up the sidewalk and knock on the door.

My hand barely leaves the wood before it opens, but it's not my mother staring out. No, it's a girl, roughly my age, with blonde hair and dark eyes and the unmistakable scent of a faerie. There isn't even a moment of registration in her expression. She's known I was coming all along. Of course she did. She's the changeling that replaced me.

"I was hoping it was a mistake," she says. "But here you are." She shakes her head, looks me up and down. Clearly isn't impressed by what she sees. "Fuck." Then she opens the door wider and steps away, leaving me to enter on my own.

Four

My mother's house doesn't smell like home.

My own room carries the scent of cinnamon and cardamom and smoke. Even Mab's kingdom—desolate though it is—has a tang to it, the sharp scent of snow and crisp air and fallen branches.

This place is vanilla and lavender and cloying as hell.

The girl walks down the short hall, and I click the door shut behind me, my nerves at full alert. Her footsteps barely make a sound as I follow her, and no one else in the house is moving about, either. For some reason, I keep expecting her to turn around and try to stab me, but then again, what else could I expect? She's my replacement. Even if a part of me wants to try to treat her like a sister, the other part knows she's been living the life I was supposed to.

And I hear humans say *their* home lives are fucked up.

I walk down the hall slowly, cataloging everything. The family photos that I want to stop and stare at for hours, the painted landscapes in modest frames, the vase of fresh irises on the side table. *This could have been your life,* I think as I take it all in, as I look at photos of picnics and graduations. And I'm surprised to find that not one part of me wants it.

Maybe that's why my changeling replacement looks pissed. Maybe she is envious of *me*.

"Why are you here?" she asks when I enter the kitchen. At least in here there's something familiar and comforting: the scent of fresh-brewed coffee. She holds a mug in her hands and studiously refuses to offer me a cup.

It's one of those fancy modern kitchens with an island sink in the center and granite countertops and chrome everything. I sit at a high stool on one side of the island while she leans on the other side. We watch each other for a few long moments. Studying. Waiting.

She doesn't look anything like me. At least, she doesn't anymore—maybe her child form had similar hair or features, but she's no longer my doppelganger. She's shorter by far, and it's clear her life doesn't involve killing or being a weapon. She just looks . . . normal. Average size, average face, average hair, average clothes. Her makeup is smooth and her expression is blank and her nail polish is a clear lacquer. Nothing about her stands out, and maybe that's why she's been so good at pretending to be me. Nothing about her is remarkable. Nothing would tell you that something is amiss.

And I know it's all faerie glamour, know that with a snap of her fingers she'd probably be some Kali goddess archetype with flaming eyes and severed heads. But in this disguise, she's downright disappointing.

"You're supposed to be me?" I ask. No point trying to be friends. It's clear we're never going to be on the same page, even if we are employed by the same matriarch.

She doesn't say anything, doesn't twitch her lips into a frown or grin. She might play a human, but she's Fey through and through. No other creature is so completely emotionless when they want to be.

"Why are you here?" she asks again.

"I'm just going to help myself to the coffee, then," I say. "Mugs are?"

She doesn't move, so I slide off the stool and rummage through the cabinets, finally finding a thick terra-cotta-colored mug. Normally,

I take my coffee black, but I want to piss this girl off as much as I can, even though I know my issue isn't with her. So I brush past her and open the fridge and pull out the creamer, then open a few of the jars lining the counter and find the sugar. I figure it would be rude to search for a spoon, so I reach around her and grab the one from her mug, doling out two heaping spoonfuls of sugar into my cup before pouring in the creamer and coffee. She doesn't say a thing throughout the entire episode, barely even looks my way. But I can feel the energy radiating off her; she might be pretending to be an emotionless twat, but she's actually quite pissed.

Good.

When I'm done, I sit back on the stool and take a long inhale over the mug, making sure to do a complete "Mmm" after. It's cheesy and we both know it, but I'm okay playing this game as long as it takes. It kind of feels nice to be the one toying with someone else. At least it's a change of pace.

I take a sip. It's not nearly as strong as I'd like, and it's clearly not single-origin, but whatever. Beggars can't be choosers.

"Much better," I say. "As I'm sure you know, Winter sucks at making coffee. Or maybe you don't know. I haven't seen you around before."

Yes, her current appearance is just glamour, but I can sense her energy like a calling card. I would have remembered it. I have a mind for faces and energies; Mab ensured it.

Her eyes tighten. Oh yes, she clearly feels that pretending to be mortal is a jail sentence. Most Fey do. Being in the mortal world might give them direct access to Dream and playthings, but it cuts them off from Faerie. There's a magic in that world that infuses everything. Being away from it for too long? Things feel flat and empty. It's like a greyscale nightmare you just can't escape.

"So, how's life? How goes pretending to be me?"

She says nothing for a long time, which means I just take another drink of coffee and look around the kitchen. Rooster artwork on the walls. An orchid on the kitchen table. But all I can really focus on are the presences I feel upstairs, the two sleeping bodies slowly spiraling Dream into the ether.

For a moment, I wonder if they have one of Laura's figurines. She might have tried to crush me with her stone creations, but I have to admit, using kitschy décor to harvest Dream from sleeping mortals was pretty ingenious. The Pale Queen chose her vassals wisely. I still managed to kill all of them, though.

"Queen Mab did not say you would be coming," the changeling finally says. "But I knew your energy the moment you crossed our threshold. Which Mab assured me you would never be allowed to do. So why are you here?"

She sounds like a broken record, and I'm tired of listening to the skip.

"I'm here because Mab sent me here. How else would I have found you?"

Because that was another thing I'd noticed when standing outside the house—it was blank. Not a trace of magic or anything unusual, nothing to give it away. But now that I'm inside, I can see the traces of power and runes in the walls, the wards and protective circles. This place was made to deter unwanted visitors, but the devices used were expertly hidden. Basically, a shit ton of magic to hide that this place houses a shit ton of magic. Faerie glamour and misdirection at its finest, which means this girl is no pushover.

"But why did she send you?" she asks. "I have everything under control. You are not supposed to be here—it is a threat to Vivienne's well-being, and thus a threat to my purpose."

She still hasn't taken a sip of coffee, and I'm suddenly struck with the question of whether or not she makes herself sick eating human food all the time. Then I wonder what it is that she's supposed to have under control and feel like an idiot for not jumping to that question first.

"That's none of your concern," I say. "I need to see her."

It's the first time there's been a hint of a chink in her armor. Her knuckles are white on the coffee mug; I'm impressed it doesn't shatter.

"You cannot."

"I can and I will," I say.

"The only reason I let you in here is because they are asleep. It is against my orders to allow her to see you."

"And it's against my orders to kill you," I say, idly stroking the rim of the mug. "But one of us is going to crack, and I can assure you, it's not going to be me. I've already killed a few dozen of your kind in the last twenty-four hours. Adding one more to the mix won't hurt."

And no, it's not actually against my orders to kill her. I just find lying much more amusing.

She opens her mouth—hopefully to disagree with me—but then there's a creak upstairs. We both go silent, looking up to the ceiling.

"You must leave," she says. She doesn't sound cool and collected anymore. She sounds terrified.

"Like hell," I say, still not looking at her.

"I said leave!"

The coffee cup smashes, and I don't know if she's dropped it or if she actually did break the thing with her bare hands. I don't look. I shove off the stool and start heading toward the stairway in the hall.

Her hands are on me before I take two steps. She's strong, much stronger than I gave her credit for, but I'm stronger. I shake her off, and when she tries to grab me again, I spin around and have an iron blade to her throat before she can blink.

"Give me one good reason," I whisper, staring into her dead eyes. "You've stolen my life for the last eighteen years. Give me one reason, and I'll steal yours."

She doesn't say anything, doesn't move a damned muscle—*good girl*—and I back off as I hear footsteps coming down the stairs. Don't want to meet my mother while smeared in faerie blood.

"Claire?" the approaching figure calls. Feminine voice. *My mother.* My heart leaps in my throat at the sound of my name. And then the changeling girl steps forward, and it takes all my self-control not to shove my recently sheathed knife between her ribs.

"Yeah, Mom?" she asks. Her voice is different. I'll be damned if it doesn't sound more like mine.

"I thought I heard something. Everything okay?"

"Yep. Just dropped a mug." She hesitates, looks back toward me while my mother reaches the end of the stairs. "We have . . . company."

"Company?" the woman—*No, your mother, get it through your brain*—asks. But then she rounds the corner and sees me, and I expect the world to stop.

She stands there in sweatpants and a baggy T-shirt, her blonde hair pulled back in a loose ponytail, the golden strands streaked with grey and white. I can see the trace of her, the girl from my visions—it's in the angle of her cheekbones, the length of her neck. But that is where the similarity ends. This woman is in her early fifties, and there isn't the slightest hint of power to her. She doesn't glow with energy, doesn't carry herself with any sort of kick-ass charisma. She looks like she's spent the last twenty years of her life sitting at a desk. And, to be fair, that might be precisely the case.

I want to kill Mab.

When her eyes lock on me, I expect to feel something. Anything. Or for her to feel something. For there to be the slightest iota of a registration of familiarity. But there is nothing, and that hits harder than being shot in the chest.

Trust me, I know.

"Good morning," she says. She looks from me to the changeling. "Um, is this your friend?"

"Yeah, sorry," I say. I step forward, trying to cover up my wounded feelings by staying on the attack. "I'm Melody. Claire's friend. From work." I wonder briefly if the changeling stole my middle name as well, but if she did, neither she nor Vivienne take notice. At least there's some part of my history that's actually mine.

Either that or Mab wanted to ensure there was absolutely no reference to the Immortal Circus in Vivienne's life—even the name of Viv's former best friend.

The changeling's eyes flicker to me, then back to her mother. My mother. Not her mother. Jesus, this is confusing. Does the name Melody make anything click in my mother's head? Some memory of a life once lived? Melody had said that she and Vivienne were best friends in the circus, which was probably why my mom subconsciously named me after her. But the name doesn't seem to register, and the changeling doesn't give her a chance to process.

"Yeah," she says, picking up my slack. "Before I got laid off. Melody and I worked at the office together. I thought I'd mentioned her."

My mother shakes her head.

"Sorry, I didn't remember."

Clearly she's still confused as to why I'm here at six in the morning, so I make up the first excuse I can.

"I just got back into town for a vacation," I say. "Early flight. Claire said I could stop by for some coffee."

"Oh, that's just like my Claire," my mother says, and I want to punch the changeling in her face. I want to punch her every time my mother says my name. Every second that goes by without her realizing who I am. Why had I not considered this? That my mother wouldn't even recognize me, that Kingston's magic would be so ironclad? I'd figured Vivienne would see me and there would be recognition and tears and magic. Instead, the woman stares at me as though I'm an unwanted stranger, and I have no idea how I'll ever be able to change that.

Screaming *I'm your daughter, and this is just a faerie* before stabbing the changeling in the back probably wouldn't work. Even if the faerie bitch did explode into leaves, or whatever, in the process.

Something tells me Vivienne isn't wired to recognize magic. Not anymore.

Mab wanted me to coax out Vivienne's power, said that my spark would bring hers to life or something like that. But the woman doesn't become some glowing magical figure at my appearance, doesn't start prophesying the end or the location of the Pale Queen. She just looks confused as shit and a little miffed that I'm here before she's had her coffee. I consider handing her the pendant to see if that does anything, but for some reason I don't want to do that with the changeling around. That's what I tell myself. In reality, I'm not ready for the consequence.

"Speaking of coffee," I say, looking to the changeling. I refuse to call her Claire, not unless I have to. It feels like holding on to a piece of myself. "I could use another cup. We have *so much* to catch up on."

The changeling glares at me, and I smile back widely. Then I look to Vivienne, who misses the entire exchange, and try to find some hint of emotion toward me in her eyes. This shouldn't hurt. I shouldn't care that she acts like I'm nothing, that I don't belong here. But deep in my heart, in the shadows I've let frost over, there's a hint of something there. Something that tells me that the little girl who'd grown up with this woman for seven or so years is crying out with recognition and longing. I can't let myself feel it, though. I shouldn't. Yet it's there. Scratching its way out.

I *want* her to love me. To recognize me. Because a part of me I've long forgotten is trying to recognize her. I might not feel it, not fully, but the glimmer of it is there. Like a ghost limb. Even with the emptiness ringing between us, a part of me is scrabbling for recognition.

That's when I realize it: she's not the only one I wish would wake from this magical illusion. I want to feel this as well. I want whatever magic is binding my own memories to shatter with hers, for this to be a reunion. Rather than a very awkward dance where neither of us knows the right steps.

I sigh inside. That's not going to happen. I know it in my gut—this won't be as easy as I'd hoped. I try to think of cover stories, elaborate lies to explain why I'm here and why I have to stay in their lives until . . . until whatever is supposed to happen, happens. As the changeling leads us into the kitchen, I watch my mother's retreating back and remember what Mab said.

I might have to kill her to get this information out of her.

For the first time in my life, I might actually not be lying when I say that would hurt me more than it hurts her.

$$***$$

We spend the morning talking about trivial things. Or, they do. I lie through my teeth the entire time, telling them I am back here to visit family (at least it's partly true). Vivienne's husband—my father—is asleep the entire time. Apparently he works in a factory and didn't get home until three in the morning.

I want to scream at the two of them as they sit at the table over their mugs of coffee. They sit the same—the same slight hunch, the same rise of their shoulders, the same flicker of their eyes to the corners of the room when talking. The changeling has done her research. She's fit herself into this world, this life, without breaking a sweat. And I . . . I feel like I'm that one dancer in the chorus who just can't get her steps in sync. Everything I do feels clunky around them, wrong. I should be in the changeling's shoes—my traits should mirror my mother's, my habits ingrained from years of watching her interact with the world. Instead, it takes focus not to fuck up, not to give any tells that I was raised far from human, that every inch of me yearns to fit into this pattern that I was made for but not conditioned to. The pattern someone else fit into before me.

"So what do you do now?" she asks, sitting at the table with her black coffee and tired gaze. It's clear she's not used to being up this early. And also clear she doesn't enjoy it.

"I work for a few philanthropic organizations," I say, because—like Mab—I've never been able to resist the irony. "You know, general charity work. I just got back from some time in Uganda, feeding orphans."

"And yet you're still so pale," the changeling mutters.

"SPF eighty," I retort, and look back to my mother. "I love helping people. It makes living worthwhile."

Vivienne smiles. The hint of something glows inside me, as though I've said something that makes her pleased. Or proud. And I want to feel it again.

"I'd love to travel like that. Sadly, I just never seem to be able to leave the city. Something always manages to pull me back."

"You don't say. Well, maybe I can bring you along sometime. We're always looking for extra help."

Another smile, and I realize I actually mean it. *Pull yourself together. She's not going to join you on your escapades.* But I kind of wish she could.

"I doubt she'd enjoy falling into *your* line of work," the changeling says. "Seems rather dangerous, don't you think?"

I shrug. "Not if you stick with me. Besides, I'm sure Viv is more than ready to see the world. Something makes me think she'd do great on the road. You know, nomadic. Circus style."

I watch Vivienne's expression the entire time, but despite the small twitch of a smile at the word *circus*, she doesn't give any tell.

"That could be fun," she finally says. Her eyes flick to her imposter daughter, as if she's scared to be admitting this. Okay, maybe I'm projecting the *scared* part, but there's definitely some strange power dynamic going on. "But I don't know if I'm cut out for that sort of thing. I've never really been good with travel."

"I find that hard to believe. I'm sure somewhere, deep down, you've got the spark."

"Mom's busy," the changeling butts in. "She has to work overtime a lot, and it's hard for them to get replacements. No one is as good at her job as she is."

"Which is?" I ask, somewhat hoping it will be something really cool, like stuntwoman or even a damn marine biologist.

"I'm a substitute teacher at the elementary school."

Bang. It's like a fucking punch to the chest. Vivienne Warfield, savior of the faerie and mortal worlds, now working as a substitute teacher. Mab couldn't even swing it so Viv was tenured at a college or something?

It's so unfair, I want to punch something. Preferably Mab. Instead, I take a drink of my coffee and try to keep my eyes on the prize. I'm not here to make small talk or reconnect, even if a part of me really wants to. There's a little girl inside me screaming out for my mommy, begging for a hug or a handshake or a meaningful smile that says *it will all be all right*. I squash her down, along with all the other negative things in my life that are best forgotten. Like Roxie. And emotions in general.

"Well then," I say. "Sounds like you're a busy woman. Tell me, though. What do you dream of doing? You know, if you weren't working with kids?"

I expect a quick answer, an *I don't know* or some other ingrained BS. Instead, she looks into her mug for a long time.

"It's stupid," she finally says, and it sounds as if she's trying to convince herself.

"Try me."

If the changeling could kill me in front of Viv right now, I'm sure she would. She's glaring daggers. That's fine. I have dozens of daggers in my coat to throw right back.

"Well," Vivienne says, "I *have* always thought about taking dance classes. Maybe trapeze. It just seems so graceful and elegant, you know? Like magic."

"Like magic," I repeat. "Tell me more."

She shrugs, eyes once more flickering to the changeling. "I guess when you work every day, you start to wonder if there's something else. Something more glamorous. Not that I'm not grateful! It's just, you know . . . I wonder if there's another world out there I'll never touch." She laughs and shakes her head and looks at me. "But what am I saying? I'm way too old for dreams like that. I've got a loving husband and a great daughter. That's all I need."

The changeling beams at Viv. Then, when her mother isn't looking, she glares once more at me.

"What about you?" I ask her sweetly. "It's been so long since we worked together. What do *you* want to do next with your life?"

Again, that glare that could peel paint.

"I'm perfectly fine being close to home. You know that, Melody. Family has always been the most important thing in my life. Unlike you, I can't just leave everyone I care about behind."

Okay, I admit, the dig actually does get under my skin. I've never actually had a family to leave behind—*she* took them from me. And, as I look at Viv, I realize she's still doing everything to keep them at arm's length.

"I find that the ones I care about always come back to me," I say. "And those that cross me, I don't see again." I make sure to direct the first part to Viv, and the last part to her. If my mother notices the exchange, she doesn't say anything. She's already up and busying herself about the kitchen.

"I should probably start making breakfast," she says. "Before Austin wakes up."

I don't tell her I've already eaten, because I've decided that I will eat whatever she prepares, whenever she prepares it: it's not often I get a home-cooked meal. Come to think of it, this might actually be the first time someone else has physically cooked anything for me. Mab usually just had servants bring me dishes from the mortal world. Snap of her fingers sort of thing. I don't think the Faerie Queen has even seen a frying pan.

The changeling might not know why I'm here, but I can definitely tell she doesn't want me around. She'd want me around even less if she knew that my charge might involve killing the one she was hired to protect. But hey—take it up with our mutual employer. In any case, I don't let Vivienne's cooking stop me from prodding. If I'm going to find a way to her secret past, I need to dig. And that means I need her to start thinking about things she probably doesn't want to remember—and things the changeling *definitely* doesn't want aired.

I ask about her family. She says she hasn't heard from her parents in years.

I ask about vacations. The only ones she's taken were to visit the in-laws. Or trips to amusement parks in the changeling's early days that I'm not entirely convinced aren't made up.

I try to ask more about her circus dreams—has she seen any shows, has she taken a class, has she ever had actual dreams of any sort regarding the big top—but every time, the changeling steps in and changes the subject. It's maddening, but it's not the fact that the changeling's making this difficult.

It's the fact that Vivienne honestly seems okay with everything in her life. Maybe not happy, but okay with it.

The woman rummaging around before me should be a queen in her own right. She should be reigning in a castle with a host of servants ensuring she's happy. She literally saved the world. She's a hero. And she should have a hero's reward.

Instead, she's worrying about retirement and helping her deadbeat daughter pay off her college loans.

And here I am, hoping to get her to help Mab even more, when the bitch queen couldn't even give her a consolation prize.

I'm your fucking consolation prize. A daughter you don't remember, a relationship you can't feel. Or maybe this is my consolation prize from

Mab, for bringing the Pale Queen into the world. It wouldn't be the first time her reward was more like a punishment. And it doesn't matter—the effect is the same. I feel like shit. Both for trying to get her to do more for Mab, and for being a shitty excuse for a daughter.

Convince her your love is enough to die for, Mab had told Kingston. Was it? Was the love between my mother and Kingston enough to warrant this? A boring life with a boring family and a really boring kid? When she could be . . . what, with me? Trying to save the world? I can almost imagine it—a mother/daughter duo, two kick-ass assassins in kick-ass leather bombers with a host of weapons and countless enemies. We'd probably have secret hand signals and crazy combo moves that were part ninja, part acrobat, and one hundred percent awesome. We'd be unstoppable. We'd stomp into bars just to start shit and then make out with half the clientele before the night was through.

But that's just the image of my mother I've been harboring. Someone like me—witty and strong and fierce as fuck. When I look at Vivienne . . . it's clear she's not made for that sort of adrenaline. Not anymore. She's soft, and there's something in her demeanor that tells me she'd be the kind of woman to hand over her purse and social security number before throwing a punch at her burned-out teenage mugger. If it were her and me on a night on the town, it would probably involve a chain Italian restaurant and bland sangrias. Maybe a movie. Probably an early night in.

If we were together, my life would probably be a whole hell of a lot different than it is now. Vivienne might have been a badass years ago. But the rules of her contract have turned her into the exact opposite.

And then it hits me. I look around at the kitchen and its kitschy shit and the family photos. This could be my life, when it's all over. Mab could force me back to the human world with no memories and no future, and I would have no say in any of that. I wouldn't even know it had happened. Hell, I might have agreed to this sort of parting gift when I signed the damned contract. *Never sign a faerie contract.*

That had been my motto. Because it always led to something like *this*. Vivienne's humming to herself, and another pot of coffee is brewing, and in that moment, I can't tell if I feel at home or like an alien on some foreign shore. The entire time, I can only think *this should have been my life, this should have been my life.*

The question, though, is whether I would have wanted it.

Fuck that. She's not exiling me here, not if I have anything to say about it. Which I probably don't.

As I watch Vivienne scramble eggs and make toast and chop vegetables, I'm struck with images of my own upbringing: Mab, teaching me how to pull magic from the ether and make my stuffed animals dance; Pan, guiding me through the castle on late-night expeditions for treats I know he hid just for me to find; William, showing me how to craft rings from silver and imbue stone with memory. And sure, those memories are tainted with blood. My first kill at ten years old, stalking a rogue Shifter through the streets of Tokyo while dressed as a Harajuku girl. The countless training sessions in magic and weaponry and hand-to-hand combat. The long nights alone, and the many nights coiled amongst the naked denizens of Faerie when my body had aged and my heart had hardened.

Would I have really given all that up for this? For quiet mornings and the scent of toast and the promise of . . . watching television for a few hours or going to Pilates or whatever these women do to keep their minds off the slow march toward death?

And holy shit, what am I even thinking? What am I feeling? This spite toward her. Not because she doesn't recognize me, but because . . . because in this room, in this moment, I feel like I'm the only one who's actually alive, and no amount of screaming will ever get her to wake up from her comatose dream. My entertainment is drifting between worlds and cities, stalking prey and getting shitfaced, and playing with demons and dangerous magic. I have access to every nightclub in every hot spot in the world—and in Faerie. My cardio involves getting sweaty with satyrs or running down dragons in the Alps. Every day is a game of survival. Every night a victory dance. Even lately, after the disaster with Roxie and the Pale Queen, I feel more alive being a failure than I would playing out the role of Average Mortal Girl.

The fact that I don't just think that but *feel* it in the very depths of my gut makes me feel even more distanced from the woman playing chef before me.

Maybe I'm no better than the creature who raised me after all. I don't fit in here. I'm not built to be a mortal. I'm made to kill, to screw, to party. And I'm fooling myself if I try to convince myself otherwise.

Suddenly, I want this job over with more than I've ever wanted anything in my whole life. Not because I'm scared of what I might have to do to get Vivienne to remember her powers, but because—next to her—it's become glaringly obvious that I have become nothing more than a monster. I'm less her daughter than the faerie stealing my name. Even if I tried, I could never be the girl she would want me to be. Even if I wanted it—and, I'm starting to realize, I *do* want it—I couldn't fit into her life, or she into mine. Ever.

Stop being weak, I hiss to myself as Vivienne and the changeling chat. *Don't think of her as your mother. Think of her as a target. Mab is the woman who raised you. Mab is the woman who made you who you are. And Mab may not be a mortal, but she's the closest thing you have to a family. This is merely the woman who birthed you. She was a vessel. Nothing more.*

Gods, I wish that line of reasoning didn't make me feel like shit.

I also wish I could bring myself to fully believe it.

The changeling is halfway through telling Vivienne about her job search when the stairs creak again. I look over and am greeted by the sight of a man I'm honestly a bit impressed my mother was able to bag. I mean, I know she'd scored with Kingston, but this guy's a fox. A silver fox, too, which is probably not something I should think about my biological father.

He strides into the kitchen with bleary eyes and similar pj's to Viv's, which makes me wonder if they were some joint Christmas present from their undeserving daughter. Like Vivienne, he's in his early fifties, and his hair is more grey than dark brown. He sort of looks like a model for a European clothing company, even if he is unkempt and clearly running himself into the ground.

My father. This guy is my father. I can see it in the angles of his face and the way he holds his head up, the curves of his eyes and the curl of his fingers.

He seems to catch on to the fact that I'm in the room five seconds after stepping into the kitchen. He actually does a double take, then reaches for the mug of coffee that Vivienne's already poured for him.

"And you are?" he asks. Not at all as pleasantly as Vivienne, but not as rude as the changeling. At least I know where I get my attitude problem.

"Melody," I reply, and is it my imagination or does he actually look a little surprised by that? "Claire's friend."

And your real fucking daughter.

Even though the words itch at the back of my throat, I don't think I could convince these two short of a DNA test. Not that it would help; I can tell the magic that's looped through their brains is tight.

He reaches out and takes my hand, and maybe it's my imagination, but his grip seems to linger.

"I'm Austin," he replies. "None of that Mr. Weaver shit. Pleasure to meet you."

He lets go and turns to his wife, who smiles at him and gives him a quick peck on the cheek. "Morning, sunshine," he whispers, and her smile widens—it's the first smile I've seen that doesn't look forced. Then he turns to the changeling and says, "And good morning, sweetheart," and she smiles and returns the greeting, and I want to vomit.

Because there's something so picturesque about this, so scripted and perfect, that I can't believe any of this is real. The greeting, the matching clothes, the ready cup of coffee. It's way too normal. It stinks of glamour and deceit, even if no one else can feel it. Both Vivienne and Austin are playing roles that I don't think they're aware of, and the changeling is directing it all with a hidden hand.

I look to her. She said she had it under control. Is that what she meant? Keeping the two of them so high on magic that they don't even realize they're living a daytime TV show? I wonder if she gets off on it, making these mortals dance like that. Faeries love screwing over humans, and what better opportunity than this? No wonder she looked so angry at my arrival; I was cutting in on her fun. And most likely signaling its end.

Sorry, bitch. But you're out of a job. Back to tying knots in virgins' hair for old times' sake.

Austin leans back on the counter and nurses his coffee.

"Melody, eh?" he continues, his eyes intent on me. Like he's searching for something. Or found it. "Kind of a unique name. That a stage name or something?"

I glance to Vivienne, who's still oblivious as she butters the toast, and then to the changeling, who's once more glaring daggers at me. Then I look back to Austin, his expression this strange mix of begging and guarded, as though he wants me to press a subject we all know I can't broach. I open my mouth to mention that *yes, I once toured briefly with a troupe, the Cirque des Immortels—have you heard of it?*

"Breakfast smells amazing," the changeling intervenes, trying to change the subject. "You sure have outdone yourself, Mom."

I want to gag. Vivienne turns around and beams at her false daughter. Then she catches sight of me, and the smile fades. Which does nothing for my self-esteem. I can't tell if it's because she's unhappy I'm here or because I'm asking questions that no one has been allowed to voice in here before. I'm off script, if we're continuing that actor thing. And she's clearly not happy about having to improvise. Austin seems to be watching the whole thing with interest, and is it just my imagination, or does he look at the changeling with a hint of anger? As if he wanted to hear my answer. As if he alone out of all of them liked my disruption of their routine. Even if he didn't like being awake so early.

What do these people really know? And what do I have to do to force out the truth?

Before I can ask, the changeling goes white. Like, ghostly white. Like someone stepped over her grave white. Her eyes widen. Then she looks at me.

"What the hell have you done?" she whispers.

"Claire, language," Vivienne begins, but before either my mother or I can ask what the girl's talking about, there's a knock at the door.

"Jesus, what are we, a train station?" my dad asks. He pushes himself from the counter and walks toward the door.

The changeling is there before he gets two feet.

"No, don't worry about it. I got it."

She casts me a look. One that clearly says *get your ass over here, now.* I drain the last of my coffee and hand Austin the empty mug as I walk past him. "It's not a stage name, but I got it from a performer my mom loved," I whisper, but then the changeling has my arm and she's dragging me down the hall.

"What gives?" I hiss.

"Who the hell did you bring with you?"

I don't have time to answer. There's another thud on the door, this one louder, and I go silent as the entire door shudders on its hinges. Impressive. Whoever it is, they're going for *intimidating.*

For the first time all morning, I'm actually feeling a little excited.

"Who knows you're here?" the changeling asks.

"No one," I reply as the doorknob rattles. "Just Mab."

She curses under her breath, something in the faerie tongue that I've only heard from the lowest of the low. I'm impressed she knows it and suddenly wonder where Mab found her in the first place. Maybe this girl was doing more than knotting virgin locks . . .

Another thud, and this time I hear Austin in the back calling out "Who the fuck is it?" but we don't answer. I shove past the changeling with blood pounding in my ears and a knife in my hand. And a very big smile on my face.

"How enchanted is this place?" I ask, my hand on the knob.

"Very," she replies. "No Fey or Shifter can get in without permission. But they shouldn't have been able to get past the sidewalk."

"Perfect," I mutter. And it is; even after last night, I still have the taste for blood in the back of my throat. The changeling glances at me. She actually looks frightened and—judging from the look she gives me—my manic smile isn't consoling her. "Well then, looks like we'll have our party on the lawn. Stay back. I'd hate for you to get hurt."

Then I kick the door off the hinges and jump out into the bloody dawn.

Five

The lawn looks like something out of a postapocalyptic motorcycle movie. I mean, seriously—four guys on bikes making doughnuts in the front yard while whoever was brave enough to knock twitches underneath the fallen door. It's as if they're trying to make an impression, which is stupid, since that means they clearly don't know who they're dealing with.

But I do. I take a deep breath as I walk forward—making sure to stomp down hard on the fallen guy's face, which is greeted by a very satisfying cracking noise—and can tell these guys are from Summer. Oberon's kingdom has a very distinct taste: the magic infused in these guys reminds me of lightning and cut grass, something wild and verdant and dangerous. Which is funny, because I never imagined anyone from Summer belonging to a biker gang.

At least now I know what Mab meant about Vivienne needing protection from someone. If not *why*.

I don't question what they're doing here—this is clearly an act of aggression, which means I'm clearly in the right to counterattack. Not that I would actually give a shit if I *wasn't* in the right to attack; maim first, question later, as I always say. Before I even hop off the door, I fling two knives toward two of the bikers. The daggers hit true, and the leather-clad guys explode in a flurry of leaves and sparks before they even register surprise. I'm actually disappointed at how easy it was.

The other bikers are a little faster.

Vines shoot up from the lawn and wrap around my wrists and ankles, binding me fast. I struggle and curse under my breath, but I can't get free, can't grab any of the daggers hidden throughout my clothes. But Mab didn't teach me the lesser magics for nothing, and I didn't endure hours of painful tattoos just for aesthetics.

I send a jolt of energy down my spine, visualizing the newest runes and glyphs tattooed there, and power blooms from my palms as the remaining motorcyclists bear down on me. Fire burns the vines to ash, but the power isn't without a price—sweat and chills break over my skin as I crouch down and grab two more blades from my boots. Another flick of the wrists, and one Fey goes down as the other casts some sort of barrier around himself, the blade bouncing harmlessly to the side.

This guy is fast, and he's on top of me before I can grab another weapon, barreling me to the side. I try to roll from under him, but he's heavy as a boulder and I know it's more than meat—there's magic coursing through his veins, and if not for the runes and wards on my skin and jewelry, I'd have been crushed or blown apart from the power. He somehow readjusts, fluid as a serpent, and his knees are locking my arms to the ground and one hand is on my neck. I can't move. Can barely breathe. And for a split second, I wonder if maybe I'm in over my head. The masochism of it actually gets me more excited. I don't just want to hurt, I want to *be* hurt.

"It's a shame we have to kill you," he says as his other hand traces symbols in the air. I know a few of them. Banishment runes. He's not just going to kill me. He's going to send me to the lowest regions of the netherworld. If I weren't moderately worried for my life, I'd actually be impressed. Guy's got skill. Even if he does have a rather unfortunate green buzz cut.

But before I can twist or send a rush of power through the runes on my spine—this time for electrocution, or paralysis, or something more painful—there's a crash, and the guy topples to the side. I roll onto my knees and grab a knife and thrust it between his ribs before he can take another breath. Without the slightest gasp, he explodes in a flurry of willow leaves.

"I had that," I say coldly, standing and staring down the changeling girl. She glares at me, and it's then I realize she isn't holding a weapon—I honestly expected her to run out with a frying pan or something. Girl can fight with her bare hands; good to know. She's starting to look like she regrets saving me.

"No," she says, turning back to the kitchen, "you didn't."

I sigh and look around at the remains of the carnage. The bikes are already dissolving into the earth, nothing more than clods of dirt and grass held together with glamour. So much for having a sick ride after all my troubles. Then I look to the open doorway, and the faerie still unconscious beneath the door. I walk over to him, throw the door behind me, and kneel down hard on his gut. He grunts awake. I still slap the side of his face to get his attention. At least, that's why I tell myself I do it.

"Assassin," he snarls.

I smile.

"Obviously. Now, to business. Why the hell did Oberon send you here?"

Now it's his turn to smile, which looks rather demented with his teeth covered in viscous lime blood. Like his compatriots, his hair is green and shaved close, though this guy has tattoos swirled over his face. Almost tribal, but not as douchey—these are magicked for sure.

"We are here to thank you, assassin," he says.

"Thank me? For killing your friends? You shouldn't have."

"For showing us the way." His eyes dart to the door. "We have been waiting for the Oracle's appearance, and now, you have led us to her. The bitch is ours now."

I have a dagger to his throat before I can stop myself.

"That's my mother you're talking about," I say. I keep my words devoid of anger; I find it's more effective when dealing with a hostage. Makes them scared. "Why are you after her?"

"She belongs to Oberon," he says. "And now that we've found her, he won't stop until she's his." He laughs, or coughs, and a spray of green blood flecks my face. "Nowhere is safe, assassin. You can't hide her any longer."

Then, before I can slit his vile throat, he wraps a net of glamour over himself and dissolves into the grass, sinking back into the world of Faerie.

I look from the open door to the torn-up lawn and the street beyond, everything still sleepy and silent despite the fight. No one here knows what happened, and I don't know if that's usual faerie glamour at play or some defense set up by the changeling. I only know that defense is no longer enough to keep my mother safe.

So much for today being a simple meet and greet.

I wipe the blood off my face with the back of my hand and step inside, trying to figure out how to tell my family that it's time for them to leave home.

***

"You're not taking them," the changeling hisses.

We're up in her bedroom, and the place is just as stark as I would have imagined a faerie trapped in the mortal world would have it. A few posters on the robin's-egg walls, a few knickknacks on the dresser. But these are all slightly out of sync with the facade she's trying to uphold. The posters are all motivational BS you'd see in office buildings and schools—cats on branches and cyclists reaching a summit at sunset, with little quotes underneath. The decorations are kitschy ceramics that don't quite fit together, mismatched salt and pepper shakers, a nutcracker missing its hat, a hippo bank in a tutu. Clearly, the girl didn't do much research in this regard. And clearly it hasn't mattered for her cover.

"I'd love to see you try and stop me," I reply. I pick over the objects in her room with disinterest, my back turned to her to show that I'm not at all worried about my guard being down in her presence. I almost want her to try to stop me; I feel guilty for blowing my mother's cover, and that's not a sensation I'm okay sitting with. *Why the hell would Oberon want her? Especially since she's no use to anyone right now?*

I look back and see the girl leaning against her desk; her fingers dig into the wood, bringing up small splinters.

"I have kept her safe for nearly twenty years," she growls. "While you have been away, I have been stuck here, ensuring no harm befell her. Just as Mab ordered. And now you come here and bring hell down upon this house, and you think I will just let her leave with you?"

"Mab's orders."

"Then Mab can get her herself." The girl's eyes narrow. "I don't trust you. Not with her life. Not with either of their lives."

"She'll be safer in Winter than—"

"She cannot go to Winter!" She shoves away from the desk and stalks over to me, and it's then that her glamour starts to wear off. I can see the faerie underneath, and I'm pretty certain she's some sort of dryad, what with the coarse skin and vines twined through her hair. She grabs my arm and forces me to look in her eyes. "Don't you see? If she could have been held there, she would have been. The magic . . . the magic that took her memory is powerful, but there are holes. If she returns to Winter, she will start to remember. And if that happens, it will be too much for her. She'll die."

That's precisely what I need to happen, I want to say. But I've learned many things being an assassin, and being secretive is one of the most important. The less the changeling knows of my purpose here, the less chance she has of stabbing me in the back.

"What do you care?" I ask instead. "After all, you're just her warden. You should be relieved—I'm here to take her off your hands. Consider yourself free to do whatever the fuck you want."

She bites her lip, and the glamour slams back into place. She looks like a lost girl, for a second.

"She has grown on me," she says, then looks to the wall. "Besides, it is against Vivienne's contract: she is unable to enter the Winter Kingdom, under any circumstance. Mab couldn't risk Vivienne's magic unraveling within her own walls. The safest option for everyone was to hide her somewhere else, somewhere isolated and protected—both from her own powers, and from those who would seek them. And if she leaves here, if she goes anywhere with even a hint of magic, the powers keeping her safe will unravel. I refuse to let her die." Her shoulders square, and she looks back at me with a newfound vigor. "I refuse to let the last eighteen years of my life be for nothing. You will not undo my hard work with your ignorance."

"We can't keep her here," I reply. I'm not even going to touch on how I feel about that *last eighteen years* shit. "Not if Oberon's on her trail. He's already broken through your defenses."

"Thanks to you."

I let her comment slide. "Which means we need to find someplace safe."

"But *why?*" she asks. "Why now? What the hell do you need her for? Hasn't she already done enough for Winter?"

I open my mouth, but I can't bring myself to speak. Because she raises a damn good point: Vivienne is my mother, not this faerie bitch's. And yet she's the one trying to look out for Vivienne's well-being. I'm just, what? Playing to Mab's whims again. Hoping to use my mother like Mab used her. Which is worse in this case, since I'm technically bound to Vivienne by blood.

"I don't have a choice," I finally admit. "Mab needs her. *We* need her. I don't know why, and I don't know what I'm supposed to tell you. And no, I'm not asking for your permission or understanding here. I have to keep her safe until . . . until she's useful. And if she can't go to Winter, I'll take her to the next best thing. We're going to the circus."

I'd briefly considered taking her to the Wildness. Oberon might not be able to find us there, but the unclaimed Fey that live within don't take kindly to outsiders. Especially those from Winter. Safe from Oberon, sure, but I couldn't risk Vivienne getting stabbed in the back by a rogue pixie. I needed someplace where she'd be safe from all outside Fey. And a circus where everyone is powerful and immortal and allied to Mab is about as close to that as I could get.

She looks at me for a long moment, her eyes sharp and quizzical. She doesn't look happy.

"This will kill her," she finally replies. "Your own mother. You will kill her if you go through with this. You realize that, right?"

I swallow down the bile and push past her, taking this as her admission of defeat.

"She's not my mother," I say, keeping my voice flat, even though saying it is like a dagger to my heart. It hurts because I know it's true. "You made sure of that."

***

"We're leaving," I say the moment I'm back in the kitchen.

"Who was out there, dear?" Vivienne asks. But she's not asking me. She's looking at the changeling with a completely placid expression. I'm wondering if she or Austin even heard the fight, or if their magic-addled brains just think it was some early Jehovah's Witness or something. If she heard my statement, she doesn't acknowledge it.

"Wrong address," the changeling replies. I roll my eyes. It's the dumbest thing I've ever heard, but Viv and Austin seem to take it in stride. At least I think that until I look at my father. He may be nodding, but his eyes don't leave me.

"What do you mean, *leaving*?" he asks.

"Did you miss all of what happened out there?" I ask, gesturing to the broken-down door. "You guys are in danger."

"There's no danger," says Vivienne. I actually stand there with my mouth agape. That's a line fed directly from the changeling if I've ever heard one. "This is home. There's no danger when you're at home."

"Mom is right," the changeling says. Her expression is smooth, but I catch the glint of vehemence in her eyes when she looks at me. "There's nothing out there. But . . ."

"But?" I ask, fully ready to beat this bitch to a pulp if she dares try to keep them here. Vivienne is *mine*. My charge, I mean.

"But it would be good to go for a little vacation, don't you think?"

Austin's eyes narrow. I like this guy. His mind may be mush from all the magic used against him, but he's like one of those old guys with dementia—when clarity kicks in, it's sharp and to the throat.

"Where would we go? We haven't gone anywhere besides Grandma and Grandpa's for years. And—no offense—I don't think they'd enjoy having extra company." He looks pointedly at me while he says this.

"No offense taken," I say. I grin. I definitely know where I got my wit. "I was thinking we could go to the cir—"

"We're still figuring that out," the changeling interrupts. She actually swats my shoulder when she says it. *Try that again, bitch, and you'll be missing an arm—at least.* "But Melody's family has a time-share down south. I thought maybe we could stay there a few days."

She doesn't specify my pretend time-share, and I'm suddenly acutely aware that I'm not certain where in America I even *am*; all of suburbia looks pretty much the same.

"Don't worry," she continues. I notice the subtle wave of her fingers at her side. Magic doesn't require movement, but sometimes the motions help. "We took this week off for a vacation anyway, remember? We just thought we'd have it here at home. All we need to do is pack."

I glance at her, because that's seriously the dumbest thing I've ever heard. My parents, however, swallow it up like Communion.

"Okay then," Vivienne says. The ghost of a smile plays on her lips. "Looks like we should go and pack, hon. Isn't it exciting? A real vacation!"

I want to vomit.

Partly because she considers a trip with her housebound daughter and a stranger to be a vacation, and partly because this is far from a friendly trip.

I give them some time to pack their things, heading to the front porch, coffee and breakfast in hand. Turns out Mom is a good cook. The thought sends a pang through me, but I force it down. No, I'm not going to think about all the mornings she could have cooked for me. I'm not going to try to remember any breakfasts like this. I'm positive I don't remember anything from my early childhood because Mab erased my memory. A part of me wonders if Kingston or some other witch could undo it. The rest of me doesn't want to open that door.

"Melody, eh?"

I turn around to Austin's voice. He's standing there in the doorway, and if he registers that the door is currently lying in the churned-up yard, he doesn't show it. His eyes don't leave me, and I won't lie, it's a little creepy, this dynamic. Him looking at me the way most guys look at me. Especially since he seems to know more than he's letting on. That's the worst part about memory magic—everything becomes a minefield.

"That's my name," I say. He steps over and sits beside me. A little too closely.

"I knew another Melody, I think," he muses over his coffee. His eyes take on a distant look as he stares out at the lawn. Again, no sign that there's anything amiss beyond a bit of nostalgia. "Ages ago. But I can't quite remember her. Definitely wasn't you, though."

He looks over to me quickly, before looking back to the world.

"You look familiar," he says.

"So do you. But I hear I have one of those familiar faces. Lots of people said Claire and I could be sisters."

"I don't think that's it," he says. Again, the look that asks more questions than his words. "Where are we going?"

You're not going anywhere, I want to say. Because as far as I'm concerned, this guy is just getting in the way. It feels like he knows too much, and that might be dangerous. I need my mother's powers. Not someone asking too many questions about my past. Not until he becomes useful.

I really am no better than Mab.

Before I have to figure out an answer, the changeling comes out and sits down beside us.

"Are you bothering Melody, Dad?"

She says it jokingly, but I can tell from the look in her eyes that she, like me, isn't comfortable with his prying. Maybe everyone's been so focused on keeping Viv in the dark that Austin's been able to keep a few memories.

"Nah," he says, immediately slipping from conspiratorial tones to Cool Dad crap. "Was just asking where we are going. I mean, I figure Melody's got some great connections. She seems like she'd have friends in strange places."

I exchange another look with the changeling.

"I don't know if you should be coming along, Dad," she says.

"What? Why wouldn't I come along?"

She sighs.

Then she places a hand on his shoulder, leans in, and whispers something in his ear. I don't catch the words, but I do catch the way his eyes glaze over.

"You better go back to bed, Dad," she says. "Stay there for a few days. We're going on vacation and don't know when or if we'll be back. And you won't care either way."

He nods and stands, turning back to the hallway without even looking at me.

"The hell was that?" I ask when he disappears up the stairs.

"Memory magic."

"I didn't feel anything."

"It's a trigger phrase," she says, looking at me. "They both have one. Makes them fully believe whatever I tell them."

"What is it?"

"Like I'd tell you," she says. She looks back up the stairs. "I hate using it. It doesn't seem right."

"You've gone soft," I say. "Too much time in the mortal world?"

"Rich. I could say the same, but reversed." She pauses. "Why are you doing this?"

"Because Mab ordered it."

"But why? I have spent so long protecting her. You know what will happen if she visits the circus. The magic holding her memories together will begin to unravel—there are too many triggers there. She can't know about her past."

I shrug, grab a dagger, and begin scratching symbols in the porch step. Nothing particularly powerful, but it keeps my antsy fingers busy and gives my mind something to focus on.

"All this time, wasted," she mutters, fully sounding like a spoiled little brat.

I glance at her. Yes, it sucks that her entire mission has been to keep Viv safe. But hey, missions change.

"She'll be fine," I say. I lower my voice. "She's my mother. I'm not going to let her get hurt."

"You mortals. You lie without even knowing it. If you take her to the circus, if her memories come back . . . it will kill her. That is why I have guarded her so many years. It wasn't just to keep Oberon off her trail. It was to keep her from dying. I was Mab's final gift."

"And what a gift this is," I say as sarcastically as possible, gesturing to the house. "A shitty cardboard cutout house and a daughter that doesn't really love them. Their life is straight from the TV shows you've been watching. Hell, I wouldn't be surprised if you fully scripted them. And hey, why is Oberon after her anyway?"

She shrugs and looks away. "That information is not mine to tell."

"Then I'll be sure to bring it up with Oberon next time I see him, since Mab has her hands full." Internally, I remind myself that I *should* go meet with the Summer King. See if he knows anything about the Pale Queen. But mostly just to see what the hell he wants with my mother.

"I hope you're prepared to live with the repercussions of this," the changeling whispers.

"Always am," I say.

She stands and walks inside, leaving me wondering if I'm actually ready to live with myself for what I may have to do.

Six

When I head back inside, the changeling is in jeans and a T-shirt, and Vivienne is in much the same. I can't help but pause when I step into the kitchen and see them standing there, doing dishes in silence together. The way Vivienne hands her presumed daughter a dish without speaking, and the changeling takes it and dries it and puts it away, as if they're cogs in a machine, as if they've been doing this for years. It sends a pang through my chest, and suddenly I'm reminded of Roxie, in the kitchen while I cooked her breakfast. Before I knew she was a traitor. When I still thought she was a future I could work toward, an example of what it meant to be human. But when I watch these two, I realize that I have no idea how to be human, how to fit into someone else's life so seamlessly.

I was raised to be an outsider. And I don't know if that's a conditioning I'll ever be able to overturn.

I set the coffee mug on the table loudly, which makes Vivienne flinch and look back. The changeling doesn't register shock—I've no doubt she felt me walk in.

"About ready to go?" I ask.

Vivienne looks to me, then to the duffel bag on the counter. "I think so," she says. "How long will we be gone?"

"A few days," I lie, because I have no clue how long this will take. Or if Vivienne will even return.

Vivienne walks over, and I try to find something in her features I recognize, something that calls out and tells me she is my mother. Sure, we look similar—same cheekbones, same eyebrows—but that's where the similarity ends. She is meek, modest, and I have no clue how much of that is nature or magic.

"Are you okay?" she asks. "You look troubled."

She reaches out, takes my hand.

And I feel it. Something inside me melts, or shifts, and suddenly I remember this—the scent of lavender air fresheners and coffee, the warmth of her touch. *Are you okay, sweetie?* she asks while I sob, curled on the floor, because I swear my doll was talking to me, saying it was going to take me away.

I shake my head, force the vision or memory down. I hate to admit that there are tears forming in the corners of my eyes.

Now isn't the time to remember what it was like to have a real mother. Not when I have to use her.

You are a weapon, Claire, I remind myself. *And this woman is just another tool you must use. You can be weak when you're dead.*

"I'm fine," I say. "We should go." I give the changeling a look, one that's challenging her to say something about what I know she felt.

I turn and head toward the hallway. The changeling is right behind me.

"I won't let you take her there."

I pause. My fingers twitch toward a dagger: I don't just want to end this bitch, I want to make her *hurt.*

"Excuse me?" I whisper. I pitch my voice low, layering it in ice like Mab's. I can tell from the expression that crosses her face as I glare at her that it works.

"I'm not letting you take her." She crosses her arms over her chest in what I'm sure she thinks is an intimidating gesture.

"Are you going to stop me?" I ask. "You know that's stupid. Not only would it be treason against your queen, but you'd also be directly challenging me. If you haven't heard, I'm not exactly a pushover."

"Who are you to discuss loyalty?" she asks. She looks back to the kitchen. "This is your *mother*, Claire. Surely you have some love for her."

"Rich, coming from a faerie. You don't know what love even means."

"But I do know loyalty," she says. "I may not feel human emotion, but I understand it. I've watched it and coaxed it for nearly two decades. While you were in Winter, fighting whatever, I was here. Making sure *your* parents felt loved. Complete. And now you're here to shatter them. What sort of daughter are you?"

My fist connects with a photo on the wall before I realize I've moved. Glass shatters and digs into my knuckles. A second later, I notice it's a family photo. Something beachy.

"Don't talk to me about family," I hiss. I take a deep breath, force my pulse back to steady. Rage simmers inside me, coating everything red. No. Emotion makes you weak—even anger. Another deep breath. I won't show weakness in front of her. "You've taken away everything. *Everything.* So don't even try to talk to me about loyalty. I'm doing this for Mab. Who is—despite what you seem to think—more a mother to me than that woman in there ever was. *She* gave me up. Mab took me in. How am I supposed to feel any empathy for her when she didn't want me in the first place?"

Which is a lie, of course, because even if I shouldn't feel emotion toward Vivienne, I do.

Her mouth opens. But for the first time, the changeling doesn't speak her mind. She pauses. Looks at the picture and the glass glittering on the floor.

"You think that's what happened?"

"I *know* that's what happened. Faeries can't make mortals do anything they don't truly want to do. Mab didn't steal me away. Vivienne had to give me up."

No one's told me this outright, but I know enough about faerie contracts to know it's true. Or, at least, think it's true. The look the changeling gives me is starting to make me question this.

"Perhaps you should ask this to the queen you follow so blindly," she whispers.

I'm on her in an instant. After that little rumble on the front lawn, I know she's packing a punch. I don't care. My forearm is against her neck, and I'm pressing her against the wall.

"Give me one good reason," I whisper into her ear. "Hell, give me one *bad* reason. And I will kill you without blinking an eye. Mab wouldn't even care, not if she knew that you tried to defy me."

"This will kill her," she gasps. "Your own mother. Why don't you see that?"

"My mother is the Winter Queen," I say stoically. I make sure to look into her eyes as I say it. "And I serve her faithfully."

"Even if she's the one who forced Vivienne to give you up?"

"You're lying."

"You know I can't."

No. Vivienne abandoned me. Sold me to the faeries. That's the story I'd told myself ever since I was a little girl—it's how I stayed strong. It's what fueled me. I wasn't good enough. I wasn't wanted. It was the crux of my whole existence. But if Mab was hiding the truth . . .

Pain lances through my head at the thought, making me wince and draw back. I nearly drop to my knees. But the moment the flash of questioning goes, so, too, does the ache.

Looks like Mab wasn't kidding about my contract forbidding questioning.

I glare at the girl, who rubs her neck even as the glamour takes the bruise away.

"We're going," I say. "Now. Unless you would prefer that Vivienne goes alone, because her *daughter* had to leave last minute. Permanently."

She looks at me, as if maybe she wants to prod further, demand I rethink this plan. But she's smart. She knows I'm serious. Instead, she turns around and goes to get my mother. I reach into my pocket and pull out the chalk.

We have a show to get to, and I have a magician to torture.

***

We stand in an open field, staring out at rows of corn and a sky that seems to slump toward the ground. The clouds are thick and heavy and grey, and as I stare at them, I can't help but feel as though something's off. It's late summer, and yet there's a chill that doesn't fit the Midwestern landscape. I sniff the air, but there isn't any magic at play. Just global warming or whatever.

I glance at my mother, who's looking at it all with a dumb sort of glaze over her eyes. Does she even know what just happened? That we literally used magic to travel hundreds of miles instantaneously? My heart clenches, and it takes a moment to realize it's not for her innocence—it's for me. I want her to tell me *good job* or at least verbally recognize that I did something extraordinary. I know it's stupid, but it must be ingrained: I want her to tell me I'm impressive, that she's proud. That I'm worth paying attention to. But she just stands there and looks out at the field as if it's the most normal, boring thing in the world.

Damn Mab and her magic. Damn her and my fucked-up childhood.

"This doesn't look like a circus," the changeling says. I shake my head and walk away, around the semitruck our portal linked to.

Viv and the changeling follow.

I don't know why I keep letting my hopes get the better of me. I expect Vivienne to say something, make a noise of excitement when she sees the sprawl of the circus before her. But she is silent, still in her dazed stupor, and I look at it all with a detached sort of dejection. At least the weather mirrors my mood.

The Cirque des Immortels spreads before us, a collection of tents and trailers and booths, all crowned by the massive tent in the middle, the black-and-violet *chapiteau*. Fencing encircles the enclave, a great archway with "CIRQUE DES IMMORTELS" in dimmed neon stretched over the dirt path leading in. It's early afternoon, and the circus grounds are alive with performers practicing and vendors stocking their booths with giant puffs of cotton candy and popcorn boxes. This is where Mab harvests most of her Dream. This is the axis on which the health of her entire kingdom turns.

And to anyone else, it just looks like another dusty show.

I stride forward, not looking to see if my entourage is following. It's not until I'm past the archway that I realize they aren't.

I pause and look back. The two of them stand just beyond the entrance. Vivienne stares up at it, her mouth slightly open. The changeling's hand is tight in hers.

"We cannot bring her in here," the changeling says.

"What . . . what . . . ?" Vivienne mumbles.

"Fuck," I reply, and walk toward them. If I have to drag the woman's ass in here, I will. I need her memories to unravel, but I need to actually be prepared for it. And for that, I need—

"What the hell is she doing here?"

I freeze. Kingston's voice sends memories coursing through my veins—his breath on my neck, his hands on my hips, my mother's name on his lips after we fucked. Rage and desire battle within, and I do what I can to let the rage win out.

I turn and stare down the magician. And oh, how I want to make him hurt.

He stands there in loose jeans and a looser V-neck, his long hair pulled back in a bun and his eyes shadowed with sleeplessness. He looks like a rock star, one used to late nights partying and more drugs than his body can afford. And in spite of everything, I still can't help but find that washed-out persona incredibly appealing.

Something about train wrecks. I just don't want to avoid them.

He's not alone, either. The Melody whose name I'm stealing stands beside him, looking just as unhappy to see me as he is. We had a heart-to-heart last time I saw her. Now, with her fists balled at her sides and her eyes tight, I have a feeling the only thing heartfelt she wants to do right now is scream at me.

Kingston's coffee-colored eyes glare as sharply as Mab's ever have. If I were the type of girl to back down from a stare, I would. Instead, I just stand up straighter and return the look.

"What is she doing here, Claire?"

"Claire?" Vivienne asks, suddenly snapped from her stupor. She looks from the changeling to me. "I thought . . ."

"Shut up," I snap. I put a hand to my head; I can feel the edge of a headache coming on. I'm so tired of putting up with this shit, and I haven't had nearly enough coffee to cope.

"Answer the question," Kingston demands.

"She needs protection," I reply. "Her cover is blown. Oberon's after her, and this is the only place she's safe."

He shakes his head. Maybe he reads the lie within my words, but he doesn't say it. I'm certain he would never agree to let her in if he knew why I brought her. If he knew what I had to do to her. And what I needed him to help me do to her.

I didn't bring them here just because the circus is safe from Oberon, but also because I need Kingston to undo his magic. That might take time. I can't keep her on the run from Oberon, and Oberon can't set foot in here. This was the closest I could come to giving Vivienne a safe place to, well, unravel. Kingston just needs to help me pull the threads.

Then the memory of the cavern filters back. Maybe he wouldn't be opposed to making her powers return. He lied to her for Mab before. I'm sure he could hurt her again without blinking, no matter how many crocodile tears he's shed around me. He told me he loved my mother, missed her like hell. Was that just another line said in the role Mab cast him in? Not that that would make much sense, since there wasn't much he could manipulate me to do.

"It doesn't work like that," he says. "She's not contracted anymore. She isn't immortal and isn't safe here. She can't just walk in and—"

"She can and she will," I say. I step up to him, until we are only inches from touching. The sparks between us are powerful, almost literal. "I've brought her under Mab's orders. You will keep her safe. There will be no arguing. Do you fucking hear me?"

I keep my words low, quiet.

"She can't be here." But it's not him replying—his lips are tight, a thin line even a tightrope walker would be hard-pressed to travel.

Melody steps up beside me, puts a hand on my arm. It's proof she doesn't know me well at all. If she did, she'd know that touching me is never a good idea.

Still, I'm not about to snap her arm in two; she's the one person in this show I can somewhat consider an ally, and I'm not stupid enough to burn that bridge just yet. And as I turn my glare to her, I realize she's not the same girl I saw a few days back. There are crow's-feet at the edges of her eyes, and maybe it's the light, but I swear there are lines of grey in her pixie-cut brown hair. In a circus where everyone is expected to be hot and young forever, the small flaws are smoke signals. Especially since her life is tied to the magic keeping the whole system running. Apparently Mab's kingdom isn't the only thing falling apart.

The strange thing is, I don't actually care.

"Claire," she whispers. Her eyes dart between me and my mother. There's no doubt about it—she looks scared. "You can't bring her here. It's not safe."

"For who?" I ask. I shake off her touch. "For her? Because, reality check, her house is no longer safe." *She stopped being safe the moment I walked into her world.*

"I wonder who brought that about," Kingston mutters. I ignore him.

"Or is it unsafe for you?" I ask, poking Melody in the chest.

"What?" The fear in her eyes melts into hurt as she takes a step back.

"You know precisely what I'm talking about. You don't want to see the truth. You don't want to see the repercussions of what you've done to her." I make sure to look at Kingston for the last part, but he's studiously looking away. At Viv.

"That's not at all what this is about," Melody says. "This place . . . it was her home. It has too many memories. If she starts remembering . . ."

I take a step forward, making her back up more. I don't want to burn this bridge, but it's too late. I already smell the smoke.

"Don't forget for one moment who runs this place," I growl. "You are in no position to question me. My orders come straight from the lips of your queen. You might run the show, but I run you, understood? Now, turn around, find her a place to stay, and get the fuck out of my face before I terminate your employment here and now."

Melody opens her mouth, but Kingston has a hand on her shoulder before she can speak. I know he wants to argue. I can practically feel it. Moreover, I can feel how much this hurts him, having her here.

I'd thought that would feel so, so good after what he'd done to me. I feel no retribution. Having her around isn't a cakewalk for me, either—he's not the only one being reminded about the consequences of his actions. Mine just haven't taken place yet.

"How long?" he asks.

"As long as it takes, magic man." I reach out and pat his cheek. "Don't worry, she's only here so long as she's useful. You should be used to treating her that way."

He flinches back from my touch.

"What are you—"

"At least this time you don't have to pretend to love her," I say. Then I shove past him and head toward the food cart. If I'm around him any longer, I'll kill him. Magical immortality contract or not.

Seven

I spend the rest of the afternoon avoiding my mother and the change-ling. I should be finding Kingston, forcing him to get this show on the road. I have a Pale Queen to track, and right now, I want nothing more than her blood on my hands and her throat in my teeth. But . . .

If I'm being honest, I'm not ready. I found my mother this morning. I'm not ready to lose her again.

My chest constricts at the thought, and it's not just from the emotion of it. My contract snarls in my lungs; I need to find the Pale Queen. I need to follow Mab's orders. I need to end this. And I will. *I will.* The pain dies down.

I just need to be in the right mind-set to strike. I can't be sloppy, can't strike out of haste. It's the surest way to screw things up. No different from any other hit.

No different.

So I do what I can to distract myself as the afternoon drags by in a constant stream of grey clouds and strange magic. Even in here, in the crazy Eden Mab created, I can taste the wrongness just outside the circus's bounds—something is off out there. It's in the clouds, stuck on the wind like the scent of manure. But this is a completely different sort of shit going down. One that's staining everything a much heavier shade of screwed. Or maybe I'm just too stressed for my own good.

I watch performers practice; even though some of these people have been working for the show for decades, they still practice daily. Probably because there's nothing else to do around here. Contortionists wearing leg warmers and sweatshirts stretch beside three jugglers tossing knives to each other, while a lone handbalancer twists himself atop a stack of crates by the food truck. There are clowns in the corner practicing skits, and everywhere I go, I feel eyes on the back of my neck. No doubt it's Kingston, making sure I don't get into trouble. Waiting for me to show a sign of weakness so he can strike and demand I take my mother elsewhere.

I wander the grounds and inspect the flow of Dream, trace the threads of it from the chapiteau to a small trailer that seems to be storing it. I don't go inside. Mostly, I try to stay busy. I try to stay out of the way. I try to keep my thoughts from catching up to my footsteps. I don't want to start worrying about what I'm supposed to do or what will happen if I fail. And yet, hard as I try, the place is small. It's impossible to avoid my life forever.

Especially when retribution comes in the form of a young girl in a baby-doll dress.

"You're back," she calls. I'm out in the main promenade, idly looking over glow-in-the-dark swords and light-up tiaras at a souvenir booth. My blood goes cold at her voice. "I told you not to come back."

"Yeah, well, I suck at following directions," I reply, turning to look at Lilith. "Especially when they come from bratty teens like you."

I expect her to grimace, but the girl standing beside the psychic booth just smiles. It's not even a malicious smile. She actually seems pleased.

"I like you," she says. For some reason, that sends chills down my spine. It's like a poltergeist telling you they want to be besties. "You have fire."

"I have a lot of things," I reply, "but not one of those is time. So what do you want, Lilith?"

The smile fades. She looks like some gothic Lolita, with her black frilled dress and curly hair pulled back with a ribbon. Despite the fact that she works for a show that very clearly involves work in the sun, her skin is pale as frost.

"I like you," she repeats, "but I do not like your friends."

"They aren't my friends," I say on impulse.

"But she is your mother." Once more, I wonder how much everyone in this show knows about me. I wonder if anything in my life is secret. Besides the stuff that everyone seems to be keeping secret from *me*.

"What do you want, Lilith?"

"I want her dead."

The silence surrounding her words is like a tomb.

"What the fuck did you say?" I take a step forward, my hand automatically reaching for the dagger at my hip.

"She should not be here," she says. "She has broken so much. And she will only break more."

"She is under my protection. Under this troupe's protection. If you so much as lay a finger on her . . ."

"I would never harm her," she says. She closes the space between us, and my resolve falters. But I don't step back, even though I want to. "I would not need to." She smiles again, but it's nowhere near happy. It's the smile of a murderer twisting the knife. "There are many who wish her dead. And by bringing her here, you have put her in the spotlight. She is not immortal, not anymore—the magic that protects us won't shield her if she leaves these grounds. And unlike us, she cannot stay here forever. She won't last long. No matter whose protection you say she is under."

Despite my natural aversion to her, I lean in closer. My blade is somehow in hand, and I press the tip into her gut. Gently.

"If she so much as breaks a fingernail," I grumble into her ear, "I will hold you personally accountable. And I don't care what sort of contract you're under. I'll find a way to make your life hell."

She kisses me on the cheek. Presses her stomach to the dagger so it's *me* who pulls back.

"Don't worry, Claire. I've been in hell since the day I was reborn."

Then she steps back and tilts her head to the side, as if she's listening to something far away.

"Speaking of," she mutters, almost to herself. "I have heard you have let something loose. Something that should not be on this earth again."

"Again?"

But she just smiles and looks me in the eye.

"You won't defeat her," she says. "Even with the Oracle here, the pawns are not in their proper places. The queen will take control. You are not enough to stop her. Not on your own."

"Clearly you don't know me that well."

"I am not working as a psychic just for show. I know you better than you think. Just as I know you could never bring yourself to kill your own mother. No matter how hard you think yourself to be."

I open my mouth.

"I'm protecting her."

She chuckles. We both know it's a lie.

"At least your mother had the decency not to understand her past or powers. She could be forgiven for feigning weakness, for thinking she was merely human. But you, Claire. You are pathetic. You know precisely what you are. You know how bright you burn. And yet you will not use your power." She shakes her head as though it's the greatest shame. "Your mother understood the nature of sacrifice. You are still just a child playing at being a hero."

"You have no idea what I'm capable of."

She shrugs.

"Nor do you. What is the greater disappointment?"

She steps back and turns away, but before leaving, pauses to say over her shoulder, "The Pale Queen will not let this slide, you know. Once she is secure, this will be the first place she strikes."

"How do you know?" I ask. But she doesn't answer. She just walks away, leaving me wondering if maybe this wasn't the right place to bring Vivienne after all.

***

I hunt down Kingston shortly after Lilith's vague threats. I'd tried hunting *her* down, but she as good as vanished. Miraculous, seeing as the performers were—to my knowledge—not allowed to leave the circus grounds under any circumstance. I still have no idea what my mother did, and Lilith seems to know more about the Oracle and the Pale Queen than even Mab. I should be torturing answers out of her. Instead, I'm trying to find the magician who can make my mother's memories unravel.

According to some performers, he's holed up in his trailer; while everyone else in the show seems to double up on bunks, he has an entire trailer to himself. There's even a star on the door. I'm not at all surprised. Diva.

It takes a few knocks before he answers. And he definitely doesn't look happy to see me.

"You're still here?" he asks.

"It's your lucky day."

I hop up the step and push past him, under his arm and into the trailer. It's . . . definitely not part of the mortal world.

The interior is spacious. And I'm not talking spacious-for-a-trailer. I'm talking literal mansion. There's a sweeping staircase at the far end of the plush-carpeted hallway, and crystal chandeliers drip from the ceiling. A dozen doors branch off to other parts of the place, and the hall is lined with suits of armor and Tiffany lamps.

"What the hell?" I ask as I step inside.

"Come on in," he grunts. "Make yourself at home."

I look around, spinning slowly on the spot and using my limited abilities to trace out the corners of this place, the magic running through the walls and floor, the blueprint spreading out in my senses like a water-stained map.

"What is this place?" I ask. Because there's an energy here that isn't part of the mortal world—this is definitely in Faerie.

"My retirement plan," he says coldly, stepping up beside me. "A castle in the woods. Just like I always wanted." Despite that, he doesn't sound the slightest bit proud or excited.

"Retirement, eh? Almost at the end of your contract?"

"Not quite. But I'm no longer in the triple digits, so it feels like tomorrow. Why are you here?"

"People keep asking me that," I say, turning to him. "Can't a girl just visit?"

He smiles. It doesn't come close to reaching his eyes.

"*You* can't."

I walk deeper into the mansion. Definitely not a bad place to retire to. It would give *me* something to look forward to. Maybe I should talk to Mab.

"What does Oberon want with my mother?" I ask. "Rather, why does he want her dead?"

I glance back at him just in time to see him calculate his next words. When he speaks, I have no doubt that it's mostly a lie.

"She's dangerous," he replies. "She almost destroyed his entire kingdom before. In a way. He wants revenge."

"Right. Because he's not dealing with enough right now—he'd totally go out of his way to kill a woman with no memory or powers while his kingdom starves."

"How bad is it?" Kingston asks, his voice heavy, and I know he's not talking about Oberon or my mother.

"Bad. Mab thinks she's lost half her citizens, and more are leaving by the day." I turn and lean against a doorframe, crossing my arms over my chest. I don't know if it looks seductive or badass, but I'm hoping for a mix of both. "What do you know? About what's happened?"

His eyes dart around as though he's looking for eavesdroppers, but this is his pad. He's a witch; this place is definitely better protected than even my own. Not that I'd ever tell him that.

"Something's loose," he replies. "I felt it. Last night. Mab refuses to tell me what it was, but everyone with a stitch of magic in their veins felt the pull. Something or some*one* was raised." He looks at me, raises an eyebrow. "What did you summon?"

I want to tell him it wasn't me, that it was Roxie, but that's a line of conversation I don't want to explore with him. And it doesn't really make a difference—I was a part of the ritual that brought this thing back. Apparently, I was the one who started it. After all, I was the one gathering the blood.

"I don't know," I say. "Eli says it's some astral creature, bound to the lower levels. She calls herself the Pale Queen."

I can't tell why his features tighten—maybe it's the mention of my astral ally, or maybe the name Pale Queen rings a bell. I don't get a chance to ask him.

"And that's why your mother's here," he says. "Because Mab needs her powers back."

I nod.

"You think I can just undo it," he says. "But memory magic doesn't work like that. And this wasn't normal magic. I can't just go in and make the magic that I've spent years layering go away."

"Why not? And hell, what did you even *do*? For that matter, what did *she* do?"

He sighs, runs a hand through his hair.

"It's complicated. Like everything involving your mother. Or Mab, for that matter." Despite looking like he wants to launch into a story, he doesn't offer me a comfy seat or move from the hallway. Clearly, he doesn't want me going deeper into this place.

"I'm not going anywhere," I say. "So please, don't spare the details."

Another sigh.

"When your mother came to us, she had . . . she had done something. Something terrible that she wanted out of her life. Everyone who comes to the show is a similar story—running from a bloody past that's two steps from catching up to them. Mab offered to take it all away. But your mother was different. There was a power in her that Mab had spent a very, very long time searching for. The Oracle isn't so much a person as an energy, a singular force that manifests in different creatures. Your mother was the latest host.

"The last time the Oracle was seen, she was under Oberon's control. She was always a tiebreaker in their scrabbles for Dream. She could foresee any attack, see into the heart of any enemy, and learn how to defeat them. Moreover, she could manifest whatever power was necessary to do it."

"No wonder Mab wanted her," I mutter. *She puts my own powers to shame. Or, did.* "So that . . . thing. That power. That's still inside of her."

He nods, his eyes tight. Whatever he's seeing in memory, he doesn't like it. "For the most part, yes. But it was too much for her. I locked that part of her away when she joined the show—it was already eating away at her. But then, when shit hit the fan . . ."

"Convince her your love is strong enough to die for," I mutter.

His reverie snaps. "Where did you hear that?"

"Around," I reply. "So, what? You convinced her that letting her powers go was worth it? Letting the Oracle powers or whatever kill the woman that was left?"

Again, that short, cold nod.

"There was no other choice. She knew the risks and she took them. We let her powers go. And she saved us."

"But she didn't die."

"No. Not quite. Once the demons were gone, I stepped in. Tried to force the power back down. I nearly lost it, but I managed. And I locked those powers deep inside her."

I don't ask about the demons, because that's not relevant right now. I can't imagine the end of the world happening because of a few stray astral creatures. Then again, the Pale Queen seems to be trying for that on her own.

"She seems okay to me," I say. "A little off, but functioning."

"You don't get it. Her memories were burned out of her when the Oracle took over. Everything that made her human, gone. She lost most of who she was, and I had to fill in the rest. She's no longer the woman she once was. She's new. She's what I made her to be."

His voice actually seems to hitch when he says this, and he looks away. If he weren't such a damned good actor, I'd have fallen for it head-first. As it is, I know he's only doing it for show. At least . . . I think it's just for show. *He manipulated your mother.* He's still the asshole who ruined my mother's life, no matter what emotions for her he might have harbored.

"If you made her, then you can unmake her," I say. I realize how horrible it sounds before the words even leave my mouth. Once more, I'm no better than he is; maybe I should stop treating him like he ruined my mom's life, when I'm probably going to be the one who ends it. "We need her to find the Pale Queen. She's hiding in the Wildness, and we can't find her without Vivienne's powers. We need the Oracle. Before this bitch bleeds the kingdoms dry."

"I can't help you."

"Can't, or won't?"

"You don't know what you're asking me to do."

"I know very well what I'm asking you to do."

I step forward then, my veins filled with hatred. And no, it's not all directed at him. I'm pissed at myself, pissed I'm asking him to do this, pissed I'm trying to unravel the little bit of a life Viv was given for Mab's and my own ends. I want to let her live in peace. I would let all of Faerie die before I let Kingston hurt her again.

But I signed a contract. I'll fight for Mab until the end.

"Don't even pretend you love her," I whisper. "I know it's a lie. I know Mab had you manipulate her. Because of you, she sacrificed everything. You don't even know what her life is like now."

"I do," he says.

"Bullshit. You're safe in here with your little illusions and pretty playthings. You don't give two shits about her."

"Really? Then why do I visit her every month?"

"You're lying."

"Am I?" he asks. "She doesn't remember, of course. But I do. I remember watching her age. I remember her falling deeper and deeper in love with someone else. I've watched more of her life than you have, Claire. Hell, I even watched her bring you home from the hospital. You didn't know that, did you? That I was there for your birth."

My mind reels.

"You're not—"

"I'm not your father," he says. He looks at me, clearly remembering the night we spent together. "I'm not that sick. No, I was there in the delivery room. Faeries and Shifters aren't the only ones who can disguise themselves. I watched you grow, right up to the day Mab had me take you away and hide you in Winter. And then, I watched your mother move on and forget. Do you know what that's like, Claire? To watch someone you loved forget who you are so completely, you don't even have to disguise yourself anymore in their presence?"

His eyes are wild, and there's a breathlessness in his voice that tells me quite clearly that this isn't an act. He's been waiting to air this for a long, long time.

I step forward, until we're close enough to lean in and kiss. And maybe we will, maybe this will be one of those *I hate you so much I'll bone you* moments. Or maybe I'll just punch him. I'll get something out of it either way.

"Let's get one thing straight, *magic man*," I hiss. "I don't give a flying fuck about your feelings toward my mother. I don't care if you miss her. Or if you regret screwing her over. And I definitely don't care if you watched me grow up. You are going to help me get her powers back. No matter what it takes. You've manipulated her before to get what you want. I have no doubt you can do it again."

"I told you," he whispers, the hurt in his eyes and his words palpable. "I can't just undo it. Not without killing her outright. The magic that binds her memories in place will dissolve in time. That's why I visit. Don't think it's just out of misplaced nostalgia. I have to replenish the magic every few weeks. Left to itself, it would dissolve."

"So we let it dissolve."

He shakes his head.

"If it dissolves, she dies. Simple as that. She can't become the Oracle again, Claire."

"Mab says she can."

"Mab's kingdom is dying. She's desperate. And you haven't seen Mab when she's desperate."

"Faeries can't lie," I say, suddenly aware that neither of us has moved a step. His breath smells like coffee, and not in a bad way.

"She's not lying if she thinks it's true. If I let the magic in her dissolve, she'll simply fall apart. It's not just giving her a false personality, Claire. It's keeping her alive. The power within her is literally eating her up. I let it go, and she goes out, too."

"There has to be a way."

"There isn't."

I search his eyes for a tell, for any hint of a lie. Maybe he wants to keep her like this—a doll he can play with. Maybe he doesn't want her to remember for another reason. But if he's lying about his logic, it's not showing. *It's not a lie if she thinks it's true.*

That's when his earlier words filter through my head. If Oberon had control over the Oracle before . . . maybe, just maybe, he'd know how to reclaim her. After all, he wants her back. He has to know how to get her powers to manifest.

"I'll find a way. You clearly don't know me; I never fail in a mission."

For the first time in the conversation, *he's* the one who smirks. He edges forward, the slightest shift, and I don't like the sudden change in his demeanor.

"That's not what I hear about Roxie," he whispers. "Sounds like you fucked that one up quite well."

I grit my teeth. I want to punch him. No, I want to stab him or chain him up and torture him for a few days. Instead, I keep my face blank. *Don't let him see it's working. Don't let him see it got under your skin.*

"As far as I'm concerned," I say smoothly, not looking from his eyes, "that job is still on. I haven't failed. Not by a long shot."

"Whatever you have to tell yourself, Claire." He steps back then, but it doesn't feel like defeat. It feels like he's taking control. He walks over to the door and pushes it open. "I think we're done here. I can't force you to take your mother elsewhere. Just as I can't force you to leave. As you said, you run the show. So you call the shots. You want your mother to slowly die here, feel free. Just don't expect me to hold your hand through it."

"You're an asshole," I whisper.

"And you're sentencing your mother to a slow, painful death. Remember when I said her memories would burn her up? I meant that literally. You'll get to watch her slowly cook from the inside out. Personally, I'd rather be an asshole. At least I get to sleep at night. Ta-ta."

I bite back the curses in my head and storm out the door. If he won't be of any help, I'll find someone who will.

***

My brain is raging when I leave Kingston's trailer, and my initial response is to leave. Run. Head to a bar or to my bath and scream or fight or drink or float my way to oblivion. But the moment the idea of walking away passes through my mind, I'm struck with that same anxiety as before—I can't leave my mother behind. Not unless I'm doing it to further Mab's cause.

Kingston was lying. He had to have been. I can't let myself believe that he doesn't know what to do, that in keeping my mother here, I'm torturing her. This was supposed to be quick. Clean. It was supposed to be easy.

I wasn't supposed to care. Which is why, when Vivienne comes up to me as I storm from Kingston's trailer, I nearly break down right there.

"Are you okay?" she asks.

Damn it.

I wipe the tears from the corners of my eyes and convince myself it is anger and frustration and allergies.

I can't view her as my mother. I can't even view her as a person. She is a tool. One I will use. And tools don't have emotions or needs. Neither do I.

"Hi," I say. I know she asked me a question. I don't want to answer. I don't know if I could piece together the lie if my life depended on it.

Right now, I'd give almost anything for someone to come by and give me a reason to leave. I'd even welcome the damned changeling. Or Lilith. Because standing before Vivienne creates a gravity I don't want to fall into.

I won't fully admit it to myself, but a part of me wants to collapse into her arms and cry and be comforted. Now more than ever, I want to know what it feels like to be cared for. To have someone else try to share my burden. I can't, though. My burden is *her.*

"You don't have to pretend, you know," she says. She takes a step closer. Hugging range. Her eyes don't leave my face, and I can't meet her gaze. "I *am* a mom—these aren't the first tears I've seen. What's wrong?"

"Everything." My voice doesn't hitch, thank gods, but it's lower and gravelly and definitely sounds like I'm on the edge of a breakdown.

"Oh." Clearly not the answer she expected. People hate it when you answer that question honestly. "Do you want to talk?"

"No offense, but I don't think you'd understand."

Or maybe you would, and then you'd fall apart, so you really don't want to go down that road.

She smiles sadly. "I know what you think of me," she says.

"I don't think you do."

"Oh come on, I've known since the moment we met. You think I'm simple."

I actually laugh, it's so ridiculous. But the action just makes another tear well up. I sniff and look away and laugh again. I can't believe I'm having this conversation with a grown woman, especially a woman who can't know she's related to me. I'm not a therapist. But I'll probably need one after all this.

"I don't think you're simple."

"Really? Because I'm pretty damn sure you were bored out of your mind all morning." The fact that she cursed gains her a small point, even if it was a pretty harmless one. "To be fair, I am, too. I hate talking about my job."

"You and me both."

Her smile turns a little brighter. Then she looks back up at the tent and sighs.

"What?" I ask.

"Nothing. It's stupid."

"I highly doubt that." Wait, I actually mean that. I *want* to know what she's thinking. I want to have some insight into her life. Pain wells up inside me, sharper than any dagger. *I don't want to hurt you. I want to make you feel better.*

"You really want to know?" she asks.

I nod. I don't want it to be the truth, but it is. *Jesus, I need to get out of here. I need to kill something.*

"I want to run away."

I don't have a response to that. Thankfully, she keeps talking.

"This . . . all this. This is what I want. Ever since I was a little girl, I've thought about running away and joining a circus. Being a star under the spotlight. Falling in love with, I don't know, some dashing lion tamer or magician or something."

She catches herself in the daydream, but she doesn't apologize or say *but Austin's perfect for me.* Because that would be a lie, and somehow, I know she doesn't want to lie around me.

"Magicians aren't all they're cracked up to be," I mutter. She catches it, but the wistful expression doesn't leave her face.

"Even so . . . I don't know. I have everything I've ever wanted, and yet there's a part of me that wants this most of all. To run away. To be a part of something as big and beautiful as this. Some nights I wake up and think I have, you know? Like one of those dreams that's so real, you wake up and have to convince yourself that your waking world isn't the dream."

"So why didn't you do it?" I ask. I don't know why I ask it, because I know every answer she gives will be some prefabricated lie Kingston implanted in her. But the words leave my lips anyway.

She shrugs and looks at the big top.

"Life got in the way, I guess. I don't know. Things with Austin and me got serious. I got pregnant. Not that I regret that," she adds hastily. "It's funny. So much of my life feels like a blur. Guess it's just old age. But the moment Claire was born . . ." Her face lights up, and a tear actually forms at the corner of her eye.

Another one tries to form in mine.

"Well, I'll never forget that moment. Seeing her face for the first time. Holding her. Hearing her cry. She was such a little angel, and I knew that it was the one thing in my life I'd done right." She wipes away the tears. "It's funny. I remember that moment clearer than anything else. Out of my entire life, Claire's birth is the thing that's stuck with me. I've forgotten her recitals and graduation. But I'll never forget that. That's what changed. When I became a mom, when I had that responsibility, everything else seemed unimportant. She was my world. *Is* my world."

I don't say anything for a moment. The air between us grows thick, and she laughs to herself, looking around the show as if she's trying to find a different cue.

"I'm sorry, I don't know why I said any of that. Must just be this place—makes me start thinking things. I'm sure you've heard it all before from your own mother."

I choke down a sob and turn away, bending to tie a bootlace that doesn't need tying.

"Actually, no," I say. "I haven't."

When I've forced myself back together, I stand and look at her. She's staring at me the way Austin had earlier. As if she knows something, or thinks she knows something. As if she wants me to press a little bit harder so the truth pushes through the cracks of this lie we're all playing at.

Time to see how much she actually knows.

I pull out the necklace and hold it out to her. I'm ready to crack, but if I don't do this now, I might not have another time with her to myself.

"Do you recognize this?"

She looks at it, curiosity darting over her features.

"I don't think so," she says.

I take her hand and set the necklace within. Her fingers don't clutch around it. I expect a shock of power, for her memories to transfer. For *something* to happen. But nothing does.

"It's pretty," she says. "But it's not my style." She holds it up before her eyes, letting it dangle and glint in the muted light. Then she takes my hand and gives it back. I hate to admit how nice it feels to have her touch me, her fingers tentative.

"Where did you get it?"

"My employer," I say. "Same woman Claire used to work for. Thought . . . I don't know what I thought. It's not important."

Clearly the stone's not important, either, but I loop it back over my neck anyway. It's still something of Vivienne's. Even if she doesn't remember it.

A metaphor for yourself, eh?

The crack in me fissures deeper. I need out of here. Now. Before she sees me break down.

"I need to go chat with the crew," I say. "Thanks for the talk."

Then I turn and head into the tent. I barely make it to the first row of bleachers before the tears come. And for the first time since Mab chastised me for showing weakness, I don't try to stop the flow. I sit on the bench and sob in silence.

Because somehow, I know Vivienne wasn't talking about some false memory. She remembers my birth. Of everything else in her life, she remembers bringing me into the world, and that gives her joy. It gives her something to live for.

I want to hold on to that. I want to remember it as well.

Instead, I'm going to throw all of it away.

Eight

I want out.

Trouble is, I can't get any farther than the perimeter of the circus before my contract latches back into place. I tried a few times. One toe over. See if I could duck out for a drink, or a screw, or a kill. But I can't. I'm stuck in here just like the rest of the performers, and the only way I'll manage to escape is to come up with a logical reason to leave—something that will further my mission. Fucking faerie contracts.

I walk the perimeter, one hand on a pocketed knife and the other clutching the necklace Mab gave me. I need to speed up the process. I need to get Vivienne's powers to manifest before she dies. And I need this all to happen before the Pale Queen makes a move. Whatever move that would be.

The calm drags against my skin like nails. I know this tactic. The Pale Queen won't attack until Mab is sufficiently weakened. Like draining blood from a body, she'll wait for all of Mab's minions to leave before striking. I've used similar methods to make people talk: bleed them until they're on the edge of death, when they'll do anything to stay alive. *That's* when you make your demands.

And once they crumble to your whims, you kill them. Two birds, one stone.

Maybe the Pale Queen just wants to rule in peace, but I doubt it. It takes a psychopath to know one.

Which is why I need to find her, before Mab becomes weak. Before the Pale Queen has an army. While there's still a chance.

"You think so ill of me."

I glance around, but my surroundings are empty—just rolling farmland to one side and an expansive parking lot on the other.

"Gods, Claire. You're hallucinating."

"I am no mere hallucination."

I pause, and I can't help it—chills roll down my spine. It's not a feeling I'm used to. Slowly, I look to my left, toward the parking lot, the knife in my pocket flipped open and waiting.

There, standing a few feet away, is the Pale Queen.

Impossible.

She's standing on circus grounds.

"You can't be here," I hiss.

The woman steps toward me, raising her arms out to the sides.

"And yet, here I am."

She's in the same dress she wore in the dream, all white and cream and dripping silk. But across her face is a mask. Delicate, glittering, made of white lace and diamonds. It molds to her features, revealing only luscious red lips and eyes that smolder like embers, crackling hues of red and orange and violet.

I expect some sort of alarm to sound. The enemy is here. She is here, and she is standing on Winter's territory, and no one seems to notice. For a split second I consider screaming out, demanding someone help—the circus is filled with magical murderers—but then I remember, I'm the fucking assassin. The grip on my knife tightens.

"Why?" I ask.

"Why?" she replies. Her voice is cool, her elocution perfect. "You know *why* I am here, my dearest. We both know you are not *that* blind."

Numbers add up in milliseconds.

"You want my mother."

Those lips purse into a smile.

"I have no interest in a mortal," she says. "Only in what that mortal might *become*."

"I won't let you kill her."

"Of that, I have no desire."

She is closer now. So close I could reach out and shove my blade through her gut. It's no hallucination, no vision or illusion. She's here, standing before me. I can *feel* her presence. There's an energy around her, a static that crackles against my bones. A scent that defiles this world. It's like standing around Eli, my demonic ally. But much, much worse.

My knife stays in my pocket.

"Why are you here?"

The smile widens.

"You ask the wrong questions, my dear." She reaches out as though she's going to touch my cheek but pauses with her hand an inch away. Even there, the nearness burns like fire. "So like her, aren't you?"

"I will kill you," I whisper.

She laughs. It's not an evil, maniacal laugh. It's sweet. Almost innocent.

"We shall see about that. I had hoped you would understand by now, Claire—I am not just a queen. I am an idea. And you cannot kill an idea once it has taken hold in the hearts of many."

"Why. Are. You. Here."

"To see you. To see if you had changed your mind."

"We are enemies," I say.

"Are we? Or are we both tired of being ruled? Manipulated? Perhaps we are simply both ready to take command."

I pull out the knife then. It's a simple iron blade—only a few enchantments, and none nearly strong enough to bring her down. But maybe it will buy me time if I need it. My hand moves almost on its own accord, and I can't tell if it's instincts or the contract spurring me to action.

"You've declared war on Winter," I say. "For that alone, you deserve to die."

I'm about to go on about how she's now threatening my mother, but before I can, she laughs again. This time, there *is* a hint of madness.

"Oh, sweet Claire. I'm not declaring war on Winter. I've declared war on Faerie itself." She presses her hand to my cheek then, and the static between us turns to fire. I can't help the scream that pierces my lips. I drop the knife, but I don't drop to my knees—the stabbing heat within keeps me standing on pillars of flames.

"Actually," she continues, her voice barely cutting through the scream in my head, "I'm not declaring war. I've already won. The question is, whose team will you fight for when the final curtain falls?"

The pain stops. I drop to my knees, blink away the tears I can't hold back. My hand goes blindly for another knife. But by the time I have the weapon in hand, the Pale Queen is already gone.

***

I should tell someone that the Pale Queen was here. Something binds my lips, though, and I don't know if it's hurt pride for being bested or fear. I try to tell myself that it's all a test—in theory, someone should be approaching *me* about this. Kingston should have felt the intruder. Or Melody. If either of them had, they don't mention it to me. I watch Kingston practice his whip from a distance. Eavesdrop on Melody while she chats with another girl about ticket sales. Beyond hearing that numbers are down, and it's a good thing they're moving to a new site soon, I don't learn much. I'm the only one who knows the Pale Queen was here. I'm the only one who knows the circus isn't safe. Well, me and Lilith, though I doubt many people take her seriously.

Maybe keeping Vivienne here wasn't the right choice after all. There has to be somewhere else I could take her, somewhere that Oberon and the Pale Queen couldn't touch.

The only place would be Winter. But if Vivienne's contract forbids it . . . Well, from what I've seen, faerie contracts are impossible to change.

"What are you doing out here?" the changeling asks. I pause and realize I've been pacing back and forth on the edge of the grounds. Probably muttering to myself.

"Thinking," I say.

She raises an eyebrow, as if she finds that hard to believe. Girl is begging to be punched.

She holds something out to me. It's a ticket, pale blue and covered in swirling script.

"What's this?" I ask. But I know what it is—it's almost identical to the tickets I'd seen scattered throughout Faerie, inviting the denizens to live with the Pale Queen in the Wildness.

"Kingston gave me a few. Said we might as well enjoy ourselves while we're here."

"We won't be here long," I reply. "We need to leave."

She sighs. "And take her where? She can't enter Winter, and anywhere else would leave her open to Oberon. I know you think you can take on his entire kingdom—and maybe on your own, you could—but I don't think you've ever had to take care of someone like this before. She would weigh you down and get you both killed. I don't want her here. But there's nowhere else to go. Besides, Vivienne's actually pretty excited about this. More than I've seen her before. It's probably the last good thing that will happen in her life."

The unspoken words linger between us. *Before your actions kill her.*

***

There are a few hours to kill before the show starts, and since I can't leave and I can't make time speed up, I wander. For a moment, I almost wish I weren't such a loner—it would be nice to have someone to talk to, to at least make the time go by. Roxie's face flickers through my mind, the thought of hanging on her couch with a bottle of wine, talking about music or lovers or . . . I shake my head and keep walking. Not a road worth going down.

Music comes from the chapiteau. My natural instinct is to avoid it, because music means people, which means interacting. But boredom wins out, and I head over and stand in a side entry. I fully planned on just walking by. When I see who's inside, I realize I can't look away.

My mother is hanging from a trapeze.

Okay, she's not dangling a dozen feet in the air, or swinging with the greatest of ease. Instead, she perches on a low trapeze slung maybe five feet from the ground, a thick mat right beneath her. Spotlights splay multicolored lights over her—somewhere along the way, she found some black spandex that, somehow, suits her—and the music pulses happily. And she's laughing. She stands atop the bar with her hands high on the ropes, and the smile on her face is the first genuine thing I've seen all day.

"That's great!" someone calls, and I glance to the ring curb to see Melody sitting there. She's smiling, too, but it's different from Vivienne's. Vivienne has that look of glee that children get when they're not at all self-conscious and everything is wonderful and new. Melody looks like she's happy . . . and that that happiness hurts her deeply. "Now, I want you to hold on tight and raise your left leg up with your knee bent." Melody stands up and demonstrates the pose from the ground. "Like this. And then you'll lean forward—just slightly!—and arch your back."

Vivienne does so. Her feet are pointed and her smile never leaves her face; it looks graceful, like she's done this a hundred times before. And maybe she has.

"Beautiful, Viv. Just beautiful. Okay, now pull yourself back up to standing, and we're going to do a different trick."

My mother does so. And then, in the motion of pulling herself up, she glances over and catches sight of me. The smile widens.

"Melody!" she calls out, and it takes me a second to realize she's talking to me. I wonder what the *real* Melody is going as then. "Come in! You should try this!"

The real Melody looks my way. The smile slips; it doesn't return.

"No, no, it's okay. I wasn't cut out for heights."

The lie comes easily. But Vivienne releases a hand to wave me in.

"Oh come on. Live a little!"

She laughs again. And I know that she's supposed to just be another hit. I know she's just a means to an end. In that moment, though, she looks so fucking *happy*. My heart aches. *What sort of monster have I become?*

Despite my reservations, I step into the tent and take a seat on the bleachers near the front.

"I thought you'd said you've never done this before," I say. I glance to Melody, but she doesn't acknowledge that I exist. Apparently threatening her earlier wasn't the way to her heart. *Women.*

"Sara's a good teacher," Viv replies.

"Sara," I mutter. Melody does look at me then, and her eyes are tight. I wonder if there's a meaning behind the name. "Well, you're definitely a natural."

"It just feels so good to be up here. I mean, I sit at a desk *all day.* This feels like flying."

The smile comes back to Melody's face, just as pained as before, as she focuses on Viv.

"Okay, next trick. We're going to have you go upside down."

She steps forward and holds her hands under Viv. "First, slide down to a crouch."

Vivienne does so, and Melody guides her through the motions until Vivienne is hanging upside down from the trapeze by her knees. Vivienne can't stop laughing.

"Looking great, Viv," Melody says.

I start to clap.

Then Vivienne's laughter cuts off with a gasp, and before Melody or I can react, she drops from the trapeze with a scream.

Melody's spotting keeps Viv from hitting her head—my mother lands on her back on the mat—but the scream doesn't cut off. It curdles my blood and shoots me to my feet; I'm at her side in an instant.

"Mom, what's—" I begin, before realizing my slip. But Vivienne doesn't notice. Her screams cut through the tent like a banshee's wail. I put a hand on her forehead. Her flesh is hot as melting iron.

"Get Kingston," Melody hisses, her words frantic.

I bolt to my feet, but I'm not halfway out the tent when he runs in. He pushes past me, his eyes solely on Vivienne, and places his hands on her forehead. I follow and perch at his side as blue light spills from his fingertips, coalescing over her skin in waves as the feathered-serpent tattoo writhes around his forearm. Mom's screaming stops, but the convulsions don't. She claws at the air, and her mouth is open, the muscles of her jaw and neck tight.

I want to scream. I want to help.

"Get out," he says. He doesn't look at Melody or me, but I know whom he's directing it toward.

"I hope you're happy, Claire," Melody says. She *does* look at me. Her glare puts Lilith's to shame. "We told you this would happen. I hope this is worth it."

I don't respond. I push to my feet and head to the door. When I reach the exit, I don't look back.

***

"What did you say to him?" the changeling asks. We're in the front row, my mother on her opposite side, and the show's supposed to start any minute. Whatever Kingston did, it worked well—Viv acts completely normal, and if she remembers anything from this afternoon, she doesn't show it. I also haven't brought it up.

"Who?" I ask.

"The magician."

"Nothing," I lie.

"Then why has he been talking to her?"

I glance over to Vivienne, who's eating popcorn and watching the stage, completely oblivious to our conversation.

"What's he said?" I ask.

"I don't know," the changeling replies. "But he has always followed one rule: observe, don't interact. Now he's breaking it."

He was trying to keep her from clawing her face off.

I don't respond, and she doesn't get a chance to say anything else, because the houselights dim and the music gets louder, and then there's a flash of light on the stage and Kingston is standing there, dressed in a tight leather ringmaster's outfit, a whip in hand and a studded top hat jauntily perched on his head. He doesn't look like he just saved my mother from burning alive. He looks like he's straight out of a housewife's fantasy.

"Welcome, loves," he says, his voice carrying to all corners of the tent. "The wonders of the Cirque des Immortels await. Tonight, we have acts to ensnare and entwine, rare performances both hellish and divine. So tonight, relax, sit back, and let go. Ladies and gentlemen, enjoy our show."

He cracks his whip in time with a flash of lights and a puff of smoke, and when the stage clears, he has vanished.

But the stage doesn't stay empty for long. A dozen performers cartwheel and flip into the ring as the live music picks up and a singer begins her scales. She doesn't sound anything like Roxie, but it still makes a pang flash through my heart.

The audience claps in time with the music as the performers create human pyramids, or do handstands on top of one another, or juggle clubs. It's chaos, and for a brief moment my troubles actually begin to drift away. I feel the pull of it, the desire to dream of something colorful and beautiful. Then I blink and watch the haze of Dream filtering up through the tent like glittering smog. My job slams back into focus.

A trapeze slowly descends from the ceiling, and when it is perhaps a dozen feet from the ground, one of the human pyramids moves beneath it, and an aerialist in a glittering purple leotard climbs to the top of the mound. She smiles to the audience, her head still a good five feet from the trapeze—way out of reaching distance. Then the man holding her up tosses her in the air as though she weighs nothing. She flies toward the trapeze and grabs it at the very last second.

Even though I know she's magical and immortal, I still feel my breath catch.

It's not the aerialist that I watch while she begins her act, however. It's Viv. My mother doesn't take her eyes off the aerialist. Maybe she *does* remember training with Melody this afternoon, or maybe there's just a part of her that will always want to fly. As I watch her, I can't stop the butterflies burning in my chest. She looks so happy. So enthralled. And yet, just a few hours ago, she was curled up in that very ring, screaming like the hordes of hell were trying to claw their way from her throat.

This place is everything she's ever dreamed of.

It's the life she had. The life that still haunts her. The life that will eventually undo her.

Are you sure you can do this to her? a voice inside me asks. I know it's just my inner dialogue, but damn if it doesn't sound like the Pale Queen. *Now that you've seen how happy you can make her, now that you know how good it feels to see her smile . . . can you really kill her? Can you really watch her slowly die?*

I don't have an answer. All I can do is grip the knife in my pocket and try to stay present. Focused on the show. On the job at hand.

An explosion outside the tent shatters my thoughts; the rumble makes our seats vibrate. The aerialist screams and tumbles from the trapeze, and the audience is too distracted from the explosion to notice that she lands perfectly, without the slightest hint of injury. The stage lights dim, and a second later Kingston is onstage, the spotlight making him look like a god.

"Don't worry, loves," he says. "Someone has accidentally set off our fireworks. We'll resume the show shortly." His voice is soft and soothing, yet somehow fills the tent and makes the panic subside. I know the energy sliding over my skin—he's using magic to subdue the crowd. Thankfully, my runes prevent it. I'm already pushing myself from the seat and heading toward the aisle. I know the scent of magic when I taste it, and this shit bears the unmistakable tang of Summer. Another explosion sends tremors throughout the tent, and if not for the magic lulling everyone into submission, I know there'd be an uproar. Instead, the music gets louder, and everyone settles in for the rest of the show as I burst from the tent and into the warm evening air.

A crowd's already gathered at the end of the promenade, right at the entrance. On one side of the fence is the tent crew, and on the other is a mob from Oberon's kingdom.

Everyone looks human, even the Fey, and I know it's only because they run the risk of human observation, something that goes against the laws of Faerie. I can feel their essences, though—Oberon's army is host to dryads and sylphs and a few woodland nymphs. Our team boasts a dozen or so Shifters, all dressed like they're in a motorcycle gang and all clearly itching to change and rip the Summer crowd a new one. At the Shifters' head is Melody, her hands balled into fists. She looks so out of place amidst the punked-out Shifters, as petite and cutesy as she is, and yet her expression is strong enough to give her weight.

On the other team, the asshole who attacked me at my mother's house stands at the forefront, hands in his pockets and an easy smile on his face.

I push through the Shifters and stand beside Melody, our toes just touching the line separating Mab's territory from the outside world.

"What the hell are you doing here?" I call out. I don't ask the guy's name. He won't be alive long enough for me to care.

"Oberon just wants what's his," he says.

"She isn't yours to have," Melody responds. I look over at her, slightly miffed she stole my line, but there's a fire in her eyes I can only admire. If she's still pissed about this afternoon, she is focusing it on these guys and not me. I'm perfectly fine with that; this feels like a turf war I'm not privy to.

"I think you'll find you're wrong," he says. He looks to the Fey behind him. "We don't want a fight. We just want her back. Send her over and no one gets hurt."

"No one's going to get hurt," Melody says. "Not so long as I'm here."

I glance at her. She admitted to me that she was somehow tied to the immortality clause in this show—so long as she was around, everyone within the tent would live forever, perpetually young and beautiful.

"And how long will that be?" he asks. "Even I can see through you. You have, what? A few months left, max? I wouldn't exert yourself too much, you know. Might make you croak sooner."

I'm not the only one casting curious looks at Melody; the other Shifters stare at her openly, clearly wondering if the guy's telling the truth. The flush to her cheeks proves as much.

"You need to leave," I say. "You can't be here."

"You'll find that we can," Summer boy replies. "We may not be able to enter your grounds, but we are patient. There's nothing in the rules about waiting out here—we can easily blockade your show. Keep you from getting supplies. That sort of thing. We can wait forever, you know. But I don't think you can. In a few weeks you'll crumble, and then we'll take her by force. Give us the Oracle and we're gone—no one gets hurt, no lives lost."

"Over my dead body," Melody says.

The man just chuckles. "Exactly."

***

"What the fuck are we going to do?" she asks me.

We're back near the trailers, out of earshot of the performers and the Summer mob, who haven't moved an inch. A few of the dryads turned into trees before we left, rooting themselves down in a rather pacifistic act of defiance.

Melody's clearly frightened, which is strange, because she seemed so fiery back there. Her eyes are wild, unable to focus on any one thing; she keeps looking back toward the promenade and the Summer Fey waiting there. I think I like the assured version of Melody better, even if it was a facade.

"Mab won't let them stay," I tell her. "It has to be against the rules somehow. No meddling."

"It's not Winter territory out there. She can't do anything about it. The best she could do is try to convince Oberon to have them withdraw, but who knows how long that will take? If he'd even do it."

I have no doubt the Summer King would take his sweet time reining in his lackeys. I didn't think he had it in him to directly approach the circus—there has always been a sort of mutual respect between Winter and Summer. Sure, they play at being at war, but I think they do it just to keep themselves from dying of boredom. Attacking Vivienne's house was one thing. Being here . . . Mab would see it as an act worthy of revenge. If she weren't preoccupied with the Pale Queen and the loss of her own subjects.

"Was he telling the truth?" I ask.

"What?"

I look her up and down.

"You," I say. "Was he telling the truth about you?"

She grimaces. Answer enough.

"How long can you hold out?" I ask.

"It depends on if they try to fight," she replies. "So long as I'm healthy, they can't cross over or force their attacks through. But if I get sick, or the tents are jeopardized somehow, we're screwed."

"What do you mean? How could the tents get jeopardized if they can't get through?"

She shrugs and looks away. "Inside job."

I stare. It's against performers' contracts to harm the show. Even *I* know that. So the magic should be solid—as long as Melody's healthy, we're safe. Why does she look so worried? Like it's happened before.

Suddenly, I wonder if I should try to get Vivienne to Winter anyway. First the Pale Queen, and now Oberon. I can only hope Melody's powers hold out long enough for me to get to the bottom of this.

"How long?"

She looks at me. "Until I die?"

I nod.

"I can't believe you're asking me that."

"We all go at some point. How long."

She sighs. It sounds like she wants to cry, but she holds it together. I hate myself for how cold I am right now. Before this afternoon, she was the only one in this damned show who tried to be a friend. But that will all amount to nothing if we lose Vivienne.

"A few weeks. Maybe more. Maybe less."

"Shit."

"I'm sorry."

"It's not your fault." I don't ask if there's a replacement queued up; it seems in bad taste, even for me.

"Can you keep her safe?" I ask.

"I did before," she replies sadly.

"Then you'll have to do it again." I reach into my pocket and pull out some chalk. "It looks like I have a date with the Summer King."

Nine

The warehouse looms up around me like the ribs of a dragon, all dusty and decayed in the moonlight. I should know. I've been in the ribs of dragons before.

It's not Summer territory. Far from it. I'm still in the mortal world, somewhere in southern Vermont. I come here not because of the mountains like a dark rip of paper on the horizon, or the sky studded with stars. I come here because this is where a few ley lines converge, which means more power, and an easier way to access the worlds between and beneath the ones I frequent.

The silence here is almost deafening, and there's an openness I haven't felt in a while. Here, so far from magic and the circus and faerie plots, I feel as if I could just lie down and let the world rush by. I don't, though I do crouch down where the ley lines touch and begin sketching out a perfect circle. If I'm going to the Summer Kingdom, I'm not doing it alone. Not because I'm afraid, really. But because it helps to have some cannon fodder when going against the big guys.

And Eli is the best fodder I have. I don't even feel guilty when he gets sent back to whatever astral plane he resides on; he's annoying enough that I'd happily send him back there myself.

It's hard to focus on what I'm doing. I can barely admit it to myself, but there's a tug in my awareness, a hitch in my breath. I can *feel* my mother out there, beckoning like true north. I know she's safer with Melody and the circus than she would be out here with me. Especially where I'm going next. But it still feels like negligence.

I try to convince myself it's because I'm worried about the mission falling apart. The truth is, I'm worried about *her*. Every time I blink I see her, curled on the mat below the trapeze. Every solitary gust of wind is her scream. Even the silence haunts me—it reminds me of the moments when she looked at me as though she knew something secret, as though we were both in on the same thing, but unable to voice it.

Does she recognize me?

I force the question down. Today's been a roller coaster of emotions I'm not supposed to feel. My mother recognizing me has nothing to do with my mission. It doesn't change the outcome. All it changes is my guilt level after.

Once the circle and sigils are drawn, I stand up and step outside the ring, pulling a dagger from my coat and cutting a long line across my palm. I barely feel it, I'm so used to getting cut. Kind of screwed up.

There's no invocation, not anymore. Just an offering of blood. I press my hand out and meet resistance along the circle's perimeter. My blood drips down along the invisible wall, but it doesn't fleck against the concrete. The drops get sucked into a vortex, dark blood turning to flames as they spin, creating a small inferno that rushes up into the night sky and becomes a pillar of silent fire. Eli: always so damn dramatic. At least this time he isn't that hungry—normally he feeds off my blood and energy like a leech.

A few moments later his hand slaps against mine, and the flames get sucked into his body, revealing a tall, lithe Japanese man in a white suit. He looks like a rock star, with his sunglasses and choppy hair and cocky demeanor.

"Claire," he says, his voice somehow both human and . . . not. There's a gravelly tinge to it, as though his throat is full of embers. "Fancy seeing you again."

"You haven't changed," I say, nodding to his current body. Normally, Eli switches skins like I'd switch underwear.

"You haven't given me enough time." He smiles. "You make a girl feel so wanted. You even chose white."

I know it's weird, but astral creatures can only appear in whatever colors they were summoned with. I hadn't even noticed I picked out white chalk. It's his favorite. He says it makes him feel angelic.

"So why am I here?" he asks. He looks up at the stars, the Milky Way glinting off his lenses. "Barely a day has passed since you last sent me home. That was quite rude, you know. You didn't even let me say my good-byes."

I'd sent him back right after Roxie betrayed me. His snarky questions were the last things I wanted to deal with. His palm is still pressed tight to mine, my blood making soft pats on the ground when it hits.

"You know the drill," I say. The next words come out by rote: same contract, every time. "I need you to be my ally and follow without question. I need you to do exactly as I say and nothing more. You will be bound to me and only me, to serve as I command for as long as I need you and no longer. And I need you to not be a dick."

The last line is less business and more for both our well-beings. He can be a prick without the clause.

"Someday, you'll deviate from that, and I will never let you live it down."

"Maybe. Your terms?"

"I'm tired," he replies. I know it's an outright lie—astral creatures don't tire. "All of this back and forth. I grow weak . . ."

"What do you want?"

"Four."

I grit my teeth. "That's double our last rate."

"Four. No more, no less. And yes, I'll let you help pick."

I open my mouth but he cuts me off.

"No children. I know." He shakes his head. "Their souls are boring anyway."

For a moment I seriously consider just how much I actually need Eli's help in all this. Four human souls in exchange for his presence is hefty. But I can't think of anyone else I trust to bring into Summer, and after the week we've had, I know I'll need the extra firepower.

"Fine," I say. "Deal."

He pulls off his glasses with his free hand.

"What's wrong with you?" he asks.

Normally, this is the point where he would twine his fingers around mine to seal the deal. I try to do it for him, but the barrier is still in place—I can't budge my grip past it. Which means I can't blow past this interrogation.

"I'm fine."

"You're lying."

"You're right."

His eyes narrow. Everything else about him is human, save for the eyes. They glow blue azure in the night, almost brighter than the moon. You could see hell in those eyes if you looked deep enough.

"You're still hung up on the girl," he says. Then he pauses, his eyes searching mine. "No. It's not that, is it? What has changed since I saw you last?"

"Parental issues."

"Mab?"

"Just close the damn deal, okay?"

He chuckles. Because he's not the one losing blood here. Or getting the second degree. But he doesn't drag it out any longer. His fingers close around mine, and the familiar jolt of heat and pain and power flashes through me, from my heart to my toes. Then he releases my hand and wipes his on his coat, leaving a smear of red that fades quickly.

I pull a rag from my jacket and wipe off the now-cauterized wound. I don't speak and neither does he. Not for a while.

"So," he says, "what's new?"

I almost chuckle. Almost.

"We're going to Summer. I'll tell you on the way."

"There we go," he says. "I like it when you take charge."

***

I can't portal directly into the Summer Kingdom. It's against the rules, and oh, do the two monarchs like playing to their made-up little rules. The portal instead leads us to the boundary between the kingdoms, to where the Wildness brushes up against Summer.

We stand at the base of a large tree. When I say large tree, I mean it—the thing is as thick as a house, its branches reaching hundreds of feet into the air. Runes and sigils are engraved in the trunk; I'm not the only traveler who's marked this out for portals.

"So we're here to stop the Summer King from killing your true mother," Eli muses at my side. "Which you still might do. Accidentally or intentionally, depending on what's necessary. Have you considered that maybe we should just let him have her?"

"Have you considered I could summon you missing certain appendages you prize?" I ask, looking to his crotch.

"I did not. Though you have my mind racing now."

I shake my head and start walking forward. It's easier not to get into emotional topics with Eli. He's about as far removed from human as one can get—which, coming from me, is rather rich, seeing as I barely know what it takes to be human. With him, your best bet is to stay lighthearted and cocky. I've learned from much trial and error that astral creatures respond better to wit than anything remotely heartfelt.

"We need her," I say. "Whatever powers she possessed, they're the key to finding where the Pale Queen is."

"And we failed so spectacularly on our last mission," he mumbles. "Why not try the same thing again?"

"Shut it. This time we actually have a lead. We just need to get her powers to manifest."

"You still haven't mentioned how we do this."

"Because I still don't know."

Unlike Winter, the Summer Kingdom is one of the most inviting places I've ever set foot in. Rolling fields and forests as far as the eye can see, the scent of fresh grass and the song of birds in the air, everything caught in a perpetual sunrise. A cobbled path winds from the forest's edge and into the heart of the kingdom and Oberon's castle. Obviously, it sets me on edge immediately—anything this open-armed has to come with a price.

Eli follows close behind me. And, despite that whole "not being a dick" clause, he doesn't shut up.

"Have you considered that perhaps finding the Pale Queen is not our best tactic?"

"What did I tell you about serving without question?"

He stops, which causes me to pause and look back at him.

"Think about it, Claire. Mab has us running headfirst to find the Pale Queen. But I've not been static while at home. There are ripples in the astral world, you know. The creature we unleashed has more power than you and me combined, and more hatred than any demon I've met. Even without an army, she is a force to be reckoned with. And I do not mean to be rude, at least not in this moment, but I don't think you could take her."

"What are you suggesting?"

"That perhaps rushing in to confront Oberon is not the best tactic. The Pale Queen poses a threat to more than just Winter, and it will take more than Mab's forces to take her."

"So you think I should, what? Get Oberon to sign a peace treaty or something?"

"I think it would be better in the long run than a threat."

"Mab would kill me if she thought I was trying to make peace behind her back. You know that."

"Perhaps, but your Winter Queen is not so blind as to underestimate this threat. Perhaps she is already trying to work with Oberon."

I shrug.

"Beyond my pay grade."

"But you will admit I have a point."

"I will only admit that it doesn't matter." I sigh. "Look, I'm not saying I get this, either. Mab wants me to get Vivienne's powers to unleash. Supposedly to learn where the Pale Queen is. Do I believe that's the only reason? Not for a second. But I can't question. My contract prevents it."

"I still think the irony of you signing a contract is hilarious."

"Yeah, well." I keep walking.

I'm not blind, either—Eli's right. Mab has never been one to show her hand, and I have no doubt there are more reasons behind accessing Viv's powers than simply finding the Pale Queen in the Wildness. *Especially* since the Pale Queen seems to have no problem seeking me out. And yes, she and Oberon should probably be working together to fight off this threat, rather than squabbling over a single person.

But I'm not a diplomat. I'm an assassin. And Mab's already flung me on my course. I'm here to get Oberon to back off, and maybe reveal a bit more about the Oracle's nature in the process. And tell me why he seems to think he owns my mother.

We walk in silence a bit longer, the fields around us dotted with copses of trees and glades of flowers.

"I know why we're here," Eli says after a while.

"I'd hope so, seeing as I already told you."

"You already lied. We aren't here just because of Oberon and your mother. We're here because you're trying to cope. It isn't healthy, Claire."

I glare at him, and I actually do laugh at him this time.

An astral creature who feeds off innocent souls telling me that I'm not coping properly?

"I don't even know how to respond to that," I say.

"Because you know I'm right."

"Because you're ridiculous," I say. "I'm not coping."

"Clearly."

"Do you want to go back?"

He grins. "That would break our contract. And you know that's not something you want to deal with right now."

True. I already have one rogue astral creature to deal with. I don't need another. Especially since, outside of the bounds of our contract, Eli could and probably would kill me without a second thought.

"You're avoiding your problems," he says softly. "And that will get us both in trouble before long."

"I don't need a counselor—I need an accomplice. So shut up and keep your eyes open. Oberon won't be too happy when he finds out I'm here."

I know Oberon already knows I'm in his kingdom. Like Mab, he can feel when magic is used on his turf, especially travel magic from a Winter denizen. Especially mine. He and I have never been on the best of terms. Probably because I've killed off so many of his spies and Dream scouts. By my count, I only have a few more minutes before the welcoming committee arrives and I'm either handcuffed and bagged or turned around.

I'm fine with either option. I could use a fight to get my mind off things.

Damn it. I hate it when Eli's right.

More often than not, he is.

After a while, the fields turn to houses. The place has changed a lot over the years I've been trespassing here. When I was a kid, the houses were more like ramshackle huts, everything dilapidated and smelling faintly of shit. But the Trade has flourished in Summer, and the houses now rise above me like some sort of elfin wonderland—wooden huts dot rivers, and bungalows dangle from copses of trees, rope bridges spanning between everything in a beautiful maze. It surprised me when I first came here, the difference between the kingdoms. In Winter, everything is hidden behind the castle walls—to keep out the wild winds and the wilder creatures roaming in the woods. And that's not to say the Summer Kingdom is unguarded—I can feel the runes and glyphs that glow on stones dotting the road, wards against true enemies, and runes probably hiding some dormant Fey beasts—but it's definitely not as contained as Mab's. Which has always made me wonder . . .

Which kingdom would be the easiest to overthrow? Mab's, where everything is enclosed but could be taken out in one fell swoop? Or Oberon's, whose citizens sprawl for miles in the open? Mab would topple the moment the walls were breached, which is an impossible feat. It would take ages to track down every citizen of Summer. Even if they are out here like sitting ducks.

Not that there are many Summer Fey left to track.

The last time I was here, even the outer reaches of Oberon's kingdom were swarming with Fey. It was never as seedy as the brothels and bars of Winter—instead, there were sprites dancing in circles or dryads planting trees. It all looked like some pagan hippie love-fest.

But now the houses are empty. Just like in Winter, every place we pass is a shell, an open-air crypt. No rubble in the streets, no clothes hanging on lines. It's not like some third-world disaster. The place is just empty. Like a museum exhibit without its mannequins, everything plastic and perfect and waiting.

"Are we missing a party somewhere?" Eli muses.

"Like I said, the kingdoms are dying. Fey are flocking in droves to the Pale Queen."

"I wonder why. What could she promise that's more appealing than this?"

I can't tell if he's being sarcastic—his voice is perfectly dry as he says it. He knows what I know; he saw the ticket the Pale Queen had delivered to the denizens of Faerie, promising a life of untaxed Dream and no monarch supervision. But even that . . . I can't say it feels like enough. I could understand Fey leaving Winter. I mean, who wouldn't want to get out of that frozen hellhole, especially with the drought of Dream? But Summer was thriving. The Trade was lucrative. Why abandon a perfectly good ship?

We keep walking. The mound that is Oberon's castle slowly rises from the landscape up ahead. The structure is squat and sprawling, with low earthen walls and turrets and towers made from trees as large as redwoods. It's simple in its elegance, understated and smooth. Mab might be all imposing angles, but Oberon is lush and organic. Earth tones everywhere.

Which, to my senses, is a clear sign that he's packing a mean punch somewhere beneath it all. There's no way he could run a kingdom on kindness alone. One must be ruthless to rule. Which explains the assassination party he's sent after my mother.

My resolve tightens as the thought floats through my mind. I can imagine her, back in the circus. Is she being kept under close guard? Is Kingston with her right now, making sure that she's comfortable even as her memories slowly burn through his magic? Or is he dueling it out with the mob of Summer Fey lingering on his doorstep?

I kind of wish I were there to see it go down. I'd love to see Kingston go all Alpha Male on some Fey assholes. Just as I'd love to see what the Shifters can do under pressure. Have the Summer Fey let the showgoers leave? Or is everyone trapped in the complex, like some carnie sleepover from hell?

I should be there, protecting her.

"Penny for your thoughts?" Eli asks.

I don't answer, just nod toward the crowd on the horizon I know he felt coming long before I did.

"Ah, yes," he says, his cane tap-tapping on the cobbles. My imagination, or did he just manifest that thing? It seems to be his weapon of choice, the ivory shaft capped with a golden figure of a screaming child. "Let the fun begin."

Ten

Oberon is not pleased to see us.

I mean, he's never pleased to see me, obviously, but this time he seems even less so. He sits on his throne of curving branches and lichen and stares down at us, his dark eyes burning. He is the antithesis of Mab: he is dark to her pale skin, his clothes light to her black. He wears pale-tan robes, his rusty hair curling around the antlers stretching from his head. And he hasn't spoken. Not once. He just sits there with his hands clenched on the arms of his throne and his jaw tight.

I can't exactly be the one to make the first move, though. Ropes bind my arms and mouth. Tastes like straw and manure. I would *not* be surprised if the guards picked these up from the floor of the stables before shoving them between my lips.

Star treatment right there.

Finally, after staring daggers at us for another few moments, Oberon leans forward and speaks.

"Why have you brought this thing here?"

Instantly, someone rips the rope from my mouth. I lick my lips. It's not exactly coy, but it's not exactly *not*.

Oberon's a hornball if I ever saw one. The austere, self-controlled ones usually are.

"He's my partner," I say, nodding to Eli. He kneels right beside me, looking for all the world as though he's perfectly comfortable being roped up. I know for a fact that he is. Just as I know he could escape if he wanted to. "Now, my turn: Why are you after my mother?"

A small smile plays over Oberon's lips.

"I was wondering when Mab would let that little cat out of the bag."

"Answer the damn question."

Faeries can't lie, but they sure as hell can stretch the truth like taffy. When they aren't just spinning circles around it.

"Because she is mine," he says. "And I am taking her back."

"She's not yours. She's not anyone's. She's a mortal."

"That is where you are wrong," he says. "On many counts. Your mother swore herself to me. Before you were even born. Just as she swore you to Mab in order to get her powers back." He smiles. "And your current goal is to get her to remember her powers, is it not? The irony is not lost on me."

I barely hear his final words. My gut is somewhere far beneath the floor, my skin cold. I feel heavy as death.

She gave me away. No, she bargained with my life.

I'd always thought that I was the bad end of a deal, that Mab had manipulated Viv into giving me up. But to hear that, to have it confirmed, to know that my mother willingly gave me up, for what? For power? She was willing to sacrifice her own child for magic.

And look at you. You're willing to sacrifice your mother for that very same power. For that very same leader. Looks like you two have more in common than you thought. You're both horrible people.

Oberon seems to read my inner thoughts.

"Ah, she never told you?" He stands and walks toward me, then crouches in front of me and puts one rough hand on my cheek. "Mab never mentioned that your own mother deemed your life so unimportant, she could barter it without fear? Well, of course she could—Vivienne knew that with enough magic, she could forget the whole thing. Your mother has done a great deal of forgetting over her short life. She's made it an art."

I stare up at him, and it's like looking through frosted glass. Everything is blurred around the edges, and for the longest time I wonder what sort of magic he's using on me.

Then I realize he's not. I'm crying. Second time today, and I can't even mentally berate myself for it.

"I wouldn't take it too personally," he says softly. His hand hasn't moved from my cheek. "You weren't even conceived when she made the deal. How could she have known she would be giving up such a perfect child?"

In some small corner of my mind, I know he's manipulating me. He's called me many things in all of our encounters, but *perfect* was never one of them. Unless it was followed by something particularly derogatory.

"Why now?" I ask. "Why are you telling me this now?"

He's had me locked up on many occasions. Many opportunities to share this secret.

"In life and war, timing is everything." He smiles. The grin is vicious, just as cold and calculating as Mab's.

He pats my cheek and stands.

"So you see, there's very little you could offer me that would make me call off my dogs. Vivienne has already given you up once, so your life is no good as an exchange. And you have nothing I desire." He shrugs. "I'm actually rather disappointed in you, Claire. You were raised by one of the best manipulators in the world. And yet here you kneel, with no plan and no way to bargain. What did you hope to do? Appeal to my humanity?" His voice drops. "You forget what you're dealing with."

He waves his hand, and the guards that brought us in—rather hunky humanoid dryads with vines in their hair—lift me to standing. My body is numb. It doesn't want to move. It doesn't want to feel.

"You asked why I'm after her," he says as his guards turn us away. "Your mother swore her next life to me, and those words were binding as iron. That is why I will have her killed. She is no use to me as she is in her current state. Even if her powers resurface—which I know you think they will, I'm not blind as to why you'd seek her out after all this time—her body can't support the magic within. She would be a simple spark before burning out entirely. But when she dies, the powers of the Oracle will find a new host, one at the height of her power. And in that new life, she will be mine."

"But the Pale Queen," I mutter. My brain slowly kicks back to life. Too slowly.

"The Pale Queen is no threat to me," Oberon says. The guards pause at the door while Oberon continues to speak. "She may take those who are disloyal. She may even try to raise an army. But she is nothing against the Oracle, not when the Oracle is restored to power. Was that your ace? Thinking I would perhaps band with you to fight her? No, Claire. It serves me more to kill Vivienne and have the Oracle returned to me. That is better than any peace treaty. Though it does please me greatly to see you begging for my help. Does Mab know you are here?"

He smiles.

"No, of course she does not. And what will she think when she learns her one ally has gone behind her back in hopes of striking a deal?"

"The Oracle just tells the future," I say. I try to shrug off one of the guards. If I keep him talking long enough, I can figure a way out of this. He has to see reason. *I can't just let him kill her.* "Why do you want her so much?"

"She does much, much more than that, my dear. Your sweet mother is the greatest weapon the worlds have ever seen. Once she is mine, I will show you just how powerful she is, and how far those powers extend.

By my estimation, that should be quite soon. Your circus won't stand forever, not with Mab's attentions diverted as they are. You see, for Mab, this Pale Queen is a true threat. But to me, Mab's distraction is worth losing a few peons. There are much greater players at stake."

"I won't let you have her," I say.

Oberon waves his hand. The guards resume dragging me away.

"You've already shown me where she is," Oberon calls. "Just as you've unleashed the Pale Queen. By my estimate, Claire, you've already damned the woman you swore to serve. Forgive me if I'm not terrified by your empty threats."

The door slams shut behind us, and I'm left wondering if Oberon meant Mab, or my mother.

***

"All things considered," Eli says, "I'd say that went exceedingly well."

I don't laugh, even though I know he's trying to make light of the fact that we're currently locked in separate cells in the lowest part of Oberon's dungeon. I don't trace the walls and look for a weak point in the magic running through the stone. I don't even stand up. I just sit there against the wall and look out the bars at the empty hall beyond.

What's the point?

I could just stay down here, let them take my mother—

Pain shoots through my body, so hard and so fast I gasp and fall over, clutching my chest. I can't breathe. Can't breathe . . .

And then it's gone.

"Let me guess," Eli muses as I gasp and push myself up to sitting. "You thought of going against your contract."

"Something like that," I reply. I drop my head back against the wall, taking some small delight in the painful thud. For some reason, that pain is enough to root me down into my body again. Not that I *want* to be here. But I don't really have much of a choice apparently. "So how are we going to get out?"

"I assumed you already had a plan. After all, it sounds like you've been here many times before."

I look around. The cell is barely bigger than a closet, and every inch of it is covered in runes.

"I have been. But the bastard's learned from his mistakes."

"So do we bribe a guard with our bodies?" Eli says with a hint of excitement.

This gets a chuckle from me. He's trying to make me feel better, which is really strange. But I'll go with it.

"You can try," I say. "Don't know if it will do any good."

"Oh, it would do *some* good."

I shake my head and close my eyes. I try to force out the images of my mother bargaining me away. How does that change things? Does it make my next move easier? After all, if she never cared about me, I can't exactly bring myself to care about her. I'm not *that* masochistic or starved for familial love.

"Was that really your grand plan?" he asks after a moment. He actually sounds tentative, which means this isn't a joke—he's worried about my response.

"What? Getting locked up?"

"No. Using the Pale Queen as a bargaining chip."

I don't bother mentioning that it was his idea.

"I thought he'd see reason. You know, back off, focus on the common enemy. I didn't know about my mother's vow."

"So I gathered. Which means we are locked away with nothing to bargain with and no way to fight. I must say, of all the expeditions I've agreed to go on with you, this is definitely the least thought-out."

"Shove it."

"I'm just saying, I would have thought you'd have a fallback."

"I don't have *time* to craft a fallback."

"And here we are."

I roll my head against the stone. If I had known I'd be locked in a cell, I wouldn't have summoned Eli. Solitary confinement is a much better fate.

I hate that he has a point. I should have thought this through. I should have had contingency plans in place. I had gone in with only one ace up my sleeve, but Oberon was playing a different game. This is what happens when you get sloppy: you get caught. Trouble is, I truly had thought that he'd see the Pale Queen as a mutual threat, that he'd be hurting enough to put down his quest for my mother. Instead, I've just buried the point home for him: the sooner he has my mother killed and reborn, the sooner he can rise to greater power.

"Are we going to kill him?"

Eli's question makes my eyes snap open. I half expect a platoon of guards to storm us the moment the words leave his lips. The fact that they're met with silence only hammers in just how empty the kingdom is.

"What are you talking about?"

"He refuses to bargain," Eli says. "Your mother's life still hangs in the balance. According to your contract, you must use any means necessary to keep her safe until she divulges the location of the Pale Queen, am I correct?"

"Yeah."

"Well then, if Oberon won't pull back, you must kill him. It's the only way to keep her safe. Especially since there's no telling how long the circus's protection will last."

"How do you know all this?"

"I may be bound to the lower planes, Claire. But that does not mean I can't watch what you do on high."

I sigh.

"You can't kill Oberon. Just as you can't kill Mab."

"They are Fey. They may be immortal, but even immortality can be brought to an end."

"It doesn't work like that," I say. "It's not like in the circus, where they're only immortal because of a contract. They're forces of nature. Manifestations of winter and summer, light and dark."

"Good and evil?"

"Those lines are blurred," I say. I rap a fist on the concrete. "Obviously."

Eli doesn't say anything for a while, and it makes me believe he's lost interest in the conversation. I close my eyes again and try to figure a way out of here. About the only option I have is letting him loose from his bonds, but there's no telling whether he'd help me and no telling whether it would work. The wards on these cells are ironclad. So I guess we just . . . what, wait? Until Oberon gets my mother.

Pain shoots through me again, sends me reeling to my side. It's only when I convince myself *okay, okay, I'll get out of here* that it releases.

Fucking contracts. This is why I spent so long freelance.

"She has to know we're here," I say, trying not to pant. "Mab will force Oberon to let us out."

"And what makes you think he'll listen?"

I shrug. "He has to."

"I don't think he and Mab are as infallible as you are led to believe. Or as immune. You must remember, Claire, that I come from a completely different plane of existence. We exist without Summer or Winter. So, too, could your world."

***

Oberon never comes down to gloat. Not like all the other times I've been locked away in here. No one comes down. No one brings food or water, and it becomes immediately clear that the cell I'm in isn't made for a human—no toilet, for one thing. Thank the gods the runes on my spine allow for more than just a little extra magic or power; a quick flash of magic and my metabolism slows to a near halt. It's not a fun skill—the fallout on the other side of it is pretty nasty—but it's saved my ass on more than one occasion like this. I should be able to go at least a week without eating or sleeping or . . . anything else. But once the magic fades, I'll basically be a zombie.

Just what I need.

Trouble is, I'm bored to tears, and I can't sit here much longer wondering what's happening in the outside world. Is my mother still safe? Have her powers resurfaced yet? It kills me, knowing I'm sitting here twiddling my thumbs while she's in trouble. But I'm trying to figure a way out. I trace the runes and glyphs and magical seals in the walls. Oberon's covered everything, from astral travel to radio waves to shape-shifting. Clearly he's not taking any chances this time around.

I close my eyes. I might not need sleep, but I can trick my body into it, just to pass the time. Oberon *has* to come down here. Eventually. What's the point of holding me captive if not to taunt me about it? It would be easier to just kill me and get it over with. He knows I'm not one to crack under pressure. The thumbscrews he tried out on me should have been proof enough of that.

Sleep comes slowly. My body grows heavy; my thoughts begin to diffuse. I feel the room drop away, feel my body dissolve into something more spacious.

But I don't lose consciousness. I don't forget that I'm dreaming. Instead, I watch the room blur and shift with a distant sort of interest.

Until my body congeals again, and I find myself standing in a forest.

I know this place.

I saw it in the vision from the Pale Queen's ticket.

The woods shift around me in shadow and light, nothing truly solid, everything red and orange like the world is bathed in sunset. Or maybe it's not the sun at all, but the Dream. It fills the air like ribbons of smoke, so thick even I can feel the high of it, the power that floods through my veins. So much Dream, so much power, and it isn't bottled or woven or sold as in Mab's kingdom. It floats freely, ripe for the picking. Intoxicating. Delicious.

"This is my kingdom," comes a voice. Feminine and old, pulled from the depths of the sea. "This is my rule."

And the world shifts. Suddenly, I'm not in the mess of trees; I stand on a pillar overlooking a field as vast as Winter is cold. Fey flood below me. Some laughing and dancing. Some building with stone and wood, coaxing trees to grow as arches or simple huts. There are streams of glittering water and hills of slate-grey ice. Even from here, I can see that there are no boundaries between the Fey of Winter and Summer: snow drifts against hot springs, saplings rise from patches of ice. It's as though the seasons hold no sway here. As though no one cares about the age-old rift.

Above it all, above the trees and the ice and growing monuments, the sky flutters like a crimson aurora, the Dream so thick it nearly blocks out the sun.

And then I realize, it's not a pillar I'm standing on, but a tower of a castle that stretches behind me like a maze, everything within glittering and gorgeous in the light. How could she have built all this so quickly?

"My followers have known I would rise for ages. And they have been preparing for my arrival."

"Why are you showing me this?" I ask. My voice is hollow, and I wonder if I'm talking aloud in my sleep, if Eli can hear my question from his cell. "When you know I'm just going to kill you."

"I believe we are after the same thing," she says. "A world free from tyranny. A world of balance."

"I'm only after your head," I respond. "And trust me, if this wasn't a dream, you'd be dead already."

"You will understand, in time. You will see how truly alike we are. When freed from the shackles of your monarchs, our kind can flourish."

"Our kind? What the hell are you talking about? I'm a mortal."

"And yet so much more. Your mother is in danger, is she not?"

I don't answer. I'm not negotiating with terrorists. Even in the dream world.

"I could keep her safe, you know. In my kingdom, neither Mab nor Oberon could trespass. And I have more than enough magic at my disposal to ensure she lives comfortably, for as long as she likes."

I can't help but stare at her. Her mask is back on, and her crown glitters like the sun. Despite the glare, I can tell she's smiling.

"You're lying."

"I do not lie, Claire. I have no vendetta against you, or your mother. I feel your pain. Truly. I know what it is like to be subject to the whims of the Faerie Kingdoms. Under my rule, you both would be safe."

Laughter peals from the valley below, and when I glance around, the thought actually crosses my mind: *What if I came here? What if I let the Pale Queen win?* It looks peaceful. More pleasant than Mab's kingdom, and definitely better than the life Vivienne had been living in the mortal world. Here, she could have a future. That's more than I can offer her.

I fully expect my contract to lash the thoughts from my brain. It doesn't. It can't; I'm still dreaming.

The woman reaches out, gently places her hand on my arm. It still burns like fire, but the pain is muted. Someone else's pain. In someone else's dream. "Soon, you will have to choose. I can be forgiving, but I will not be patient forever. Bring your mother to me and lay down your arms, and you and I shall rule side by side. Consider this my final gift. A reminder of who actually has your back. Remember whose side you're truly fighting for, Claire. Faerie's, or mankind's?"

The dream fades, inks out like a stain, and then I jolt awake at the sound of metal clanking. In the hall is a figure in shadowy robes. My hands immediately reach for a knife that isn't there. Before I can try to go on the attack, the figure turns down the hall and disappears.

"The fuck?" I whisper.

Just as the door swings open.

Eleven

I can't actually believe my luck. I crouch there for a good minute, ears and eyes straining for further footsteps. Surely this is a setup. There's a faerie waiting down the hall to call the guards and have us killed. There's no way in hell the Pale Queen has plants within the Summer Court, ready and waiting to do her work, even if it's springing me from jail. And it's not like anyone within Summer could or would spring me from the dungeons. Oberon would know about it immediately and have their head on a spike.

It makes no sense, and that keeps my hackles raised.

"Are you going to let me out now or what?" Eli asks. I nearly jump out of my skin. It's so easy to forget he doesn't sleep.

"It's a trap," I whisper.

"Of course it's a trap," he says, not even caring to drop into a whisper. I wince.

I can't hear or sense anyone, but that doesn't mean there isn't a faerie or golem or something waiting just out of range. It feels like a test. One where those who stay in their cell get rewarded and those who sneak out get punished. Badly.

Good thing I've never cared about a little rough play.

I creep from my cell and over to Eli's. It's not locked with a normal padlock. Instead, there's a long copper plate along the locking mechanism, the surface smooth.

"What the hell is this?" I whisper.

Eli leans against the wall of his cell, arms crossed, as if he's there of his own volition. I can just see his outline, though his blue eyes burn bright.

"I'm pretty certain only Summer Fey can open it," he says.

"Of course." Because simple just isn't the name of Oberon's game.

I glance around. The hall is empty, but I know the upper dungeons are swarming with Fey. They have to be—what's the point of a dungeon if there isn't a guard?

"Give me a moment," I say. "I'll be right back."

Oberon took all of my weapons, and the dungeons are pretty much warded against all magic—not that I have much at my disposal anyway. But I'm still a weapon unto myself. An assassin who relies entirely on her blades is worthless. And I will never let myself be worthless.

Eli wishes me luck as I creep down the hall. At every turn I expect to stumble across a guard, but there's no one. Not around the next corner, and not up the first flight of stairs. Oberon's kingdom is just as empty as Mab's. And that means even his guard is depleted. Suddenly, my plan seems a little more impractical. Not because I don't have the skill to pull it off, but because there might not be anyone to pull it off *on*.

Then again, I *could* just leave Eli there . . .

I'm about halfway down the next hall when I hear someone coming my way. I stop and curl up into the shadows along the wall, slow my breathing to a whisper. The figure rushes past me. Am I that lucky? They don't see or sense me, and the robe they wear gives nothing away. I can only hope it's the same faerie that released me, the one that works for the Pale Queen. I have a lot of questions to ask, and this would kill two birds with one very convenient stone.

I slink behind the retreating figure, and it's only when my arm goes around their neck that I realize that if it *is* the person working for the Pale Queen, they're going the wrong way. And when my arm tightens, their flesh doesn't give. Because it's not flesh at all.

I curse my luck at having jumped a golem when the creature lets out a yelp, and I let go immediately. It crashes to the floor, and I rip off the cloak. I don't know whether to start cussing him out or kissing him.

"Pan," I gasp instead. "What the hell are you doing here? *How* are you even here?"

The satyr statue sprawled at my feet looks back at me, one hand to his smooth chest as though he's fending off a heart attack. He's one of those cherubic faun statues, complete with dimples and nubby horns. Except he's clearly been around the block; there are chunks missing from his marble skin, and one of his horns has been sheared off to the base.

"Claire?" he asks. "What are you doing out? I'm here to rescue you."

I laugh. Then I realize he was serious and feel really bad for a half second. But seriously: *him* rescue *me*?

Pan's been at my side ever since I was sent to Mab's kingdom, my mentor and watcher and glorified babysitter. And yes, he's come to my aid a few times. Last time I saw him, he'd been helping me protect Roxie. But making his way into the heart of Summer to free me? That's a level of badassery I didn't think the guy had. Or stupidity. I mean, who wears a cloak when trying to seem inconspicuous?

"How did you get here?" I ask.

He pushes himself to standing. The fact that he doesn't answer right away tells me he really doesn't want to talk about it.

"It is a long story," he says. "But we must get you out of here. Now."

I grin. "Clearly already ahead of you on that one. I need to get Eli, though. Did you pass any Summer Fey along the way?"

He doesn't ask how only I escaped. I know that will come later.

"Why do you need a Summer faerie?" he asks. He looks at his feet.

"To open the lock. It's magicked or something. Only opens for someone from Summer."

Pan is many things. A good liar isn't one of them.

"Let us go, then," he says, still not making eye contact.

"Pan, what aren't you telling me?"

He doesn't answer. Instead, he starts walking down to the dungeons, from where I'd just come. I shake my head. Statues suck at small talk. This one in particular.

Pan doesn't speak until we're back at the lowest cells of the dungeon. He stops in front of Eli's door and looks to me.

"There is much you don't know," Pan says. Then he glides his hand down the copper plate, and the door unlatches.

"Clearly," I respond.

Eli steps forward, looking between the two of us as if there are a dozen questions he wants to ask but probably won't until he has me on my own again.

"Well then," he says instead. "Shall we?"

Pan nods and turns away, but I force him to a halt.

"Hold on." I grip his shoulder tight. "How do we know this isn't a trap of some sort?"

He actually looks as though I've stabbed him through the heart— his eyes go wide and his mouth forms a tiny little O.

"Why would you even think that?" he asks.

"Because you show up in the nick of time, somehow magically able to get Eli out of his cell, and now you're promising a hasty retreat? It's too easy, Pan."

"This is not the time or place," he responds, looking up and down the hall. But no one's coming to recapture us. Oberon's complacent in his guard.

"And this isn't a place you should be," I reply. "So you're going to tell us how you're here. Now. Or I'm going to lock your stony ass in one of those cells for Oberon to find."

His expression goes from shocked to angry in a heartbeat.

"After all I've done for you."

"Trust is hard to earn and easy to break," I reply.

"I was created in Summer," he says. "It is here I served Oberon and your mother, through many of her incarnations. Until I learned about you. About what happened to you. I left Oberon and forswore my oaths. Mab took me in as your caretaker. That is how I know Summer, and that is how I know the secret ways in and out. Now, if you'll follow me, my *stony ass* will save yours. Once more."

Then he turns and storms off.

I glance at Eli, who grins in an impressed sort of way. "I like him," he says. I shake my head and follow Pan through the halls.

I've been through the Summer Palace many times. And it *is* a palace, whereas Mab's place is definitely a castle. Hers is built for defense and awe. Oberon's is built for luxury. Once we leave the dungeons, we're in a grand hallway twice as tall as it is wide, the arched ceiling dripping with tapestries and chandeliers that frame massive stained glass and picture windows overlooking fields and gardens. We pass pedestals with suits of armor (I keep expecting them to attack, but these must actually just be for show, which proves how confident Oberon is in his exterior defenses) and priceless vases and other décor that's so gaudy and baroque I actually long for the starkness of Mab's decorating. Despite the extravagance and false sense of safety, I don't let my guard down. There might be a softness to Oberon's style, but that doesn't mean he's stupid.

Mab uses sex appeal to lure people into thinking she's pliable. Oberon uses aesthetic indulgence.

Pan brushes aside a tapestry and leads us into a narrow passage, the light in here coming only from what peeks through the velvet on either end. He doesn't speak, and he doesn't lead us toward the light. Rather, he ducks into the shadows of a side corridor, this one even narrower than the first. I follow by dim sight and the sound of his hooves clopping against the marble. Eli is silent as a wraith behind me; if not for the pressure of his gaze between my shoulder blades, I might have thought he'd vanished.

I don't ask where we're going. Pan leads us along one corridor and then another, down a flight of stone steps, and into a passage so dark, even my rune-enhanced vision can't see a thing. If not for the glow of Eli's eyes, I would probably be following by sound alone. Finally, after a good twenty minutes of walking through colder and darker tunnels, we come to a dead end.

At least, that's what I assume from Pan's sudden halt.

"This is just past Summer territory," Pan says. His voice echoes in the hall. "Right on the edge of the Wildness."

"And a dead end."

Silence. Yes, yes, I know I could portal here—I'm not that stupid. But Oberon took everything I was carrying. I don't have a single nub of chalk left.

I don't mention this. Because I have no doubt Eli would make some quip about hiding things in other places, and I don't have the energy to punch him.

Thankfully, Pan saves me from saying anything. He bends down and picks up a small piece of chalk. "I brought in extra," he says. "I am well prepared."

"So you are, old friend," I reply. I hope that's enough of an apology for doubting him earlier. Probably not. He hands me the chalk, and I start sketching, the white lines practically glowing in the darkness. I draw out the rectangular doorway, then the glyphs and sigils for travel: equations and words and symbols. As much as I don't want to be going there, I trace out the coordinates for Winter. I need more weapons, and Pan—helpful though he is—wouldn't be much use in an actual mission. I won't tell him that, though. I'm not that much of a bitch. Most days.

"Thanks again," I say to Pan as I crush up the chalk and blow it over the door. Magic swirls down my arm and through the dust, cementing the portal in place.

"You are welcome," Pan replies. I can tell he doesn't mean it.

***

My room isn't empty when I arrive there.

Which should be impossible. So the moment I see the hearth fires burning, I know who's there before he turns around from his spot on the sofa.

Kingston.

He's no longer in his ringmaster attire, just his usual jeans and baggy T-shirt, his hair back in a scraggly man-bun I sort of want to chop off and sort of want to yank on.

"Guess that answers whether or not I fixed that flaw in my room's defenses," I mutter, throwing my coat on the sofa beside him.

He doesn't smile.

"It's still glaringly obvious," he says. He pauses, looks me right in the eye. "Why are you doing this to me?"

Not *where have you been?* or *how's the good fight?* but *why are you doing this to me?* I want to laugh. Instead, I head to the liquor cabinet and grab a bottle of bourbon, take a swig, and begin rustling through my weapons case.

"Doing what?" I ask, shuffling through butterfly knives with one hand while the other holds the bottle. I grab a few blades that are specifically enchanted against Summer Fey and begin sliding them into my various pockets and belts.

"I'm not your enemy," he says. And oh, he sounds as though I've kicked him in the nuts. It's so pathetic I laugh again. Then I take another drink, because I don't have the mental or emotional capacity to handle this. I just learned my mother's next life is bound to Oberon. On top of everything else I have to handle, now I have her future incarnations to worry about.

"What the hell are you talking about?" I ask.

I slide open a drawer filled with rapier-thin swords. I pick one up, the blade a burning violet, and examine it in the light. Enchantments are still relatively fresh, the power good. Blade sharper than a scalpel. It'll do. Satisfied, I thrust the blade into my hip, where it vanishes in a whirl of smoke, ready to be summoned when needed.

Okay, I admit, I'm picking some of my more flashy weapons partly for show. But they're still good weapons.

"Why did you bring her to me?"

I look at him, roll my eyes, and go back to looking for more weapons. The more I can hide within my flesh, the better—I'm not letting anyone steal all my blades again. I grab a rope dart and twine the chain around my wrist, where it disappears into my skin.

"We have a dozen Summer Fey camped out around the show right now, waiting for us to crack. Waiting for her to become vulnerable. It's been three days since you left her with us. We can't move, not without risking her life. The moment we tear down, we stop being in Winter territory. Not that staying put has helped. Her . . . episodes . . . are getting worse."

Three days? Normally I could control—or at least coerce—time between the realms to remain stable. Apparently, being in Oberon's care screwed that one to hell. At least a year hadn't passed.

"Stay, then. I'm sure your troupe would love not having to switch sites every week."

He shakes his head. "It doesn't work like that. *Can't* work like that. There are rules."

"There are always rules."

"We can't stay in one place for too long without risking exposure. And we're already running low on patrons for the show. If we don't move soon, we're toast. And if we move, Viv is no longer under our protection. She isn't safe."

"Then maybe you shouldn't be here flirting with me," I reply. "You should be figuring out how to continue protecting her."

"That's your job," he says. "I've already done my part."

I turn on him. I've already ripped him a new one for *doing his part* to my mother, but I want to again. I want to rip him open until his guts are strewn about my room. Metaphorically and maybe a little literally.

"Why the fuck are you here, Kingston? To whine? Because I brought your ex into your show? Because I'm forcing you to see the consequence of your actions?"

I grab a rapier from the cabinet and shove it into my other hip as I speak, the magic unraveling into my flesh. A small part of me had hoped it would pierce; I want to feel the pain. Strike that; I want *him* to feel it.

"I'm here because she can't stay with us. Not for much longer," he says. "You need to take her."

"Where? To Winter? She can't come here, and I'm not about to go under Mab's nose on this one. Not with what's at stake."

His eyes narrow.

"You let Mab move you without even questioning it. Did it ever strike you that she won't allow Vivienne in Winter because she would rather use her to hurt me?"

"Get over yourself. This has nothing to do with you."

"It has everything to do with me. Just as it has everything to do with you. Mab's punishing us."

"You really have a victim complex, you know that?"

"Live with Mab as long as I have, and you would as well."

"Yes, well, I'm not an idiot. I didn't sign any immortality clause. Still mortal. Still have an easy way out."

"That's nihilistic."

"It's the truth."

And that's when it hits me, like a punch to the gut. My mother's no longer under Mab's contract, no longer immortal—her soul, or whatever, supposedly goes back to Oberon the moment she dies. But if Mab were to reemploy her, she'd be safe. Oberon wouldn't be able to touch her. Ever. Maybe that's the way out. If she becomes immortal, her powers can't kill her. I could still get her to track down the Pale Queen. I could still . . .

You honestly think Mab didn't already consider that?

"How long until your magic fades enough for her powers to come back?"

He shrugs uncomfortably and looks away. "A week. Maybe more, maybe less. It's not something I can predict. Some memories flare stronger than others, and they burn through the magic faster."

"And then?"

"She dies. I keep trying to tell you this. She won't become the Oracle again. She's just going to burn out and die."

"Mab said her powers would come back."

"Mab doesn't know the situation like I do." He looks to me. "It's not just that, though. We don't have a week."

"What do you mean?"

"I mean Melody's sick."

"She's not sick," I say. "She's old. And dying."

Again, the tightness in his eyes, telling me I hit my mark.

"Yes. That. She doesn't have much time left. Not if . . ."

"What? Not if what?"

"They'll attack soon," he says. "Nothing big. Nothing we can't fend off. But it's starting to wear on her."

"That's not allowed. Mab would never—"

"For now, they aren't doing anything wrong, so Mab can't intervene. But they know we're weakening, and Melody's so stressed it's wearing her thin. In a few days, she's going to crack. Maybe not enough to let them in, but enough to let them do some damage. Viv can't be there when that happens. We can't let them take her."

"No shit," I reply. I'm packed solid with weapons, but I grab a few daggers and walk to the sofa. I flop down beside him and grab my jacket, hiding the weapons within. The leather's enchanted—stronger than steel and warded against most magic. It's also studded and sexy as hell.

He actually flinches away from me. That's a first. Normally he's trying to get into my pants. Or at least pretending to be.

"But we're going around in circles," I say. I keep sliding daggers into various pockets. I should probably pack some Tarot cards, just in case I need the extra magic. "Viv dies, we don't track down the Pale Queen, and Oberon says he gets the Oracle. You're saying that no matter what, Viv's powers won't come back to her. So, what? It's hopeless?" I don't let myself consider the Pale Queen's offer. Not with Kingston around, and not when my contract could stop the blood in my veins for thinking such treason.

"If we had more time, maybe I could figure something out. As it is, it's taking all my concentration to keep the show running and Viv from living in terrible pain. This is on you."

"Isn't it always?"

"If Oberon let up . . ."

"I've already talked to Oberon. He's not interested. He wants Viv dead."

I take to staring into the flames. Kingston needs more time. I could wait outside the circus and kill off Oberon's army, but that would be seen as a blatant act of war, which means Oberon could attack the tent with his full force and not face any consequence. Mab's not ready for that sort of attack. Not yet. I need to figure out how to access Viv's powers. And if they're buried down with her past, maybe the past is where I need to go.

"I loved her, you know," he says. His voice is gruff.

"Yeah, I know."

He grabs my arm. Forces me to look at him. My initial response is to break his wrist, but when I see his eyes, I actually feel a pang of pity.

He just looks so damn helpless.

"No," he says. "You don't know. I know what you think. I know what you saw. Mab told me to convince your mother I loved her, but I didn't need to pretend. I *did* love her, Claire. More than I've loved anyone in my entire life. Do you know what it's like? To go over three hundred years trying to find someone you love enough to spend the rest of eternity with? And then to find her, and lose her. Not once, but twice. She gave everything up when she saved the show. And now, she doesn't even know what she's lost. Do you know how it feels to watch the woman you love fall in love with someone else? To have her look at you and not have any clue who you are? To have to feed that magic so she can *never* know, because it would kill her, even though it kills you every single day of your meaningless life?

"I run a show that doesn't change. I live a life that will never end. I can't even kill myself because it's against my fucking contract. The only thing keeping me together is the thought that maybe she's happy, that maybe I can move on because she's moved on. And now you've brought her back. Back to me. Back to the show. Back to being a reminder of everything I lost and can never have again."

He doesn't look away through his entire monologue. When he finishes, he looks like he's on the verge of tears. Normally, weakness is a huge turnoff. But something about this is endearing. Not that it helps his case any.

"That castle, the place you barged into . . . that was supposed to be our retirement. She and I had dreamed the entire thing, and I built it. All for her. Started when she was in the show, but I never showed it to her. I wanted it to be a surprise. Then she . . . left. And for some reason I keep building, hoping maybe one day she'll see it. Maybe one day, it will be so filled with her memory that it's like she's there." He shakes his head as if he can't even believe he's telling me this. I can't, either. He must have an angle; no henchman of Mab's shows weakness unless it's to get something.

In this case, I have a feeling it goes deeper than trying to gain my trust or get my mother out of his care. I just can't figure out what.

"And yet," I say, looking him dead in the eyes, "love her though you do, you still slept with her daughter."

He looks away then, spots of color rising in his cheeks. He lets go of my arm.

"It was a moment of weakness," he says.

"Fuck you." Just like that, all pity I might have had for him vanishes. But he isn't in fight mode. He's still wallowing.

"I missed her," he says. His eyes waver as he watches the fireplace. "So much. I'd watched her grow old. Watched you up until Mab took you away. Mab hid you from me, did you know that? She never would tell me why, but I think it's because of this. She knew I'd fall for you. Would need you, if only to feel . . ." He shakes his head. "I'm so screwed up, Claire. I slept with you because it let me pretend I was with her again. That she still loved me. I can't even begin to ask your forgiveness."

Inside, I am as cold and dead as the dagger I want to shove in his chest.

"Good," I say. "Because there's no way in hell you'd get it."

I stand and slip back into my jacket. Now that it's fully stocked, I feel a little less naked.

"You need to leave," I say. "I've got work to do."

He looks at me. Still like a lost little puppy. Still a thousand miles away from me giving a shit.

"I can't go back to her," he says. It's barely above a whisper. "I can't keep doing this, Claire. Her pain keeps getting worse. I don't know how much time she has left, how many more times I can take away her hurt. Especially when I know it's just going to kill her."

"It's your job," I say through clenched teeth. "You'll do it because you have no choice. Because it's what you signed up for. Just like I will do my job. Now, get out so I can get on with it."

He stands. Looks me in the eyes.

"I once said you took after her," he says. "I was wrong. You take after Mab."

I smile, imitating the Winter Queen the best I can. I know I pull it off flawlessly.

"That's the first nice thing you've said all night. Out." I point to the door.

He shakes his head again. But he doesn't walk away. He snaps his fingers and vanishes in a swirl of slate-blue smoke.

The moment he's gone, my smile drops. I shove my hands in my pockets and force down the weakness rising up in my throat like a sob.

My night is just beginning.

Twelve

I fully expect Mab to intercept me as I leave the castle and head back into the kingdom proper. But the halls are empty and frozen, and I nearly slip on the ice twice. By the time I make it out into the cold night air, I'm ready to be back in the mortal world. Preferably somewhere with a beach and drink service.

Just that thought is enough to take the air from my lungs. Apparently I'm not even allowed to indulge the fantasy of taking time off. I pause on the steps and take a deep breath, letting my thoughts settle back on the job.

I try not to war with myself while I head toward the Lewd Unicorn. I know, in theory, I should be with Mom, trying to get her to remember. Trying to reignite the spark. But if I'm being completely honest with myself . . . I can't. Being around her makes me feel vulnerable. Weak. And those aren't things any assassin should feel. I need to stay away, focus on other things while the magic binding her memories unravels. I need to ensure Oberon doesn't kill her before that happens.

Shivers spread across my body, and at first I assume it's just the cold. Then I realize I'm not walking alone.

The Pale Queen walks beside me, still in her gown of white, though it glows pale blue now. And still, I can't see her face through the mask.

I have a dagger out and to her throat in a heartbeat, but she takes another step and the blade passes through her as though she's nothing but mist. I stop cold.

"I'm not really here, dear girl," she says. Her voice echoes in my head like wind through a conch. "You cannot kill a vision."

"What the *fuck* are you doing here?" I hiss. I look around, afraid I'm being watched. Even though the streets are empty, Mab has eyes everywhere. She knows everything that happens within her kingdom. Everything.

"I'm not," she repeats. She pauses and turns to me, raises an arm, and taps me on the temple. "I'm in here."

"I'm going insane," I say. "I've finally seen too much, and I've blown a fuse and now I am insane."

"You are not insane."

"This is impossible," I say. Not because I don't believe in visions, but because I don't believe they could happen *here*. Mab's disconnected this place from any and all magic. There's no way the Pale Queen could be projecting herself here, into my thoughts and vision.

To think she could means . . .

Well, it would mean she has powers not even Mab can imagine.

She laughs.

"That would be correct," she says.

I don't acknowledge her statement.

"Why are you here?"

"Because you want to distract the Summer King."

"I—"

"I can hear every thought in your head," she interrupts. "I know what you think, what you desire. You wish to save your mother. I wish to destroy the kingdoms. Perhaps we can work together."

Pain shoots through my chest and I fall to my knees. I barely feel the ice that scrapes under my fingernails as I claw at the cobbled street, trying to keep myself upright.

"I will never . . . work with you," I manage. The pain subsides immediately. It takes all my self-control not to roll over into a fetal position and rock; the ache isn't there, but the memory of it lingers. Instead of showing any more weakness, I push myself to standing and glare at the figment of my imagination.

"Be that as it may," she says, completely glossing over the fact that I just buckled, "the Summer King may soon find himself . . . preoccupied. I will help you. Again."

"You know I'm bound to kill you, right? Why the hell would you help me?" Her proposition from before floats through my mind, bringing with it the sense of nails dragging across my skin. I can't let myself consider it. Any of this. She is the enemy. No matter what, the Pale Queen is the one I must kill.

"All things change."

"Not this."

"Even this."

"You're not getting anything in exchange," I say. "This isn't a deal."

"All conversations are deals, Claire. The sooner you learn this, the better. The key is whether or not you fulfill your end of the bargain. And I *always* fulfill my bargains."

Before I can ask her what she means, a gust of wind filters down the street. She vanishes like snow the moment the wind touches her.

"Shit."

I glance around again. No one there. No eyes in the windows or sneers in the shadows. No one to see me talking to myself. I should go tell Mab that this happened. I turn to go, but then stop myself. If I tell Mab, she'll dig out every scrap of truth. She'll learn that the Pale Queen is offering sanctuary for my mother and me. That alone would give her reason enough to kill me on the spot. And if she learns I unwittingly made a deal with the enemy . . .

What the hell did I just do?

"Nothing," I say, trying to convince myself. "You did nothing. She's just playing with your head."

Something I've found astral creatures to be quite good at. Speaking of . . .

I pull my coat closer around me and continue on my way, forcing down the Pale Queen's offer and what was basically her assurance that she would attack Oberon. For me. Eli is waiting. And drinking on my tab.

***

"Did you decide to take a nap?"

I sidle up beside Eli at the bar. He doesn't look up from the five empty tumblers in front of him.

"No," I answer. "Christ, man. How much have you had?"

He shrugs. He doesn't seem the slightest bit intoxicated. I don't think he actually *can* get intoxicated, come to think of it. Not even from Dream. "You can afford it. Where were you?"

"I had company. Kingston." I'm not going to mention the Pale Queen. I don't need him thinking I'm any crazier than he already does.

"Ah, the magician. Why don't you just sleep with him again and get it over with?"

In answer, I punch him in the shoulder and look around the bar. The place is empty. And I don't mean that in the metaphorical only-the-regulars empty. I mean we are literally the only two people in the bar. Even the bartender is missing. For once, my sanctuary feels less like a home and more like a, well, bad dive bar.

"Does Celeste know you've had all those?" I ask.

"I'd hope so. She poured them after all."

"Then where is she?"

He shrugs again. "Don't know. But I'm already thirsty." He looks at me then. Even behind his sunglasses, I can see the blue of his eyes. He doesn't look happy; he looks tired. "I'm going to have to ask you to pay up soon. There were more than just wards in those cells. Half of those sigils are designed to drain the life out of their captives. I'm surprised you're able to walk."

"I'm tough," I reply. I know where this is going. "We'll get you a meal later."

"Not much later," he says, looking back to his empty tumblers. "And I'll need more than a single meal. I want a couple. A couple very much in love."

"Jesus, Eli, really?"

"Really. And if you keep complaining, I'll get more specific."

I shake my head. I keep expecting Celeste to flitter out of nowhere and pour me some bourbon; if she doesn't show soon, I'm going to have to do it myself. I eye the rows of bottles behind the bar, the contents glowing in a multitude of delicious colors. Distilled Dream. The stuff is like honey to the Fey, but to me, it's more like a short LSD trip. Totally potent, totally addicting. And seriously deadly, both in the case of overdose and in the more probable case of trying to jump off a building because you downed too much flight Dream.

"When?" I ask.

"Why?"

"Because I want to go after Oberon before he has a chance to realize we've escaped."

Eli doesn't answer at first. Instead, he slowly takes off his sunglasses, folds them up, and places them in the breast pocket of his jacket. Then he turns to me, and those blue eyes are scathing.

"What the hell is your problem?" he asks.

"Uh, what? What the hell is *your* problem, Eli?"

But before he can answer, I'm made aware of the bartender's arrival by a slight purple glow reflecting off the white of Eli's suit and the clink of glass. There's a tumbler of bourbon sliding toward me before I even turn to our hostess.

"I was wondering if you'd be in," Celeste says.

Celeste is a wisp—a tiny glowing ball of purple light—but despite the fact that she has no limbs or lips, her skills as a bartender are legendary. I've seen her man the entire bar when slammed with pixie rock groups and angry sprites and satyrs on the edge of bacchanalia. She hovers behind the bar, her voice echoing within my head.

Can't keep me away, I think back.

I love this place. It's the one part of Winter where Mab almost never goes. But it also means I have to keep my thoughts controlled—Celeste can read me like a book. One with very big fonts. Which means I shouldn't be here for long, or under any sort of influence. My brain is not a stable place right now. *What is Eli's problem?*

"I've been wondering," Eli muses to his refilled glass. The liquid glows a sultry red. Whatever Dream Celeste is feeding him, it's definitely more . . . earthly delights. And his voice has a dangerous edge. I know that tone. It's his innocent, shit-starting tone.

"Yes?" Celeste responds. Her glow dims just a little bit as she addresses both of us. Probably because she wants me as backup.

"Dream." He raises his glass and swirls the liquid around. Then he tilts the glass and lets a stream of it slowly trickle to the bar. "You make such a fuss over it. Say it's what feeds you. And yet . . . you don't keep it for yourself. You work so hard pulling this from mortals, only to give it up for your queen. So you can then barter it back."

"What are you asking?" Celeste asks.

"I don't understand it," he responds. He watches the Dream, and whether it's his magic or the elixir, I swear I see shapes and bodies writhing in the flow. "You have no money. Just Dream. You give up your Dream to be sold a little bit less of the Dream you earned. You pay for Dream with Dream. You work to sell the very thing you buy. Why?"

"Because that is the way things are done." Celeste's response is quick, rote. I've heard it before, from other Fey. Not that I questioned the system too deeply. Mab didn't like it when I stuck my nose into her affairs. And for her, the Dream Trade was a *very* personal affair.

"And?" he asks. "In the beginning—because there has to have been a beginning—why? Why did Mab and Oberon take control? And why do they get the bulk of what you work an eternity for?"

Celeste doesn't answer. Not for a while. The empty tumblers on the table levitate up and are tossed in a bin beneath the counter, shattering when they hit. Eli drops his now-empty glass to the table, but Celeste catches it before it hits. Then she tosses that, too, into the bin with a crash. For a moment, I think she's cussing out Eli in private. And maybe she is. It's only when a rag appears from under the bar that she addresses us both.

"In the beginning, there was chaos. Chaos between the Fey, chaos on earth. There was no balance, no order. We nearly killed ourselves in that confusion."

"The beginning?" he asks. "As in, when the Fey first appeared, or when humans appeared?"

"They were the same," she says. *"Humans and Fey have always lived symbiotically—their Dreams fed us, and our magic fed their world. And so, when there was no order, the worlds of Faerie and Mortal were a mess. It was from this chaos that Mab and Oberon appeared. They crafted their kingdoms and crafted the balance. And when Faerie became whole, so, too, did the mortal world. As payment for this great act, Oberon and Mab declared themselves rulers and set up the parameters for the Trade. Those who sought refuge within their kingdoms did so because they knew the cost of losing the balance. They knew how necessary Mab and Oberon were to keeping order. Without Summer and Winter, the mortal world would collapse. And so we partake in the Trade. To sustain ourselves, and to sustain the worlds."*

"How noble," Eli says. He taps the bar absently, as if he's hoping for another drink we both know will never come. "A life of servitude so others may live. No wonder so many of you are jumping ship."

"Eli—" I begin, but he stands and cuts me off.

"I'll be going, now. Thank you for that history lesson. As always, *she* will pay my tab. In Dream."

He shakes his head and walks out of the bar.

For a moment, Celeste and I just sit there in stunned silence.

"What was that about?" she asks.

"I have no idea," I mutter. "But I apologize for it."

"Astral creatures," she says, and I can practically feel her raising her hands in disdain.

I stand and follow Eli out of the bar. It's only when I'm outside and jogging to catch up to him that I realize I hadn't even touched the bourbon.

"What the hell is up your ass?" I yell.

He doesn't stop. Just walks a little faster, his cane tapping in the empty silence of the street.

I don't think. I grab the nearest thing I can find in my jacket and throw it at him.

When the dagger lodges between his ribs, he stops. Then he unhinges his arm, twists his free hand around his back, and pulls the blade from his skin. There's no blood, of course. And by the time I reach him, his suit is already restitched.

"That," he says, turning to face me, "was very rude."

"So is what you just pulled." I hold out my hand for the dagger—this one was enchanted to poison Summer Fey. He's lucky the blades for astral assholes are in my boots. But he doesn't hand it back. Instead, his eyes glow brighter blue as he folds the blade with one hand, the metal instantly flaring white-hot. It drips through his fingers and steams against the snow. "What was that about?" I ask.

"That was for you," he replies. He shakes the last of the metal from his hand and pulls a handkerchief from his breast pocket to wipe away the final traces. Naked men and women twine around each other like scandalous Celtic knot work on the fabric. Classy to the core, he is.

"For me? You treat Celeste like shit and say it was for me?"

"That history lesson was necessary," he says. "You needed to understand just how ridiculous the Trade is."

"Why?"

"Because you are risking your life for a system that doesn't work. Do you not hear yourself? Go after Oberon, try to kill him. Find the 'On' switch to your mother's powers to find and fight the Pale Queen, even though we don't stand a chance against her. I understand that you are under contract, Claire. But what you are doing—"

"Speaking of contracts," I interrupt, "you aren't allowed to question me. Ever."

"And I am not. I'm questioning your friends."

I sigh. There's no use arguing with immortals—they've been around longer, and for some reason that makes them believe they're smarter.

"Why now? All of a sudden, why do you have a problem with what I've hired you to do? It's always been about Dream, Eli. Every single hit has been to secure Mab's hold on the Trade. And yet every time I summon you, you come back willingly."

"Perhaps it's because I enjoy your company," he says.

I don't answer. He folds up the handkerchief and places it back in his coat.

"Fine," he finally says. "I am questioning because *you* need to be questioning."

"I can't."

"But you should. Especially your motives. You are running headfirst into danger. You want to try and kill the Summer King even though we both know that is impossible. You are a mortal girl. You're strong, and you're a pain in the ass. But that doesn't mean you can kill one of the most powerful Fey in this realm."

"It's the only way—"

"To ignore the real problem." He takes a step forward, puts a hand on my shoulder. I think he's trying to be comforting. All it does is come off as creepy.

"Eli."

"You are hurting, Claire. It's plain as poison. You are still torn up over Roxie, and now, paired with the appearance of your long-lost mother, you are doing everything you can to ignore it."

I shove his hand away and seriously consider stabbing him again. I know it won't do any good, but it would make *me* feel better.

"I'm not hurting."

"Bullshit. You loved her. I know it."

"I didn't *love* her," I hiss. "I don't *love* anyone."

"You can lie to me all you want. It won't change what you feel. And right now, what you feel is interfering with what you should think. You're an assassin, not some lovelorn teenager. If you want to kill the Pale Queen, you need to be thinking straight."

"I *am* thinking straight. And I *am* doing something about it," I say.

"Getting yourself killed by facing Oberon isn't productive."

"Do you have a better idea? Because if I spend one more minute in that damned circus, I will burn the place down."

"I believe that's been done before," he mutters, but then he looks at me, all serious again. "You need to process. I don't say this as a friend. I don't even say this as someone who cares about your well-being. I say this as someone calculating your odds of success. You can't kill the Summer King. You can't keep him from going after your mother. You need to be thinking straight if you want to solve this. And that means facing what you don't want to face."

"Since when did you become a shrink?"

"I am serious, Claire. Everything you are doing will fail if you don't face what Roxie has done to you, and what seeing your mother continues to do to you. You have always been a cold, heartless bitch. That is why I continually come back to work with you. Now, you are confused and emotional, and that is a dangerous combination on the battlefield."

"You know," I say, "I don't think anyone has ever mansplained something to me and lived."

He smiles and pats me on the back. "That's the assassin I was hoping for."

I punch him and start walking toward Winter's exit. The tap of his cane tells me he follows close behind.

"Where are we going, then?" he asks as we leave the Unicorn's alley.

"Getting you a meal," I respond. "Hopefully when you're fed you won't be such an ass."

He chuckles. "I wouldn't count on it. After all, we both know it's the only reason you put up with me. That, and the sex."

I shake my head. It's times like this I'm grateful he has a one-track mind. Food and fucking.

My mind is similarly wired. Eli's right; I *am* hurting, and no amount of sobbing in a tub with expensive whiskey will help. No amount of *facing my past* will help. I've lost Roxie. I've lost the hope that I could live a life even remotely resembling something normal and human. I've lost my mother—both the reunion I wanted to have and the future I'll never get.

And that means it's time to make someone else feel that loss.

I'm going to wake my mom's powers up. And I am going to ensure that both the Pale Queen and Oberon pay the price.

Thirteen

I feel strange making a portal back to my mother's neighborhood. We step out into a dark night punctured by streetlamps and the distant glow of some unknown city. Once more I can't find the slightest hint of familiarity. Then it strikes me—maybe this isn't where I grew up. Maybe Mab relocated my family the moment I was taken. It would make sense; fewer emotional triggers, fewer memories to potentially haunt. Less chance I would ever find it.

The thought just makes me colder. If this isn't where I grew up, where was it? And why does not knowing make me feel more adrift than it should?

"I must say, this is the last place I thought you'd lead me," Eli says, interrupting my derailed train of thought.

Damn it, the guy's right. Why am I worried about feeling alone when I have a job to do?

Pull. Yourself. Together.

"It's as good a place as any," I respond. I grab a butterfly knife in my pocket, let the cool tang of metal and magic root me down. I look to him and try to keep my face stony. "Or would you prefer something more exotic?"

"This will do," he says. "I'm sure we can find some couple here who loves each other and isn't just pretending for the neighbors."

"I can't believe you care so much about this."

"I don't. But you do. Consider this my lesson for the night: love makes you weak. And when you are weak, you are prey."

Before he even finishes talking, he begins his stroll down the street. He doesn't speak as I jog to catch up to him. He barely shifts his gaze from the road in front of him. But I know he's searching for his next meal; there's an alertness to him that reminds me of a hungry dog. We head down the street and around a few corners, getting deeper into the trenches of suburbia. It's quiet as a tomb out here: no animals in the yard, no stray cars on the street, no teenagers ditching their curfew. I can hear myself think. And that's not a good thing.

I look around at the rows and rows of houses, and I can't help but wonder if maybe this *isn't* so bad a life. Everything is quaint and peaceful . . . and weak. The only danger here is us.

This could have been your upbringing. This could have been your future. And I can't fight off the thoughts that run through my exhausted mind: a younger me, playing hopscotch on the sidewalk, using chalk for play and not for a weapon; teenage me, stealing cigarettes and smoking in alleys with a gang of friends I'd kill for. And Roxie. With her, I have no idea what I'm envisioning. Us living together? Or being friends, visiting every weekend for wine and movie nights? Talking about the guys or girls we were falling for, the supermodels we wanted to be or bone.

I'm so screwed up that I don't even know how to categorize what I feel for her. *Felt* for her.

And none of that matters. Roxie is dead. I was weak. I will never play out that role again.

To do that, I have to give this up. I can't be normal. I can't have a life in suburbia. I can't begin to understand how the human heart works beyond start and stop. I will always be the shadow in the street. I have to be okay with that.

Gods, it can't be good when Eli—practically a demon—is the voice of reason.

He stops in front of a house just like every other.

"This is it," he says, as though it should be a surprise. Of course this is it. He wouldn't be stopping just for giggles.

"How do you know?" I ask.

"Emotions are like magic. Each has a distinguishing trace. And this place reeks of true love. I'm surprised your ovaries aren't melting."

I glare at him. He ignores me. He walks up the sidewalk, his cane vanishing into shadow the moment he steps up to the front door. I don't follow. I don't watch him eat; it's only polite.

"Are you coming?" he calls. I wince—his voice carries easily in the cool night air. But if anyone hears it, they don't act on it.

"Seriously?"

"Seriously."

He doesn't move to open the door or teleport in, and after a few seconds I realize that he won't budge until I'm at his side. He wasn't joking—he wants this to be educational. I trudge up beside him.

"Why are you doing this?" I ask.

"Because I'm hungry."

He places a hand on the doorknob. There's a faint click of magic as he turns the knob, and then he steps inside.

The place looks like a carbon copy of my parents' house, but he doesn't give me any time to ponder. He's up the stairs like a wraith, his blue eyes casting trails of light over everything. I follow, just as silently, just as smoothly. It feels like a test to see if I can keep up. Whatever. If he thinks I'm going to flinch away from this, he doesn't know me half as well as he thinks he does.

I hear them breathing before we even reach the bedroom door. Not that either of the sleeping couple are loud, but my senses are on fire from nerves and adrenaline. I don't want to be doing this. I don't want to see this. These are innocent people, about to die because Eli is greedy and wants a power boost. *Whose side are you fighting for . . . the Fey, or humankind?*

"Remember," he whispers to me, clearly reading my thoughts, "I'm here because you summoned me. Their lives are in your hands."

"You're an asshole."

He doesn't respond, and I don't move from the open doorway as he slips into the room. I don't know how they haven't woken up—the light from his eyes is blazing, the interior of the room glowing like an aquarium. Then he leans over the bed and inhales heavily.

"They've been together eight years," he muses, his voice a low rumble. I try not to look at him, but I can't help but glance over as he runs a finger along the smooth jaw of one sleeping guy. His partner—scruffy and dark-haired to his partner's blond—mumbles something and rolls in closer, wrapping himself tighter in his lover's embrace. "Recently married. Plan on having two kids." Eli looks at me. I can't see his face from the shadows his eyes make, but I can feel his cruel smile. "It's amazing what they have gone through to come to this point, the battles they've fought. The family lost. Even now, their Eden isn't perfect. There are many on this block who think these two are abominations. You can feel the hatred directed at this house. And yet, of everyone in this neighborhood, their love is the purest. Can't you taste it? It's like ambrosia."

"We're leaving," I hiss. My stomach is in knots. I can't do this. I can't watch this. I can't let these guys die. I turn to go, but Eli's hand is on my shoulder before I can take a step.

"You. Will. Watch." He doesn't let go of me. He drags me over to the bed, and I want to scream. I want to wake these guys up, because they don't deserve this. No one deserves this. But Eli is right—I can feel the energy here, the sanctuary they've carved in a place that doesn't fully accept them. And I know why he's chosen them. Not just for the love he says he craves to devour. But for that sense of shared isolation. I look down at their sleeping faces, and I know what they've gone through. I can feel it. I can empathize.

I don't fit in, either, no matter how hard I try.

"This is what you want," he says, his free hand stroking the curly-haired guy's head. Magic filters through his touch, calming them, keeping them asleep. "You want that love. That home. You want to share your heart and feel that you are not alone. You want a future that is safe from the evils of the world. But that is the greatest lie of humanity, Claire. You are each alone. You will each die in your own time. *That* is why love is weakness. You cling to it and hope it will keep the darkness away. But the darkness always comes. And it's creatures like you and me who bring it."

His fingers clench on the guy's hair, and the sleeping guy wakes with a start.

"Wha—what the—"

I barely see what happens next; Eli's face grows pale, his jaw cracking open and elongating as his eyes burn even brighter. And then my eyes squeeze themselves shut, because not one part of me wants to see. I can't block out the light. I can't block out the man's screams as Eli inhales his soul.

It seems to last for hours, and it's not just the man that I hear, it's Eli—his voice in my head, his *true* voice, promising oblivion and despair, cold suns and burning moons, eternities of darkness and eons of bitter light. Every cell in my very human body trembles from the onslaught. Every inch of me wants to run and hide, wants to have never been born.

And then it stops.

I don't open my eyes.

"I never pegged you for squeamish," he says with a single short laugh. "No matter. He tasted delicious. I kind of like having you here. It feels . . . voyeuristic."

"Get it over with." I still don't look. I don't want to see the guy's blank eyes. I've seen the aftermath of Eli's feedings before. His victims don't die. That's the worst part.

"No," he says. His hand loosens from my shoulder. "This one is yours."

"What the hell are you talking about?" I ask. I peer at him; his grin isn't gone, but it's serious.

"I demanded four souls. I didn't say I would be the one to take each of them. I can take his postmortem, you know. It's not as fresh, but it will still do the trick." His voice drops. "Kill him."

"No."

And then I do look, and I want to gag, because the sleeping partner is still coiled around his lover, and the curly-haired guy is barely a vegetable now. Two minutes ago they were in love. They had hopes and dreams. And now . . .

"Do not for one second forget who and what you are," Eli hisses. He points to the blond guy. "This man is your hit. You are the blade. You strike. You do not feel. You do not question."

"But he hasn't done anything."

"And you have no proof that anyone else you've killed has, either," Eli says. "All you have is the word of Mab. Perhaps the blood that stains your hands was that of the Fey, but how many mortals did you kill? How many times did you strike because someone was stealing your mother's precious Dream? And how many times did you question if stealing Dream from Winter truly was a crime, in the long run, or if it was simply someone else's greed?"

My blood is colder than ice as he talks. I can't tell him he has a point. I've killed, both for pleasure and work. I've made faeries turn to ash and tortured mortals to reveal their masters. All without blinking. Without the slightest hint of guilt because *of course* I was in the clear. Even when working for the devil herself, I was on the right team. I can't even begin to question Mab—it's against my contract, and it's against my upbringing.

"There is no greater good or evil," Eli says. "There is no ruling force to take the blame. Every choice you have ever made, every murder you have ever committed, has been because you and you alone decided to go through with it. There is no celestial order to uphold. You heard the barkeep—before Mab and Oberon, there was chaos. But there was still life. And I have no doubt that in the midst of that chaos, someone else would have come along to change it had those two not risen first.

"These men are innocent in your eyes. But those you've killed were innocent to the eyes of others. Don't you see? Everything is subjective. Which is why, to obtain your goal, you must be objective. You must not feel. You must not doubt. You must kill."

I can't take my eyes off the couple. I can't stop their faces from becoming the countless others I've assassinated at Mab's command. Murdered.

Eli is right. I can't be soft. I can't pretend that I've ever had some divine purpose. I am a killer. Killers cannot love, and they definitely can't be loved in return. Not by lovers, not by family. I am alone. I am death incarnate.

Yet, as I pull a dagger from my coat—this one enchanted for instantaneous death—I wish I had the ability to create Dream. To pour some liquid life into the sleeping man's throat, make him believe he's flying with his lover, that there is some beautiful light at the end of the tunnel. I want to do this, because I want to believe I'm not as heartless as the creature standing beside me. I want to believe I'm sending him somewhere better.

I can't.

And I don't.

I reach over and slit the blond guy's throat. My enchantment rolls through him, stops his heartbeat in an instant. Eli actually moans as he inhales the dregs of the man's soul. I don't listen. I slit the other man's throat and drop the blade to the bed.

I'm out the door before Eli's finished feeding.

It doesn't matter that I want to run outside and scream and rip my hair out. I don't care that my throat is twisting, that my stomach wants to vomit up the few meals it's been able to take in. Because the moment that cool air hits me, the moment I'm back in the shadows and staring at another urban sky, it all falls away.

Eli's right. There's no great cosmic good or evil. There's no force telling me right from wrong. I've played with gods, and they're just as screwed up as the rest of us. As I stand there and stare at the clouds, I realize it all with a cold sort of clarity. I've never been better than anyone else. I've never deserved to live more than those I killed. Not really.

The key was that I thought I did.

No. The key was that I acted on it.

I take a deep breath, force it to be smooth and not ragged, not torn like I feel. I force the emotions to stillness.

When Eli steps beside me, I don't feel any anger toward him. I don't feel anything.

"Better now?" he asks. I should be the one asking him.

I nod.

"So why are we here?" he asks. No mention of what we've just done. What he's forced me to realize. Like Mab, he doesn't belabor points. He knows I understand—lesson learned, next chapter.

"Because you were right."

"As always."

"Killing Oberon won't solve anything. We need to get to the Pale Queen. And that means getting Vivienne to open up."

"Yet here we stand, far away from the circus that houses her."

"Because she doesn't remember anything," I say. I take a leaf from his book and begin walking, letting him follow my lead. "Her husband, however, does. He's hiding something. And if there's a crack in his memory, we can use it to find the weak point in hers."

"Finally, you're thinking like a killer."

I don't say anything. I know it's meant to be a compliment. But a small, dying part of me feels as if it's a curse.

Fourteen

I fully expect Austin to be asleep when we get to the house. I have no clue what time it is beyond late, but there's a light on in a distant room, the glow just barely peeking out the front windows.

Here I was hoping for a slightly more dramatic entry.

"He works fast," Eli says. I look to him, and he gestures at the door and the lawn. Both are perfectly intact. You couldn't even tell a motorcycle gang had ripped through here three days ago.

Rather than break down the door, I knock. It opens barely ten seconds later, revealing Austin in all of his sleepy glory.

And yes, I know he's my father, but there's still a small part of me that finds it devilishly attractive—him standing there in loose boxers and tank top, his grey hair mussed. He doesn't look confused to see me, though he does give Eli a guarded once-over.

"Melody," Austin says. His voice is a gruff whisper.

Dad, I want to say.

"Austin," I reply instead. "Sorry, I know it's late."

He waves it away and opens the door for us to step in.

"Don't worry about it. I was up anyway. Work in an hour."

Right. Mom had said he worked odd shifts. Doing . . . whatever it was he did.

Eli steps inside smoothly, like a king entering his castle, looking loftily at the portraits and décor on the walls.

"Who's your friend?" Austin asks, nodding to Eli. "And why's he dressed like a pimp?" He looks back to me with an eyebrow raised, as though asking if I'm in perhaps a *different* business. One that requires late hours.

Despite everything I've just seen, I actually laugh.

"Business partner," I say. "And no. Not that sort of business. He's just an eccentric."

"Uh-huh."

Eli steps over and introduces himself, offering Austin his hand. Austin doesn't take it. Instead, he once more looks at me. I don't like that look. There's a great deal of hidden information in those eyes, and it's clear he isn't certain he can say any of it with Eli around.

"Why don't you go outside," I say to Eli. It's not a question. "Amuse yourself. But don't get into trouble."

I expect Eli to put up a fight, but maybe he's realized he's already pushed me too far tonight. He just nods, says "a pleasure" to Austin, and slinks off into the front yard.

"He's . . ."

"Unique?" I ask.

"Inhuman," Austin replies. My heart gives a little lurch. Was that metaphorical? He motions to the kitchen. "Come on. I've got coffee going."

"That's the best news I've heard all week." I wish I weren't being serious.

Austin hands me a mug the moment I'm in the kitchen, then leans back against the counter while I settle myself on the stool.

"I'd offer you cream and sugar, but you don't seem like that type of girl."

"You're right. I like it like I like my men: strong and bitter."

He chuckles. It's short-lived.

"Are we dropping the facade now?" he asks.

"What facade?" Because this could be anything. I'm acutely aware of the way he's been looking at me, and the fact that I'm here in leather at—according to the microwave—three in the morning, and his wife and family are away. But I'm also holding on to that *inhuman* comment, and the fact that he said I had a performer's name when we first met. I don't know what he knows. Being raised by Mab, I'm used to playing this game—who spills first?

He takes a long drink, considering his words. When he speaks, he doesn't look at me. He looks at the photo of him and Vivienne and their changeling daughter on the fridge.

"It started a few years ago," he says softly. "When Claire became a teenager. At first I thought it was just stress, you know? I thought I was getting laid off, and Claire was exceptionally moody, and Vivienne . . . she just kept retreating into herself. I didn't know how to cope. And then the nightmares came."

"Nightmares?"

"I didn't pay much attention, at first. But they kept returning. Every night I'd dream the same thing. Viv crouched over a little girl, holding a knife. Blood everywhere. Some nights I saw different faces—Viv's father, rather than the girl. And some nights it wasn't Viv at all, but this glowing . . . thing. I tried to tell her about them, but the moment I mentioned anything about dreams she would shut down, tell me they were stupid."

Dreams are many things. Stupid is not one of them.

"Eventually I stopped saying anything. The dreams would go away for a few weeks or months. But they always came back. Always. And stronger."

"Why are you telling me this?" I ask. Clearly he doesn't think I'm some sort of shrink.

He looks at me then. His eyes waver; he looks scared of himself.

"Because then they stopped being dreams. People started to . . . change."

"What do you mean?"

"I mean, some days at breakfast I'd look over and it wasn't my little girl staring back, but a monster. Or the mailman would come and he wouldn't be our usual guy. I mean, he was, but it was like I could see through him, almost, and it was someone else—someone with a snake tattoo around his neck."

Kingston. Coming in for his regular checkup.

Austin shakes his head. "I'd see people on the street, and when I looked back, they wouldn't be there. Or they would, and they'd have wings, or thorns growing out of their heads. I figured I was just going insane. I saw someone about it. Got medication. It helped a bit with the nightmares. For a time. Then the meds would wear off or stop cutting through and I'd be hallucinating again. Eventually I just stopped telling anyone anything was happening—it seemed easier than the alternative. But I knew . . . I knew I wasn't crazy."

"Maybe you are," I say. I'm not going to give ground—a lot of mortals hallucinate, and it has nothing to do with the Fey. Not that I think that's the case here. I have no doubt this guy's brain has been screwed with so much, it's practically putty. "What does it have to do with me?"

He takes another drink and makes a face. I know that face—he's wishing the drink were alcoholic.

"Do you know what it's like to wake up one day and know without a doubt that everything in your life is a lie?"

I don't answer. He continues.

"It was like something cracked. I woke up and looked at Vivienne and knew she wasn't the woman I loved. At least, not anymore. And when I saw Claire . . . I saw her as something else. Something not quite human. Kind of like that Eli guy, but different."

"Sounds like a mental breakdown to me."

He shakes his head. "That's what I thought at first. Then I started looking at my life. Really *looking* at it. Trying to remember my life before I got married, before I had a kid. And I couldn't remember any of it. I didn't have any photos or journals. My parents were useless—just kept saying I was a good kid whenever I asked about my past. It felt like a lie.

"Then, one afternoon when Viv was at work and Claire was in class, I started looking through the few photos we *did* have. Trying to remember the picnics or vacations or school assemblies. The memories were there, but it was like remembering something I'd read; I couldn't *feel* anything. And it was horrible, because this was my family, and I felt nothing toward them. Not even the wedding photos sparked an emotion. I felt awful."

Again, I don't see where he's going with this, or what it has to do with me, but it's like watching the floodgates open; I know he's been wanting to say this for a long, long time.

"There was . . . there was this envelope. At the bottom of a shoe box. And it was weird, because it was sealed with wax, and there was a *K* on the seal. I thought maybe it was just some old wedding card that got misplaced. But it had never been opened. It felt . . . I don't know, it felt forbidden, in a way. But I opened it anyway, and inside was a photograph. It was Viv and me, at the hospital. Holding our baby. The doctor was beside her, and we were all smiling."

He trails off and looks into his mug. Whatever he sees in there isn't comforting.

"Two things hit me at once. First, the doctor was the same guy I'd seen snooping around—had the same tattoo and everything. The second hit harder. I knew, the moment I looked at that little bundle, that that was my daughter. And I knew it wasn't the girl I'd raised the last eighteen years."

He goes silent again.

I wait.

"I've known there was something off about this family for years. The dreams keep changing, start feeling like memories. I remember helping Vivienne escape from her family. I remember losing her. I remember being in a circus. And then . . . I'm here, with a kid and a wife, and I don't know how I got here."

"Sounds rather delusional."

"I'm not delusional," he says. His words are very calm and very quiet. Clearly, my temper is from my mother. "I don't know why you came here, or how you're involved in any of this. But I knew the moment you stepped in here.

"You're my daughter. You're the girl I saw in that photo. And I've been waiting a very long time for you to come home."

I don't speak. I don't know what sort of response he expects. Had I not just witnessed and partaken in the death of an innocent, adorable couple, I might have had the emotional depth to break down and fling myself into his arms and cry *Daddy*. Not anymore. I take another drink from my coffee and consider my words as he considers his. What can he know? More importantly, how can I use him?

He doesn't break the silence, either, but I can feel his eyes on me even as I stare everywhere but at him.

"Okay," I say after a while. "Let's say what you're talking about is true."

"It *is* true."

"*If*," I continue, "then what are you insinuating? What you're talking about is—"

"Magic? Demons? I don't know, Claire, but whatever it is, it's happening."

I sigh. I thought perhaps it would feel good, having my name spoken through his lips. It just feels like another thing pushing us apart.

"It's all true," I say. "Mostly. The girl you've been raising isn't human, and she's definitely not your daughter. She's a faerie. A changeling, if you will—put in my place so you wouldn't know your real daughter was missing."

He opens his mouth, and I can practically feel the questions he wants to ask: *Where have you been? What are you doing back?* I don't have time or patience for any of them.

"Listen," I say before he can speak, "I'm not here to cover lost ground. I have a mission. And it involves your wife."

"Your mother."

"Yes." I shake my head. Here I thought this would be easier, him knowing the truth. Turns out it's more difficult—not because he knows, but because he doesn't know enough. And I'm just not the right person to tell him. "She's important. She has a power. One that I need to unlock. But the very magic that has kept you in the dark is keeping her powers locked away."

"That's all you have to say?" he asks. "You come home, and I've told you . . . told you all this. And all you have to talk about is some mission?"

"You wanted the truth," I say. I gesture to myself. "This is the truth. I'm not the daughter you always wanted. I'm not the answer to all your problems. Knowledge isn't power. I have a job to do, and it involves killing a lot of people so, hopefully, the rest of us can survive. So we can save the touchy-feely bullshit for later. If I don't get the key to Vivienne's powers, there won't be a later anyway."

I can tell he wants to put up a fight. He wants to know, and yes, he probably has a right to know. Where I've been, what I've done. But all he gets is what I've become. I flourish my hand, and one of the daggers I'd hidden in my flesh appears with a whirl of green smoke.

"I'm an assassin, Dad. And right now I'm trying to save the world. You either help me in that, or you get out of my way. I don't have time for anything else."

He stares from the dagger to my eyes. As though he's trying to find a hint of the daughter he saw in that photo. As though he's trying to see if there's any humanity left.

"What do you need?" he asks.

Clearly, he didn't find it.

Fifteen

Interrogating Austin isn't nearly as fruitful as I'd hoped. As far as he knows, Vivienne has never had any sort of flashbacks or flares of power. She's never been exposed to any trigger, has never registered anything beyond bemusement toward life. My heart drops with every answer he gives, not just because I'm not getting anywhere, but because her life truly sounds miserable. And with every bit of despair comes a hint of rage. Toward Mab for doing this to her, for making the rest of my mother's life as exciting as tapioca.

By the end, all I've learned is that Vivienne has always become a little nostalgic around the circus, which is why they haven't gone in years. And that the changeling daughter has barely ever left the house. She went to a local college and lived at home, and even though he swears she moved out at one point, he can't actually remember when, or for how long. Which just has me believing that that was another implanted memory. I have no doubt the faerie has never left my mother's side.

"What do you need her for?" he finally asks, when both of our coffees are cold, and it's clear he's missed work.

"It's complicated."

"All of this is complicated."

I stare at him. I'm starting to understand why Vivienne chose him over Kingston. Sure, Kingston's flashy, but Austin's hot in a different way. Beyond good looks, the guy seems steady. And if my mother is anything like me, stability is something she probably desperately lacks. Not to mention, his ability to deal with this is incredible. He should be a blithering idiot by now. Instead, it's as if he's known about this shit his entire life.

Maybe he has.

"Viv has . . . powers. She can tell the future, that sort of thing. And I'm looking for someone who is very, very good at hiding. I can't find this person on my own. If Viv could tap into her powers, I could find my hit."

"You can call her 'Mom,' you know," he interjects.

No, I can't. My mother is the woman who raised me, and she's the icy queen of a kingdom you've never heard about. I can't tell if that's the truth, or if I'm just trying to convince myself of it.

"That's complicated, too," I say. I wish I didn't sound so defeated by it. I really, really need a full night's sleep. And a meal. And probably a really good lay, just to get my mind off of things.

"What . . . what will happen to her?"

"The woman I'm after? I'll kill her. Obviously."

"No. Vivienne. Your mother. What will happen to her?"

"Why would anything happen to her?" I counter.

"If what you're saying is true, these people have gone to a lot of effort to keep her in the dark. No one does that for nothing. There has to be a risk."

I open my mouth to tell him that there's a good chance she'll die in the process. Then I see his face. He might not know the full extent of his partner's past, but he still loves her. I know that look; he'd be crushed if something happened to her. I can't even imagine how he'd feel if he knew I might kill her in the process.

"Nothing," I say. "She's a bigger risk to those around her. That's why her powers were hidden."

"If that were the case, why can't whoever hid them just undo it?"

"Complicated."

I set down the mug. The tone in his voice says he's looking for an argument, and I don't blame him. This would be frustrating as hell, to know you've been right all along but to still be kept in the dark on why. I look at the clock. Already wasted an hour here, and who knows how Eli's entertained himself.

"I should probably go," I say, rising from the stool.

"What happens next?" he asks.

"What do you mean?"

"I mean, they're going to come back. Viv and that . . . that *thing*. What do I do, now that I know the truth?"

"I don't know," I lie. "But we'll figure it out."

His scenario won't happen. No matter what. Because if Viv *does* live through this, I'm going to ensure she doesn't come back to this life. As for Austin . . . I look him up and down. There's a resilience to him I admire. Something in his face tells me he'd go through hell and back again for his wife. And for me.

He can't remember this, though. Not for his own good.

I walk over and give him a very awkward, very brief hug.

"We'll work it out," I say. *Or, rather, Kingston will.*

***

Eli's waiting for me outside, sitting on an elegant wooden chair that I'm positive doesn't belong here. The moment I step out, he stands, and the chair vanishes with a crackle of blue embers.

"Well?" he asks, gesturing to the house.

"Nothing," I reply. Just like last time, when hunting for answers about the mysterious buyer of all the Dream, this feels like grabbing at crumbs. I know Mab knows more than she's letting on. I also know she'll never divulge until she absolutely must. Or wants to. *Maybe she should be the next person I interrogate.* But no. I can't risk the interrogation going the other way. "He knows absolutely nothing. Save my identity, which means Kingston's not as in control of his own magic as he thought."

"And yet you stayed in there for so long." He pushes up his glasses to give me an appraising sort of look. "You didn't . . ."

"No!" I say, pushing him aside as I walk around the house. "You're sick, you know that?"

"I do. So what were you discussing?"

I grab some chalk and start sketching the portal as I talk.

"Just telling him what he already suspected—his wife isn't who he thought she was, his daughter isn't even human, and he's not as crazy as he'd hoped. Viv's been completely static. No slipups or memories as long as he can remember. He has no clue how we'd undo it, and even less clue how her powers could be brought back. The magic binding her is tight."

"And yet, his slipped."

I shrug, complete a constellation of Draco, and turn to him.

"Everyone's been focused on keeping Viv's memories stable. It's not surprising that Austin's slipped—he's not a threat to anyone."

"So where are we going?" he asks.

"Back to the circus."

He sighs. "I feel like you're just going around in circles here. Weren't you just at the show?"

"Yes," I say, crumbling the chalk in my palm. "But that was before you gave me your little lesson. You were right, Eli—I *was* weak. My mission is getting my mother's power back. And that's going to involve getting a little dirty. Mab said I was the key, but I've been too afraid to get close enough to examine why." I blow over the chalk, watch it billow and swirl into the portal I've drawn. "I was scared to hurt her.

But you've reminded me. Hurting people is what I do best. Maybe that's why Mab put me on the job in the first place—she knew I'd do whatever it took."

Before I can see his reaction, I place a hand to the wall and step through.

***

I don't teleport into the circus itself, but to an abandoned shed a few hundred feet away. Not because I'm worried about breaking a rule or being rude, but because I want to get a good look at the guard Oberon's placed around my mother.

Sure enough, the moment the world clears and I'm facing the darkened big top, I smell the unmistakable tang of lightning and cut grass: Summer. The clouds are still there, the sky heavy, and it feels like a storm is about to break. In more ways than one.

Eli's at my side a moment later, swirling into focus like a cloud of white ash. His sunglasses are gone, and his blue eyes take in the field with a slow burn.

"How many?" I whisper. I might be able to sense the Fey, but getting an exact count is difficult.

"A few dozen," he replies.

I glance around, funneling a small bit of magic into some of the runes along my spine. My vision clears despite the late hour, and suddenly I'm able to make out the trees jutting from the landscape, their silhouettes vaguely humanoid and their auras glowing neon green. They spread around the circus in a wide circle, like a faerie ring of oaks and elms rather than little mushrooms. Between the trees, hiding in shadows or curled into grassy mounds, are the other Summer Fey. Wisps and goblins, Shifters and dryads. A small army.

I fully expect one of them to attack us; they don't. Nothing moves as Eli and I walk toward the darkened sprawl of the circus, the sky on the eastern horizon just beginning to glow with dawn. The light is thick and diffused through the clouds. For some reason, I know the clouds won't burn off in the light of day. There's a magic settled up there, one that seethes and refuses to shift. It even tastes wrong. I keep my hands in my pockets, fingers tight around the knives stashed there. I don't trust these calm interludes. They usually spell disaster.

And yet, we make it to the unlit neon sign over the promenade without any interruption.

We don't make it through, however.

I'm so distracted by my focus on the Summer Fey that I don't even notice the charms and wards over the entrance until I slam right into it. Like a solid glass windowpane stretching across the iron arch, the wards hold strong. No flash of light, no sparks of magic. Just an invisible barrier I can't step through.

"What the hell?" I mutter. I refocus my attention on the gate surrounding the circus. Sure enough, countless glyphs and runes are twined through the iron and buried in the grass. It's not Summer magic—that would be a violation of the rules. No, this is Kingston's work. He's ensuring that no one gets in. And the Summer Fey are imposing enough that no one will want to get out.

"Apparently things have worsened in your absence," Eli says. "The martyr is no longer enough to keep the monsters at bay."

"Her name is Melody," I reply. My gut drops. Kingston said she had maybe a week left. What if it's worse than he was letting on?

"If the Summer Fey have been attacking," Eli says, hitching onto my train of thought, "her health will be failing. The tithe is far from perfect; if she is healthy, the magic keeping the circus safe is healthy. But she also receives the full impact of any blow. If she is already beginning to fade, they would definitely have need for such reinforcements as these."

"How do we get in?" I ask. I'm already running through the dozen or so counter-runes and spells I could place on the gate to make it all come crashing down. But that seems a bit extreme. Especially if it will weaken Melody further.

"You ask nicely," Kingston says from the shadows. "Or else you're invited."

He walks down the promenade, a few lights flaring to life as he passes them. He's in loose gym shorts and a hoodie, his serpent tattoo twined around one calf. He definitely isn't happy to see us. Well, me in particular.

"Why do I have a feeling I'm not invited?" I ask. I rap my knuckles on the ward between us to emphasize my point.

He doesn't answer, but his weak smile is enough.

"I didn't think you were coming back," he finally replies. He stands only a few feet away, but doesn't make a move to remove the magical barrier.

"We got delayed," I reply. I look to Eli. "We're both perfectly respectable people. Well, *creatures*. I don't see why we don't get warmer welcomes."

"No one likes inviting in Death," Eli responds. He doesn't take his eyes off Kingston.

"And yet here I thought we were trying to save everyone," I say.

"Blood still trails in your footsteps," Kingston replies.

I actually laugh. "Oh please. Like you're any different? I know about your history. Accused of witchcraft in Salem, sentenced to burn. And what did you do? You kill everyone there, and Mab takes you on, demanding a year of service for every life you took. Salem was an awful long time ago, Kingston. Don't even pretend you're all high and mighty."

"People change," he says.

"Not our kind of people," I reply. "Now, let me in before I break my way in."

He sighs and makes a few hand gestures that I know are more for show than spell casting. The glyphs at his feet fade, and he gestures us inside. The moment Eli and I step in, he waves his hand and the wards buzz back into life.

"How's she doing?" I ask the moment the seals are in place.

"Who? Your mother? Still alive. Though I have to be at her side practically every minute now. She's in a lot of pain."

"Actually, no. Melody."

This makes him pause.

"What?" I ask.

"Nothing. She's fine. I'm just surprised you actually care."

I want to defend myself and say I'm not that coldhearted, but after tonight, that would be a lie I can't even convince myself of. I also don't want Eli to think he needs to give me another lesson. It's going to take a lot of alcohol and magic to get those guys' sleeping, peaceful faces out of my head.

"Just wondering why you need all the extra defenses."

"There we go," he says. "She's fine, thanks. Tired, but fine. As for the wards, well, you saw our little entourage out there. They grow by the day. They can't get through, but they could seriously damage us. So I've reinforced things. Discover anything useful out there?"

I shrug. I should tell him about Austin, but I want to wait. I want to ensure the blow comes at the most opportune moment—if I've learned one thing about magic users, it's that they hate learning their powers are faltering.

"Where is she?" I ask.

"Sleeping."

"Then wake her."

"Why?"

"Because we need to talk."

"She doesn't know anything, Claire. Don't you realize that? I already told you—she can't just become the Oracle. It doesn't work like that. And you can't force her to make a prophecy. It will kill her."

I round on him.

"Mab sent me on this mission because I could pull that spark out of Viv. I thought maybe it was a metaphor, you know? Just be in her presence and she'd remember. But that clearly hasn't worked, and unless you're fucking *blind*, you've realized that there's no way out of this. I can't bring her to Winter. We can't get her out of this circus. And in a few days, Melody's going to die, and all your defenses are going to go down. And then Oberon gets in." I point to the field where the Summer Fey wait. "If you think those Fey out there will be nice to her because she's important, you're wrong. They want her dead.

"There's no way out of this, Kingston. She's going to die no matter what. At least if she dies at my hands, it will be for something important. She'll save a lot of people because, hello, there's clearly some serious shit going on out there." I point to the sky. "If *I* can feel it, so can you. The Pale Queen isn't just raising an army, she's disrupting life on earth. Which won't bode too well for ticket sales, I can assure you."

He stares at me like a shocked fish.

"What are you saying?" he asks.

"I'm saying I've tried everything I could think of. I've confronted Oberon. I've talked to Austin. I've even begged the Pale fucking Queen. But there's no way out of this besides my dagger. Mab chose me for a reason—not because I'm related, but because I'm a killer. That's why she sent me on the job. She knew that no one else would be—"

"Heartless enough?" Kingston asks. "To kill her own mother? Just on the chance it could help find this Pale Queen?"

"I was going to say ruthless, but sure. That works, too. Now. Where is she? I want to get this over with."

"I told you. She's sleeping." He looks me over. "Please, Claire. Just give her one more night."

"Why?" I ask. "It's not like she remembers any other nights, thanks to you."

"That's not fair."

"None of this is." I look to Eli. He watches the whole thing as though he's watching a tennis match, a slight grin at the corner of his lips. Then I turn my attention back to Kingston. "She's my mother. Or was. But this is bigger than both of us. We have to be what we were raised to be, not what we were born to be."

"What?" Kingston asks.

"I wasn't born a killer," I respond. I may not remember my childhood before Mab, but I know enough from Austin and Viv that I know it's true. "That's what Mab made me. Just as she made you into . . . well, whatever you are. So don't hate me for following through with my orders. I don't have a choice. I'll give her another night. Make your peace or whatever you have to do. In the morning, she and I talk. And I'm not leaving this show until I know how to find and kill the Pale Queen."

Kingston shakes his head and looks as if he's about to fight, but then stops. Because his eyes land on someone beside me. I glance over.

The changeling stands in the shadows, arms crossed before her chest.

"That goes for you, too," I call out to her. Then, before she or Kingston can try to change my mind, I grab Eli's arm and begin walking away.

"That was inspiring," he muses when the others are—mostly—out of earshot.

"I learned from the best."

"Will you really torture her? Your own mother? Just to get to this Pale Queen?"

I think of what the Pale Queen showed me—her land of bliss and harmony amongst the Fey. Her offer to make that mine. And Vivienne's. I think of Mab's empty kingdom, and Oberon's slipping reign. Most of all, I think of my damned contract, and the simple fact that I can't back down from this, even if I wanted to. Mab has me snared. Right where she wanted me all along.

I never played an exalted role in Mab's eyes. I see that now. I was just there to do her dirty work. The illusions of grandeur were all on me. As were the illusions that I deserved something more.

"Yes," I say. "I am the weapon. And I will do what weapons do: kill."

***

Despite my exhaustion, I don't sleep. The runes on my back have me wired, and that's not a magic I can just shut off. At least, that's what I tell myself. I know it's more that I don't want to sleep. I don't want tomorrow to come, to have to interrogate my own mother as if she's another traitor to the throne. Moreover, I don't want to dream. I know the Pale Queen would be waiting. Or, worse, my own treacherous imagination.

Instead, I roam the halls of Kingston's mansion. It should feel strange, but I'm used to going into places and making myself feel at home. He's nowhere to be seen; he's probably hovering by Vivienne's bed, creepily cataloging the face he'll never see again. I feel horrible thinking that. I should be doing the same. She was my mother after all. *No. She's not. Mab is.*

Clearly, being in a place on my own isn't healthy, even if there is a great deal to distract me. The place is sprawling, at least four stories tall (it's hard to tell, as some of the staircases loop around) and too massive to keep track of. Red-carpeted hallways and grand ballrooms; indoor pools with glass ceilings enchanted to look like an arctic sky; kitchens straight out of a medieval castle, save for the top-of-the-line appliances; and bedrooms. So many bedrooms.

Including the wing that was clearly for the children he'd never have.

I walk this one slowly, my heart thudding heavily in my chest. It makes me feel like an intruder, but I explore anyway.

The halls are painted in pastels—pinks and blues and greens—and enchanted balloons float about the low ceiling. I pass under dirigibles and teddy bears and a glowing sun that plays soft music as it drifts. I glance into a few of the rooms as I go. One looks like a tree house in a jungle, complete with vines draped from the ceiling and clockwork monkeys slowly doing acrobatics across the beams. Another is the command center to a spaceship, the full cosmos swirling outside the window. There's an undersea sand castle with stingrays drifting through the sky and a true medieval castle with a dragon latched to the ceiling, the flames from its maw dancing over the brickwork and providing an eerie light.

Then, at the very end of the hall, is another door. This one locked.

"That was yours, in a way," Kingston says from behind me. I nearly jump out of my skin.

"How did you sneak up on me?" I ask.

"My home, my rules."

I look to the door. If my insides were knotted before, they're a total mess now.

"What do you mean, this was mine?"

He steps up beside me. He's in his pj's, but in here, in his own castle, he looks regal. If not a little sad.

"I was stupid," he says. "When your mother was taken away from me, well, you already know I kept a pretty close watch. And when she had you . . ." He sighs and looks at me, then back to the door. "I imagined that maybe I could convince Mab to let me take you. I mean, both of you. Bring you guys back to my castle so you could live as queens. She wouldn't have any of it. Said it was against Viv's contract and mine as well. I didn't tell her I'd already built this place for you. I'd watched you, those first few years. I even came dressed up as Santa once."

He chuckles to himself, and in the far off corners of my mind, I can almost picture it, this red, jolly blur of memory. But it's also rather creepy. He was still stalking us, well-intentioned or not.

"Anyway, that never happened, but I never could convince myself to get rid of the room. Or the wing. Who knows? Maybe I'll still get my happy ending." I study him for a long moment, at the way he stands there, hands shoved in his pockets and his eyes wavering over the door. It's easy to convince myself that he's an asshole. But it's also easy to convince myself that he really did love my mother.

"Why didn't Mab let you two stay together?" I ask. I know it's dangerous territory, but my entire life is dangerous territory right now.

"She didn't. I mean, she didn't decide that. I did."

"What?"

I mean, okay, Austin's charming and hot and reliable. But Kingston has *magic*. He has a fucking *castle* waiting for her.

"When the time came for her to sac— to save us, I told her it would burn everything out of her. If she lived, I'd be nothing more than a memory. But she gave that up to save the world. After, I was able to contain a little bit of her life, keep the power from destroying her completely. But I knew I had to keep her away from any sort of triggers. The circus. Magic. Me." The last word comes out as a choke. "I gave her up. Because if she stayed with me, the chances of her remembering her true past, of burning up . . . they were too great. So I crafted her a life with Austin. He's a good guy; they'd been high school lovers, and he would have followed her to the ends of the earth and back. He even came to the circus to find her once. Which is impressive, since I personally made him forget she existed. He's not good enough for her, but he tries. And that's more than I could hope for."

He sounds bitter as he speaks, but he shakes his head and changes the subject. I feel I should mention that Austin is once more remembering things—the guy must have some sort of magical brain to be immune to Kingston's literal charms.

"I know you're going to go through with it," he says. "I'd hoped . . . I'd hoped there was another way. But you're right—there isn't. And Mab *did* choose you for a reason."

"You don't need to tell me I'm heartless again," I mutter, glancing at the row of rooms. I could have grown up here. It feels more like home than Mab's castle or Vivienne's house.

"No. It's not that. You're necessary."

I glance back to him. His words drag from his lips, as though he doesn't want to admit to any of it.

"When she gave birth to you, a small piece of her power transferred." He doesn't look me in the eyes when he talks. He doesn't take his gaze from the door. "It's part of the reason Mab kept you two apart—when you're together . . . you amplify each other. If you'd grown up with Viv, you both would have died before you hit fifteen. The power is too volatile. It doesn't like being restrained."

"Why didn't you tell me this earlier?" I can't tell if I'm pissed or sad.

He blinks. It's not my imagination; a single tear drips from his eye and falls to the ground.

"Because I wanted to believe there was another way. The Oracle can't exist in two bodies. The fragment in you is weak—it's what grants you your strength, your ability to sense magic and the Fey. It wasn't all training, because you aren't entirely mortal."

"So, what? She dies, I become the Oracle?"

"No. No, you're not conditioned. The Oracle is born into a body—it can't just fully transfer to an existing one. You'd die from the power flux instantly."

"So what's the problem here?"

"She's going to need your blood," he says. He *does* look into my eyes. "She's going to need to drink it. That's what the Oracle feeds on, and moreover, your blood should transfer that little spark within you back to her. She *should* get her powers back. But I wasn't lying earlier. The magic restraining her powers and memories is strong. You're going to have to weaken her enough that the bonds break entirely. Once that happens, she'll start burning up. Fast. That's when you have to feed her."

I've seen and done many terrible things in my life. This is the first time I've actually felt queasy.

"That will do it?" I ask. "That will bring the Oracle back?"

"It should. For a moment. That much power will kill her pretty fast. So I guess . . . ask your question quickly."

"Will it kill me?"

He shrugs. "Does it matter?"

I don't say anything after that, and neither does he. Not for a long while. He's right. It doesn't matter—my life is Mab's, and I will do this no matter what. I just need to ensure someone is there to pick up my slack.

"What about my mother?" I finally ask. "When the Oracle is reborn, is it going to be my mother again?"

"I don't really know. But I don't think so. Human bodies, souls . . . those are something apart from the Oracle. I don't know what I believe. But I think that when Vivienne is gone, she's gone for good. Whatever is reborn in Oberon's kingdom will be something, or some*one*, completely different."

The small hope I'd had—that maybe I could rescue the Oracle from Oberon's kingdom and somehow have my mother back, at least by proxy—vanishes. Coldness creeps over that spark of hope. When I do this, I lose whatever's left of my mother. Forever.

After a bit, he sniffs and wipes his nose, then steps forward. He puts his hand on the door and sends a small current of magic through it. Locks click away on the other side. Then he steps back.

"I don't think you'll like it," he says as he walks away, his voice cracking and his eyes avoiding mine. "You've changed a lot since I met you. But I guess it's yours all the same."

When he's down the hall and out of sight, I turn my attention back to the door. My fingers itch to touch the handle, to see inside. To get a glimpse at the child I once was.

Then I remember Eli's lesson.

Remembering the girl I was won't help me now. If anything, it will only make it harder for me to do what has to be done.

I close my eyes and turn away from the door, leaving whatever remains of my childhood behind.

Sixteen

Eli wakes me in the morning. Normally, that would entail him slipping into the bed and being all creepy while he wished me good morning. But today, he seems to catch on that I'm not in the mood. I'm curled up on the massive velvet sofa in one of Kingston's many living rooms when he comes in. Whatever dreams I'd been having vanish the moment he knocks on the doorframe.

"I didn't think you'd sleep," he says. "You actually looked peaceful."

"Doesn't happen very often. The sleep, or the peace."

He waits for me to push myself to sitting, then comes over and sets a mug of black coffee in front of me. The fact that he's being this kind is frightening. Either he realizes last night crossed a line, or he knows that today will leap over a dozen others.

"Are you ready for what you must do today?" he asks.

"Are you suddenly worried about my well-being?" I eye the coffee but don't take it. I learned early on not to take any gifts from the Fey—especially food-related ones—and Eli's only a few degrees separated from them.

"I'm worried about your mental state, yes. But not necessarily because I care about your well-being. Remember, I only get fed if you live. The moment you're gone, I'm sent back to the netherworld."

"I don't think this will kill me."

"True. But what you're about to do might unhinge you."

I take the coffee and inhale. I don't smell any poisons, and Eli's right—he needs me in sane mind and sound body; otherwise his contract is nullified. When I drink it, I'm honestly surprised—it's the best thing I've tasted in days.

"Thanks for the vote of confidence," I say.

"Any time."

He waves his hand, and the fire in the hearth roars back to life.

"Eli?" My voice has lost its usually cocky tone. I hate to admit it, but I sound scared.

"Yes?" he asks. He actually sounds mildly concerned.

"Am I doing the right thing?"

It comes out as a whisper, as though maybe my contract won't hear it. But save for the fear of his answer, I don't suffer any pain. Maybe because I'm not considering bailing. I'm just asking about morals.

He doesn't answer right away. He stares into the flames for a long while. I take another drink of coffee. He flicks a finger absentmindedly, and the mug refills.

"I told you earlier," he finally says. "There is no such thing as right or wrong. Good or evil are based on perspective." He looks at me. "You know I don't give two shits about duty or family. And you know I've been around much longer than your world, so what happens here is of little consequence. But. You and I have been through many terrible things, Claire. I'm hoping we encounter many more. You're doing what you can to serve out your contract and serve your queen. You aren't doing the right thing. You're doing what you must. To you, that is the right thing. Between you and me, it seems to be the only thing that will allow us to continue these happy adventures of bloodshed and misery.

So yes. I will be self-serving with my answer: you are doing the right thing."

I take another drink. I can't laugh, not at what I'm about to do, but I appreciate the gesture.

"If you're saying it's right, it's probably wrong," I mutter.

"Yes. Probably. But if I remember correctly, we've had a *lot* of fun doing the wrong things."

"There won't be any pleasure in this, Eli."

"Perhaps not. But imagine how avenged you will feel when slitting the Pale Queen's throat."

"Which you say I can't do."

He shrugs.

"I was being hypothetical, and you are just being difficult."

"I have to kill my mother today."

"Let us be honest, Claire. Your mother died to you the moment she gave you up."

"You're right." Except he's not. Because a part of me is still holding on to her image. And I don't think I can ever let it go.

I shove down the doubt and nerves and fear. It doesn't take magic to calm the nerves that threaten to make me shake. I've killed thousands of times in the past. I've trained for this. The only thing I don't have training for is to be a good daughter.

Today, that serves me well.

I drink the rest of my coffee and stand.

"Let's go," I say. "We've got an Oracle to crack."

He stands by my side and offers me his arm. I take it. If he's being chivalrous, I'll milk it for all it's worth; it won't last long, I'm sure.

"There's no going back," he says as we leave. "The magic binding her was faulty at best. Now that it's unraveling, there's very little chance it can be stopped or mended. This is the only way forward."

"I wasn't planning on going back," I say. "That's never been a choice."

"You speak as though you have one."

I can't fight him on that one. I don't have a choice in what I do. Not this time. But I do have a choice in how I go about it. I'll try to make this fast. For her sake. And mine.

We leave the mansion without sight of Kingston and step out into the bright light of afternoon.

"I thought you said it was morning?" I hiss at Eli as we hop down from the trailer.

"Colloquialism," he replies. "I thought I'd let you sleep. You looked like you needed it."

I shake my head but don't reply. Nor do I head over to the food cart to down any leftover breakfast. I don't think my stomach would take it in. I want to get this over with.

The grounds are crawling with performers, but there isn't the usual hustle I'd seen before. It doesn't click until we round the corner of the trailer and see the promenade: normally, at this hour of the day, there'd be a line of some sort, people coming to collect tickets or check for open seats in the matinee. And sure, there are a few people milling about the booths and vendors, but not nearly as many as there should be. Kingston was right—staying in one place definitely isn't good for business.

We reach the trailer that Viv's held in. And this time, there's no changeling girl waiting for me outside.

"The first blessing of the morning," I mutter. "I don't have to put up with *her*. Though I thought the changeling bitch would be keeping better guard."

"Perhaps she got bored?" Eli replies. "I can't say I blame her. There are much prettier things to look at in this show than the back of another trailer."

I shrug and knock.

"Hello?" The voice is timid, but it's definitely Viv's.

"Vivienne?" I ask. "It's Cl— Melody. Can I come in?"

There's no response, just the shifting of the trailer as Vivienne comes over and opens the door. When I see her, it's clear that the magic is starting to fade; she looks . . . well, she looks as if she's coming apart. Dark shadows ring her eyes, and her skin is oddly pale and flushed, splotchy. She looks Eli and me over.

"What is it?" she asks. Her voice is raspy.

"Are you feeling okay?"

"Really bad headache," she replies. She winces when she says it, as if the words are painful. If she thinks it's bad now . . . "Did you need something?"

"Yeah. Could I talk to you for a moment?"

"It's not a good time," she replies.

"Just a minute. Please? It's about . . . it's about Claire."

"Claire? She just left a few hours ago. Said she needed fresh air."

I glance to Eli, who shrugs back. *Fresh air my ass. What is the faerie up to?*

"Right. Well, I just . . . Can I come in, please?"

It's the last time I'm going to say *please*, but of course I don't tell her that. I take a step forward, making it impossible for her to shut the door without slamming it in my face. I know her well enough—she won't do anything that rude. *Just let me get this over with.*

"Okay. But it's awfully cramped in here. Can he wait outside?"

Eli shrugs again.

"Of course. It will only be a moment."

I hope.

She steps back into the trailer and lets me come inside. The door clicks shut behind me, and this time, it's not like stepping into Kingston's trailer. No, this place is definitely a part of the mortal world, and definitely no larger than it appears on the outside; there are narrow bunk beds on one wall and, across the foot-wide path, a closet and desk. Barely room for one person, yet apparently it's built for two. Vivienne sits down on the bottom bunk, gesturing for me to take the chair. When I sit, our knees are inches from touching. Already, the heat in here is unbearable, and even with the shade drawn I can feel the sun burning against the roof and walls. Go figure—I have plenty of magic for personal warmth, and none for cooling.

I look at the woman sitting in front of me and let all the emotions bubble up: the misplaced nostalgia, the desire for love. The need to be held in those arms and told it will all be okay. My heart aches as I stare at her darkened eyes and sallow skin. My mother. My mother. *This is the only way.*

"Melody," she begins, "what's wrong?"

It's only then that I realize there are tears in my eyes. Thank gods Eli's outside.

I take a deep breath, and when I force the tears down, I stab back each of those emotions. Each one makes me weak. Each makes this situation dangerous. I am the only danger here. I am the only threat.

"Vivienne Warfield," I say, the words heavy on my tongue and her maiden name curling with power. "We have a lot to discuss."

Normally, when I take on that tone, people start to quiver. She just looks more confused.

"O . . . kay? What about?"

Kingston said I needed to break down the magic binding her memories. And one of the triggers Mab had kept her from was magic. Which, by my estimate, is probably the swiftest way of bringing this about, short of physically torturing her. If she sees magic at work, it should begin to break the seal. I flourish my hand toward the door, which immediately locks. The tiny window over the top bunk slams shut. And suddenly, the room is very, very silent. She can't see the invisible wave of magic I've sent through this place to keep out prying ears and still outside noises, but she can feel the effect. It suddenly feels as if we're the only two people left alive.

"What was that?" she asks.

"Magic," I reply.

She laughs.

"Melody, you're being ridiculous. There's no such thing as magic."

I'm not a witch—I can't just summon fire or make pretty lights appear. The magic I have is all geared toward a purpose. Which means my next trick is a little more hands-on. I press a small bit of magic through the runes on my spine, and when I cast my hand forward, ropes appear from nowhere and bind Vivienne's arms to her torso.

She gasps.

"What . . . what is—"

"Vivienne Warfield," I say again, my tone going deeper. "It is time you remember who and what you are. You know magic is real. You know this, because you are the Oracle."

I don't really know what I expect. Maybe for the words to trigger some latent knowledge, some spark of power. Instead, she just stares at me, dumbstruck. I continue.

"Your husband says you've always felt nostalgic around the circus. Have you ever wondered why? Why all of this feels so familiar? It's because you once lived here, Vivienne. You once worked and fought for this circus. And then your memories were burned away. But they're still there. Hiding. And right now, we need those memories to come out."

It feels so, so lame when I say it, but I have no other clue how to begin piercing the walls that Kingston put up around her mind. Still, she says nothing. Just stares at me as if I'm insane. Which, really, were I in her shoes, I'd be thinking as well.

I don't think my usual tactics will work, but they're all I have to fall back on. So I grab a butterfly knife from my pocket and flourish it open. This one isn't designed to kill. The enchantments woven through the metal are meant to inflict pain, excruciating pain, but it's relatively nonlethal. Plus, it has a happy little charm hidden in its midst—it will dispel magic. Maybe not the full extent of Kingston's work, but it's a start.

"I didn't want to have to do this," I say. "But I need you to remember. I need whatever magic is holding your frail memory together to crack. I need you to know what you once were. And that means you're going to have to hurt."

I lean forward, gently press the tip of the dagger to her thigh.

"I'd say this will hurt me more than it hurts you, but I don't like lying."

"You're actually going to do this?" she asks. Way too calmly. I look at her eyes then and see that there isn't the slightest note of fear. "You're actually going to harm your own mother?"

"I have to," I begin. Then my voice catches.

Your own mother?

"I never said anything about you being my mother," I whisper.

Vivienne smiles.

"Not as stupid as I thought," the woman says. "But not as smart, either. Do you really think I'd let you do this to her? Let you harm the one woman who's shown an ounce of tenderness in all of this?"

"Who are you?" I ask. I don't move the dagger away. My other hand is already going for the sword I'd shoved in my hip earlier.

"You should have seen right through," Vivienne says. Only it's not her voice now. It sounds like the changeling's. "Really, Claire. I thought Mab had trained you better. She'd be ashamed."

"I said, *who are you?*" I jab the blade down, through the woman's thigh. It doesn't slice into flesh, however—it goes right through, as if I'm stabbing cloth wrapped over air.

"I will never let you hurt her," the changeling's voice says. I watch in horror as my mother's flesh unravels, as the magic of the blade unknits the spell that bound her together. Threads fray from her clothing, flesh fades to twigs. And as her body crumples in on itself in a pile of dead leaves and spent magic, I hear the changeling's final words: "I will never let her get used by the Fey again."

It's over in seconds.

I sit there, staring at the leaves and rope littered over Vivienne's bed. A fucking Construct. The changeling made a Construct to take Vivienne's place. Which means the both of them are . . . somewhere. I chuck the knife at the wall and wave off the enchantments sealing me in.

Eli's waiting for me right outside the door.

"I take it things aren't going well?" he muses.

"It wasn't her," I say through gritted teeth. I fully expect him to say something sarcastic as I storm away from the trailer toward the outer rim of the show. The fact that he doesn't make a witty comment speaks louder than words.

We've lost our only lead. The changeling must have snuck her out in the middle of the night after overhearing my conversation with Kingston. After all, Kingston's wards only kept people out. I don't know how she dodged the Summer Fey and their runes, but I fully plan on asking her when I have an iron dagger to her chest.

I know where they're going. The one place where, if you don't want to be found, you can't.

If they're in the Wildness, though, I'm going to need a way to find them.

Seventeen

I don't head into the Wildness right away. Time might be ticking, but I'm not going in there blindly. If I'm going to find my mother, I need help.

I practically run through the streets of the Winter Kingdom. It's only when I'm halfway to the castle that I realize something's wrong. My footsteps are far too loud, and the night air far too dark. Despite the panic in my chest, I pause and look around. Sure, the streets of snow and black ice are empty, but that's nothing new. But there's something about the stillness. The cold. The dark. It's no longer a winter chill. This is beyond frostbite and malice; this is emptiness. I glance up, and the sky—usually studded with stars—is black. Void. For years, I thought the Winter Kingdom was a miniature underground city, since at times I thought I could see a cavern arching overhead, studded with glowing jewels. But tonight, all I feel is a vastness, as though at any moment gravity could release and I would tumble end over end into that gaping oblivion. No one around to even hear me scream.

Pull yourself together.

I wrap my coat tighter around me and continue my jog. Eli's waiting for me back at the gate—he's not allowed where I'm going. Which just makes the sense of being alone more potent.

I don't head into the castle itself, but down one of the many side alleys that cobweb their way from the central hub. This one is usually desolate, but even now there's a greater emptiness hanging in the corners; the shops I pass, once filled with mysterious potions and charms, are shuttered or dim, the only light coming from the rare flickering lamps strung over the street. And as I wend my way lower down, the emptiness grows. *Has everyone gone?* I wonder. My heart sinks. *Has William?*

"What are you doing here?" Mab's voice echoes.

I nearly slip on a patch of black ice as I about-face to confront her.

"The changeling. She took her."

Mab's eyes narrow. She isn't in a sleek black dress tonight. She isn't wearing a crown or ruby lipstick. She is bedecked from neck to toe in black armor, overlapping panels of leather and silver that look like dragon scales. Her hair is twisted up into a high bun, held in place with a stiletto. The dagger, not the heel.

"What do you mean, took her? Took her where?"

"I don't know," I hiss back. "But I can only assume it was the Wildness. Which is why I'm here. To see if William can make me something to find her."

I reach into my jacket and pull out the pendant Mab gave me earlier. It feels like months ago. Was that really just a few days?

"You said Mom had this last. It has a trace of her energy. I can't sense it, but maybe William can amplify it. Use it to track her."

"You lost her. You are slipping up."

I laugh. I woke up thinking I was going to kill my mother. I am so over this shit.

"Look around, Mab. I'm not the one slipping up here. Looks like you've already lost most of your kingdom. Is this what I'm fighting for now? Some empty real estate?"

Her slap is swift, and the sting of it pierces with the cold night air. Rather than rub my jaw, I smile.

"That's what I thought. I know why you sent me after Viv. Not just because you needed my blood, but because you couldn't face it. You failed her. Just as you're failing your kingdom."

"When this is over," Mab says slowly, "we are going to have a long talk about your employment."

"I don't give a fuck. Throw me away when I'm useless. Just like you did to Viv."

I pull out a dagger and stick the point to my throat. "Don't worry," I continue. "I'll do it myself. I'd rather die than live with your retirement package. At least if I fail, you won't have to put so much energy into forgetting me."

"If you fail, there will be no one left to remember."

As if to accentuate her words, a tremor ripples under my feet. Icicles crash from nearby buildings, and my hand slips just enough that the blade grazes my skin, drawing blood. Thankfully this one was only enchanted against Fey.

"Faerie is dying, Claire." She looks around. "Not just my kingdom, but the realm. As my subjects leave, my power fades. Without Winter, the balance will be thrown off. And I know Oberon fares no better. If we fall, Faerie falls. And if that happens, the mortal world will be soon behind." The gaze she gives me is withering.

"I know the Pale Queen has approached you. I know she promises you freedom and glory. But that is a lie."

"How did you know?"

"I know all that you do and see, my child," she says. The runes along my spine warm in that moment, and not from any magic of mine. "Those markings bind you to me just as strongly as your contract."

"I have a job to do." I know she thinks this will scare me into doing her bidding. But I'm beyond being scared.

"Yes. And everything rides on your shoulders. Find her, Claire. And do not shy from what you must do. The Oracle will tell you the Pale Queen's location, just as she should be able to tell you how to kill her."

"I know. I already figured that out. Now, get out of my way so I can do my job."

Her lips tighten, but she doesn't slap me again. She turns and vanishes into shadow.

"Bitch," I mutter, and then continue on my way.

My footsteps echo like gunshots as I race to the workshop door. I fully expect the place to be boarded up. But when I knock on the metal door—the paneling so dexterously made that it looks like aged wood—a small window slides open before I finish the third pound.

"Heffy," I sigh in relief.

The golem's burning eye stares out at me, unblinking and unwavering. Normally, he'd ask me a question, like why I was there or whom I wanted to see. This time, the window just slides shut and the door opens.

"Come," he says gruffly.

I don't know who made Hephaestus, but they were definitely playing God. The golem's hulking shape barely fits in the hallway, his form entirely made of cogs and ticking gears of brass and copper and steel. Deep within his chest, a red flame burns, the heat of it pressing through the cold that seems to linger over my skin. The golem isn't chatty by any stretch of the imagination, but I have no doubt that he could single-handedly defend the entire workshop, if it came down to it.

He moves slowly, lumbering his way down the hall and past a few different rooms, the heat and scent of sparks and metal growing with every footstep. I want to brush past him; I know where I'm going, and I don't have time for this pace. He'd crush me if I tried, though. Every slow step makes me wonder just how far my mother is getting from me. I can only hope the Wildness is interested in reuniting family.

Is it my imagination, or is it quieter down here as well? I never saw much of Mab's jewelers—they always kept to themselves—but today, especially, the workshop seems unusually still.

"Where'd everyone go, Heffy?" I ask, not expecting an answer.

"Mutiny," he responds, and then goes silent.

I honestly didn't think that was possible. Mab's ensured that none of us can go against her—it's written into everyone's contracts. Maybe Hephaestus doesn't fully understand the word?

We reach our destination before I can try to interrogate him. The golem gestures me toward the workroom and then turns, disappearing back into the shadows of the hall.

I beeline toward William, who sits alone in the massive room at a table in the corner, hunched over something small and glinting. No one else hammers or solders or rivets in here. Just William, patiently working in the cavernous silence.

"I need something," I say when I near.

He glances up with a start, his pallid skin looking thinner than ever, and his eyes shadowed with sleeplessness.

"Claire?" he asks. His voice is shaky, as are his movements as he straightens. Not that that's any different than usual. But something in his voice . . . He's always viewed me as a daughter—I know that. And I've tried not to use it. Now, he actually sounds frightened of me. It's not the most heartening.

"Hi, sorry. Yes. I don't have time to chat."

I pull out the necklace.

"I need you to make me something. Something that can trace the last owner of this. And I need it five minutes ago."

He looks from my eyes to the pendant. When he catches sight of the heavy obsidian, his gaze goes from distracted to focused like a hawk.

"Where did you get that?" he asks softly, yet forcefully.

"Mab," I say. "She said it used to belong to my mother."

He holds out his hand, and I drop it into his palm.

"Your mother, yes. It has been handled by many powerful women, and she one of them." He turns it over, and I swear it doesn't glint in the light—the obsidian consumes it, like a hungry shadow. It suddenly looks less like a memento and more like a threat.

"I don't have time for rhetoric, William. I'm sorry, but I'm already in a bind. My mother's been taken to the Wildness and I need to get her back. Can you help me find her or not?"

I know I should ask who had the necklace before. I should definitely ask how he recognizes it. But there isn't time.

He nods slowly, transfixed by the stone that he turns over and over in his hands.

"Yes," he finally mutters. "Yes, I think I can."

He pushes off from the table and heads to one of the many shelves along the wall, rummaging through who knows what as I stand by the table and try not to tap my foot impatiently. He finally finds what he was looking for and returns, carrying an assortment of saws and files.

Immediately, he sets to work, propping the amulet in a vise and taking a small pick to it. With delicate precision, he hammers a tiny chip off the obsidian before I can even think to stop him. A second later he produces a simple silver band ring and a torch. I watch with fascination as his nimble fingers manipulate prongs and pliers, unravel a spool of thin silver thread, and delicately solder a bezel on the ring, then set the obsidian flake within. The metal doesn't tarnish under the flame, nor does it seem to retain heat—the moment the torch is removed and the stone set, he plucks it up with his bare hands and examines it in the light. It shines faintly, and it looks wholly unremarkable. Which is how I know it's powerful.

"How does it work?" I ask.

"Intuition," he replies. He hands it over and places it in my hand. Despite having just been under the flame, the ring is ice-cold to the touch. "The ring will amplify the energies of the stone. If you focus on your mother, it will resonate with her energy and guide you toward her. Like attracts like, in this case."

"And this will help me find her, even in the Wildness?"

He shrugs. "It will help you find her, yes. But I cannot promise anything in the Wildness. That is a land without rules. If the bond between the two of you is strong enough, yes. You should be able to follow her to the ends of the Earth. But I can only promise potential."

"Good enough," I respond, and slip the ring on my middle finger. "Thanks, Will. Gotta run."

"What about the necklace?" he asks as I jog from the room.

"Keep it!" I shout back. And then I'm gone.

***

"What did Santa Claus give you this time?" Eli asks when I rejoin him at the gate. I flip him the bird, effectively conveying my emotions and showcasing the ring in one convenient motion. "Pretty," is all he says.

I'm used to facing blizzards outside the walls of Mab's kingdom. After all, that's part of the reason the castle wall was built—to keep out the elements and the threats of a bitter winter and the bitter creatures that lived on the fringe. Which is why, when we step through the great glass gate into a still landscape, I feel as if we're entering alien territory.

"Well, this is unusual," Eli mutters. He almost blends in to the crystalline blanket of snow that stretches up the castle wall in great drifts and out to the shadowed forest of the Wildness on the horizon. Not a single flake of snow falls from the sky; no breeze filters over the swaths of white. It is silent and static as a photograph.

From the front gate, laid out in the snow like a blueprint, is the trail of footsteps leading to the forest.

"Come on," I say. "This doesn't feel right."

We follow the trail at a sprint, my boots occasionally slipping on the ice resting beneath. I focus on the ring as I run. *Where is she? Where are you taking her?* I feel it, like a tug in my chest—this knowing, this affirmation that I'm heading toward the right place. My mother is in there, somewhere, and I will bring her back.

Bring her back so you can hurt her, whispers a voice, but I shove it down. This is for the greater good. If I don't find the Pale Queen, everything will suffer—and that means my mother will suffer, too.

"What I said earlier is still true," Eli says at my side, his voice easy. I don't think I've ever seen the bastard pant or break a sweat.

"What are you talking about?" Despite the magic and adrenaline coursing through me, my teeth chatter and the words are a near stutter.

"Your mother. The magic holding her thoughts in place. It is still weakening. Even outside of the circus, away from the triggers, I don't know how much longer she has."

"What are you saying?"

"I'm saying that if we don't find her soon, we may miss our opportunity to recover whatever knowledge the Oracle might possess."

"Fuck." I hadn't even thought of that—my focus was on getting my mother back. I'd managed to forget I still had a time bomb ticking at the edge of things. "Do you have any idea how long?"

"No clue. But if I did, I would guess you wouldn't like our odds."

I run faster.

It's not my imagination: I know that it's taking longer to get to the forest's edge than usual. No matter how fast I run, the dark blur doesn't get closer. After about ten minutes, I slow to a jog.

"What the hell?" I ask.

"It knows," he responds.

"Knows what?"

"That you wish to harm someone within."

"I don't—"

"No matter what, that is your intent, even if not malicious."

"So, what? Am I supposed to think happy thoughts or something?"

"Or something." He nods to the forest. "You can't trick a magic this old. But perhaps there is a part of you, somewhere deep down, that longs to see your mother as something other than a hit."

"You just told me to view her as one!" I yell. "Make up your damn mind."

"No," he says. "I told you to operate as a weapon. And a good weapon knows how to aim."

I stop running.

For once in my life, I want my emotions to make sense. I mean, I'm used to not having emotions, to shoving them down or bottling them up or killing them on the spot. It just makes this much more confusing.

I close my eyes and think of my mother. I push back, back through the images of Mab in her cold castle, past the lies and the blood and the emptiness. And there, in the far reaches of memory, is a spark. The slightest image of blonde hair and a warm smile, of my mother saying my name. It's a memory I've frosted over more times than I can count, but the heat of it still lingers, an ember in the snow. I hold on to it. Breathe against it, try to let the heat build.

Mom. Mother. More than anything, I want this to have been real. I want to know what it felt like to be loved without obligations. What it meant to be more than a tool to someone I cared for. I want you to tell me everything will be okay, and I want to believe it. More than anything else, I want to believe it can be okay. I can be okay. Somehow, once this is over, it can all be okay.

And I know it should feel like a lie: I've spent my entire life telling myself I didn't need or want this. Yet it's there, burning inside, and the moment I let myself remember it, the heat of longing is almost overpowering.

"Well done," Eli whispers at my side.

I open my eyes to darkness.

The Wildness stretches before me, an arch of trees beckoning with black branches and whispered breezes. Lights drift and glimmer farther in, and I swear I can hear a strain of music.

I wrap my hand over the ring, continue focusing on my mother, on the path I wish more than anything else I could walk.

"Let's be off," Eli says, stepping out of Winter and into the world between.

Eighteen

The moment we step into the Wildness, all sense of time and space vanishes. Winter falls from sight with the shuffling of trees, and when I glance around, I realize there are no paths here, not anymore. Just endless black trunks and a sky that seems to fluctuate between grey and green. Eli stands at my side, and for the first time since I've started working with him, he looks uncertain.

"What's wrong?" I ask. He actually twitches when I speak, then looks back to the woods. His sunglasses are gone, and his eyes cast a pallid light over the trunks.

"I don't like this place," he whispers.

"Oh come on, you're a scary astral creature from a scary astral plane. You're afraid of the woods?"

He reaches out and touches a tree. "These aren't woods," he says. "Just as these aren't trees. This is chaos manifest."

"I thought you enjoyed chaos."

He looks at me as he withdraws his hand.

"My world was built on chaos, yes. And the rules of my plane are much different from yours. But there are still rules. The chaos itself is simply a state of being. This place . . . this place has an intent. A sentience."

I look around for some sort of trail, my fingers brushing over the ring.

"So you think the woods are alive and out to get you?" I ask.

"No, Claire. I know the woods are alive. And they've already gotten us." He gestures to the path that was, technically, behind us, but I'm not so sure anymore. "Or do you feel you could easily return to Winter now?"

I shrug. "That's what magic is for."

"A force, I fear, that holds even less sway or logic here. I'd be wary of spellwork. You channel magic through rules and runes. Here, without such framework, even the magic is wild and untamable."

"And you didn't think to tell me any of this before we came in?"

Now it's his turn to shrug, but he doesn't look at ease. It looks as if he's trying to slough off his fear.

"You are the Winter assassin," he says. "I assumed you already knew."

"Surprisingly, Mab doesn't tell me everything." I mean, yes, I knew that the rules of physics and nature didn't really apply in the Wildness. But I also knew it was a magical place, a part of Faerie, so I'd just assumed magic would work like always.

He grins, but he still looks uncertain. I wrap my fingers around the ring and try to visualize my mother. The image is there, and my gut tells me to go toward the right. No path appears at the thought, and the woods to the right are thick and covered in thorns. My gut clenches. What if the ring doesn't actually work? What if William messed up?

"Uncertainty will kill us in here," Eli says. "And that's not a metaphor."

"This way." I try to sound as if I know what I'm doing, but as I push my way through the underbrush and thorns, it's hard to keep the illusion alive.

He doesn't question, however, and I do my best to keep my thoughts focused on my mother and the ring and that nagging sensation in my chest that tells me I'm going the right way. The trees seem to thicken around us as we walk, and the brambles grow higher, vines twisting around trees like thorned serpents, thick and black and glinting with poison in the half light of the sky. A part of me wants to use magic to summon a ball of light or something, but if Eli's right, I don't want to risk it—no use creating a spark that ends up exploding in my face and taking out half the forest. Instead, I rely on the power in the runes on my back and the years of training in the dark of Winter. It's not night vision, but it's close enough. If nothing else, I can always just have Eli lead and use his eyes as a flashlight.

"And you're sure she's in here?" Eli asks.

I nod.

I'd thought for an instant that perhaps the changeling would take Vivienne home, but that's a rookie mistake. And that faerie is far from a rookie—the Construct proved as much. No, the Wildness is where you go when you want to hide. Maybe she's taking Viv to the Pale Queen; maybe she's just trying to find sanctuary in here. I have no clue. Once I find the changeling bitch, I'll torture the answer out of her.

I try not to think about that, lest the Wildness redirect me. Instead, I focus on happy things, like reuniting with my mother, and saving the world, and having a happy ending. Somehow.

That's when I hear it. The still air shifts, becomes a warm breeze. One entwined with threads of music and laughter. It's impossible to really tell, but it sounds as if it's right in front of us. I can't see anything through the trees, however, and besides the music, nothing has changed.

"Please tell me you hear that," I whisper, turning to look at Eli.

"The screams for help?" He smiles at me. "Just kidding. Yes, I hear the music. Which, in the world of Faerie, isn't usually a good sign."

He's right. So many faerie tales involve mortals getting lured to their deaths by song. Despite this, we keep walking forward, toward the strain of violin and flute and drum. It sounds so cheery, so at odds with our dreary surroundings. And right now, I don't want dreary surroundings. I want to feel happy again, to taste sunlight and drink in joy . . .

"Claire," Eli mutters at my side. "Keep your head in the game."

"What?" I shake my head—what had I been thinking about?

"You were smiling. It was highly unlike you. Remember where we are."

"I wasn't smiling," I say. But then I realize, as I take another step, that I hadn't been focusing for a few moments. I bring my attention back to the ring, to thoughts of my mother. The pull is there, yes. At least, I think it is. It's hard to hear it over the music, over the urge to follow it to something better. Surely that's where my mom went—she likes music. And being happy. Yes, that's definitely where I should be going.

I keep my smile to myself as I head toward the melody. This is going to be the reunion we were hoping for. I know it.

Eli's saying something at my side, but I can't hear it over the song. I can't feel the cold of the woods or the crunch of dead white branches beneath my boots. Just the song, intoxicating me, lifting me up. Until it's not dark trees around me anymore, but boughs of verdant leaves and filtered sunlight, everything smelling of cedar and willow and lavender. The trees themselves spread out, until we are in a glade of small purple flowers and streams of light, tiny motes of brilliance dancing through the air like dust.

"Isn't it beautiful?" I ask, spreading my arms.

There's no response.

"Eli?" I ask. I look behind me, to where I know Eli was following closely. He's not there. I stand alone in the glade, warmth dripping from the branches, my lungs filled with sweetness. And I feel good. Really, really good. Like a great weight has been lifted from my shoulders, a responsibility . . . Why would I feel responsibility here? Why in the world would I feel anything but joy?

I laugh and dance around to the music that drifts through the branches. I could stay here forever. In fact, I *should* stay here forever. I have everything I need: music and sunlight and happiness.

"You *could* stay here," comes a twinkling voice. I stop mid-pirouette and look up into the trees. There, sitting in the branch of an alder, is a tiny faerie the size of my hand. She glows a faint pink in her dress made of rose petals, and her butterfly wings flap lazily.

"Hello there," I say. "Who are you?"

"I am Princess Meadowsweet," she responds.

"Pleased to meet you." And for some reason I feel strange saying that, as though the words aren't right on my tongue. But why would I say anything else? That would be impolite. "My name is Claire."

The faerie hops off the branch and drifts down toward me, small motes of light scattering about her as she flies.

"I know your name, Claire Warfield. I know very much about you."

For some reason, that makes me feel a little uncertain. I glance around. Wasn't I here with someone? Someone else who wanted to dance with me?

"I also know why you're here."

Her words bring me back to the moment and away from the music inundating my thoughts.

"Here?"

"Yes. Here. In the Land of Milk and Honey."

I look around again, but I see no milk or honey. Just emerald trees and rich sunlight.

She giggles, and it sounds like wind chimes. "No, silly. It is just a name. Though we do have both milk and honey if you so desire it. Whatever you wish, here you will find it. This is Tír na nÓg. And I am the ruler of this land."

I open my mouth to ask why she is a princess, then, and not a queen, but decide it would be rude and say nothing.

"What am I looking for?" I ask instead.

"For home."

Home . . . I shake my head as images swirl around in thick molasses-like currents: sitting in a living room reading a book by the fire, watching Roxie cook me breakfast, saying good night to my mother when she tucks me in . . .

"No," I say, and it sounds like a question. "I was looking for someone. I think."

"No, my child. I know what your heart desires. You seek a home." She waves her hand, and with that movement the glade ripples with golden light; when it settles, it's no longer a scene of lush trees and grass but a living room with overstuffed sofas and thick quilts and the rustle of someone making breakfast in the kitchen. The scent and sound of percolating coffee. The faerie is there, hovering by my shoulder.

"See?" she whispers like a breeze. "This is what you yearn for. A place to call your own. A haven from the world."

I look from her to the kitchen door. I can't see who's in there, but my heart feels it, that tug. Just a few feet farther and I can fall into that familiar embrace, be loved and held.

She's right. This is what I wanted. To be home. To relax. To be loved. I take a few steps forward, but there's a knock at the door.

"Could you get that, sweetie?" comes the voice from the kitchen. So achingly familiar, yet I can't find the name.

I nod and turn, and the princess is gone—wait, princess? Why would there be a princess here? I must be more tired than I thought. Good thing coffee is brewing.

I go to the door and open it to see Mom standing there, arm in arm with Dad. They're both in thick winter coats and hand-knit hats, both smiling the moment they see me.

"Hey, guys," I say, giving Mom a quick hug and kiss on the cheek before Dad wraps me up. "How was the trip?"

"It was amazing," Mom says as she steps inside. "You'll have to come with us next time. You'd love it."

Dad takes off his coat and helps Mom unzip hers.

"Brunch is almost ready," I say as I take their coats. "You'll have to tell us all about Dublin. I want pictures."

"Of course," Mom replies. "Just as soon as I'm caffeinated."

I chuckle as I hang up their coats in the closet. Some things will never change. As if anyone ever needed proof that we were related.

"I think we might get snowed in," Dad says, and I look back to see him staring out the window. "This has been a really weird winter . . ."

I nod. Something about his words sends chills through me.

Winter. Winter. Something about winter.

"Everything okay, hon?" Mom asks. She puts a hand on my shoulder, and it at once feels comforting and wrong, and I can't figure out why.

"Yeah, Mom, fine."

But you're not my mother. Not really.

I shake my head. What in the world am I thinking about? I close the door and look back to ask them about the castle they stayed in, but it's not my parents and my living room I see. It's a forest, the leaves bright green and the sun buttery yellow.

"What the hell was that?" I ask the faerie fluttering at my side.

"What could be," she replies. "Or, what could have been."

"Who are you?" I respond as the previous conversation unrolls in my memory. "And how the fuck did you brainwash me into being polite?"

She laughs, but it's not the light twinkle it was before. This one is tinged in bitterness.

"You truly are Mab's child, even if you bear different blood. I told you, this is Tír na nÓg—we are the land of dreams and potential. I thought you should see how good it feels to be civilized, especially when speaking to royalty."

I bite my tongue. Civilized my ass.

I've heard of this place. By that I mean Mab's mentioned that there was a collection of pixies in the Wildness that considered themselves her equal—and by her tone, I knew just how little she thought that to be true. But, pissed as I am for this princess bitch brainwashing me, I know better than to make her angry. I'm in her territory. The last thing I need is for her to think she has to teach me a lesson.

"My apologies, Princess," I say instead. "But I'm looking for my mother. And my companion. Asian guy, white suit, demonic blue eyes—seen him?"

She shivers and makes an audible sigh of disgust. "We do not allow *his* sort here."

"Jackasses?"

She clearly doesn't get the joke.

"We have sent him back."

"Back? Back where?"

"To the beginning," she says. "He is not important, Claire. What is important is why you are here."

"To find my mother."

"No. To find yourself."

I pat myself down. "All here, thanks. Though many have tried to change that."

"You try so hard to hide yourself in steel and wit," the faerie says. "And yet, at your core, you are vulnerable as a child."

Immediately, I'm reminded of the couple Eli had me kill. *Love makes you weak. And we prey on the weak.*

"It doesn't matter what I am deep down," I say, staring into her cold blue eyes. "What matters is what I've made myself to be. I'm not here to walk down memory lane. I'm here to find my mother."

She doesn't say anything for a moment. Instead, she examines me just as intently as Mab ever did. It makes my skin crawl.

"Your motivations are unclear," she muses. "Your heart is torn. One part of you wishes to save your mother, and another wishes to use her for another's ends. How interesting."

I glance away, toward the trees that stretch out into oblivion. I don't know what it means when even a faerie—usually so good at discerning emotions—can't figure out what's going on in my head.

"I wonder . . . ," she says.

Before I can ask her what she's wondering about, there's a ripple of light, the feeling of falling into gelatin, and then I hear a familiar voice.

"You've done well," Mab says.

She sits atop her towering throne of ebony and ice, her long dress of black silk and fox fur trailing the two stories from peak to floor.

I kneel before her. Snow drifts lazily from the rafters, but I no longer feel the chill. As a true Princess of Winter, I'm no longer affected by such trivial things as cold. Or fear. *Or even,* I think, glancing at the woman bound and kneeling at the base of my mother's throne, *of love.*

"What will become of her?" I ask, nodding to the captive.

"Your flesh?" Mab asks. "We may do with her as you wish, my daughter."

I look at the woman who bore me and abandoned me. The woman who helped us bring down the Pale Queen and restore balance and order to the kingdoms. She stares at me with dull eyes, her memory burned out of her like ash in a husk.

"She is of no worth to anyone anymore," I say. "Not even to herself. It would be the greatest honor for her to die here, now. As a hero."

My mother nods from atop her throne and gestures me forward. I oblige and stand, walking slowly toward the bound woman. She doesn't flinch when I withdraw my dagger, nor does she tremble when I bring it to her neck, the tip barely pressing her flesh.

"Vivienne Warfield," I intone, my voice ringing through the chamber. "You have given the greatest sacrifice to the cause of Winter, and for that, we give you the greatest honor. To die at the feet of our beloved queen, at the height of your service, in full knowledge of your deeds. May your memory live for eternity."

The cut is a simple flick of the blade, enchanted steel slicing through flesh like air. Vivienne doesn't gasp. She doesn't even bleed. The magic stills her heart and seals the wound, and she crumples to the floor.

"We have much to celebrate today, my daughter," Mab says. As she descends her throne, the body of Vivienne fades into the floor, becoming nothing more than a pile of snow.

Mab places her hand on my shoulder, and I look from the snow to her cold green eyes.

"Today, our kingdom rises anew. And you, my daughter. You are my prized warrior, my chief in command. It is time you moved into your rightful place by my side. Help me rule, and together, we will make both the worlds of Faerie and Mortal our gardens."

She squeezes my shoulder. Ice shatters across my garb at her touch, but it doesn't burn or freeze. It transforms. Magic cascades over my beaten jacket, turning cracked leather supple, silver studs to shards of ice. My torn jeans become whole, and even the weapons I bear are transformed, gilded, empowered. When the magic is done, she waves her hand and the snow that had once been Vivienne whirls up before her and becomes a sheet of mirrored ice.

The woman I see is not the girl I'm used to. She stands before me looking every inch a regal princess, one to inspire fear and respect. The shadows under my eyes are gone, my charred platinum hair is once more lustrous, and my clothes befit a queen. But it's not the physical changes that make me stand in awe of myself; it's the bearing, the poise. The pride. Shoulders back, chin high, expression cold.

Mab smiles at my side.

"Yes, my daughter. You are now my equal. And I am proud to let the world see it."

"Interesting," comes a high-pitched voice behind me.

I turn, and the illusion shatters like ice on a pond. I'm back in the woods, back to staring at the damned pixie.

"I do not think that is something Mab would ever say," Princess Honeybutt, or whatever her name is, says. "To care so much for someone's praise—no wonder your heart is torn. You yearn for two things you truly cannot have."

Okay, it's one thing to think that, and it's another to have an annoying faerie confirm it. I start walking. I don't know where I'm going, but I do know I'm not staying here.

"Why do you run?" she calls, flitting to my side.

"Because I'm on a job."

"But it does not sit right within your heart," she says sadly. "Why would you do what you do not desire?"

"Because I'm contracted to do it." I glare at her. "I have a responsibility."

"Not here, you don't."

I pause.

"What are you talking about?"

She floats in front of me, a sad smile on her face.

"In Tír na nÓg, you may do or be whatever you dream. This is the land of your heart's deepest calling. Here, you are not bound to duty."

"This is a faerie contract. It's not something I can just duck out of."

"Mab's magic holds no sway here," she says. Is it my imagination, or is there venom in her voice at Mab's name?

"Are you serious?"

"I am Fey. I cannot lie."

I close my eyes and brace myself for the pain. I envision just staying here, calling off the hunt. Letting my mom drift away and the Winter Kingdom fall into emptiness. Letting myself give way to dreams and fancy.

The agony of going against my contract never comes. I'm not struck to my knees by a blow to the heart. My lungs don't contract with fear and pain. Instead, the image floats through my mind like golden silk—the idea of staying here forever, of letting my responsibilities drift away to be picked up . . . maybe by someone else, maybe not. And not giving a shit. About any of it. Because in here, I could live any life I wanted.

"Mab cannot offer you anything like this," the princess whispers in my ear. "You know it to be true. Even if you succeed, you will be naught but her assassin. Is that truly the life for a mortal child? One who lives and breathes and bleeds to be loved and admired?"

I feel her hand lightly on my cheek, and when I open my eyes, I'm not in the forest, but in a fancy restaurant, the kind with dim lighting and candles on white-linen-covered tables. Roxie sits before me, swirling a glass of red wine in one hand while she laughs at whatever joke I just told. Her black dress hugs every curve of her body, the candle making her dark skin dance. When her laughter settles, she looks into my eyes and her smile deepens.

"Thank you, for this," she says.

"For this?"

She gestures with the wineglass. "This, all this. You didn't have to. It's not like it's a special occasion."

"*You're* a special occasion, Roxie," I reply. "Besides, you deserve to be treated like a queen."

"And you do so splendidly."

I feel myself smile and blush and have to look away before I get too lovesick. We've already gone through a full bottle of wine. And although that's normally barely enough for me to feel a buzz, being with Roxie is a whole different type of intoxication; around her, everything is amplified. Everything goes right to my head.

"We should be celebrating you, fool," she says. She reaches over the table and clinks her glass against mine. "It's not every day you get a promotion."

I shrug and grin at her. "It's my mom's company. It's not a big deal."

"Vice president is a pretty big deal," she says. "It doesn't matter if your mother's in charge. She sees something in you. The same thing I do. You have talent and promise, and you're going to take it far."

"This, coming from the girl who's about to leave me for a month."

She rolls her eyes and takes another sip of her wine.

"I'm coming back, and you're coming down for the Cali leg."

"I wouldn't miss it for the world. Even if I do now have a bunch of extra important vice president responsibilities. I'd travel to the ends of the earth to watch you sing. Call me your Oedipus."

She laughs again, and then the waiter brings over the chocolate torte and sets it between us.

"It's *Orpheus*, my dear," she says. "Oedipus is a completely different story. In any case, we'll have a much happier ending. To us."

"To us. And happy endings."

She smiles, and I feel that blush come back, but I don't fight it off this time. I look her right in the eye until it's her turn to look away, feigning sudden interest in the dessert.

"You're amazing, Roxie," I whisper.

"Not half as amazing as you."

I reach my hand across the table, and then the table is gone, and I'm reaching out into empty air.

"You love doing this, don't you?" I growl at the faerie hovering beside me. I fiercely will away the tears that are trying to form in my eyes. I will not be weak. Not here. Not now. Sweet as she may pretend to be, this faerie isn't on my side.

"Doing what?" she asks sweetly.

"Torturing me."

"I didn't realize I was harming you," she replies. She actually seems a little shocked.

"Please. Showing me all these illusions, tempting me to stay. You get a real high out of this, don't you? Let me guess: you thrive off the broken dreams of mortals."

"We do no such thing. We live off the truest dreams mortals have—the dreams closest to their hearts. And here, in Tír na nÓg, you can live those dreams. You can spend eternity in whatever life you wish. In fact, you can try as many lives as you like."

"And what, waste away while you suck out my soul? Wait here while the rest of the world dies? Just so I can live a lie?"

Her small eyes narrow. "You of all people should know that dreams and reality are one and the same. Who is to say if we wake from the dream, or into it?" She holds up her hand. "I could give you any life you wish, Claire. Whatever your heart desires, it will be yours. Fame? Love? I could give you a life of luxury or one steeped in blood. It's yours. All you need do is cease this petty war and stay here."

"Wait. What?"

"I told you, you could have whatever you like—"

"No, you mentioned the war. What stakes do you have in this?"

She goes silent.

I take a step toward her and she flutters away. It's taking a lot of control not to reach for a dagger. It would make her talk, but it wouldn't improve my chances for getting out of here alive.

"Answer me, Princess," I say. "Why would you want me to stay here when finding my mother is what's supposedly going to save all of Faerie?"

And then things click.

"She made a deal with you, didn't she?" I *do* go for a knife then. One specially made to kill Fey.

Again, the princess says nothing, which tells me everything. When you can't lie, direct yes or no questions are a bitch.

"That's why you guys aren't struggling." I glance around. Sure, it's just woods, but I can tell the place is thriving. In Faerie, the world around you tends to change when things get bad. This place definitely isn't hurting from the Pale Queen. Which means . . . "The Pale Queen was here. You talked to her. And she told you to keep me occupied.

I was told Faerie would die and the mortal world would collapse if I didn't kill the Pale Queen. What's *your* story?"

She shakes her head. "We do not fall prey to the intrigues of Winter and Summer. That is where the path of Tír na nÓg aligns with that of the Pale Queen. But that is the only involvement we have in her crusade. We are not fighters. We live on—"

"On Dream, yes. Just like the rest of the Fey." Now that I can question my charge, it's hard to do anything but. "So if the Pale Queen succeeds in overturning Winter and Summer, what do you get?"

"Long have mortals been bound by the rules that Mab and Oberon created, and long have we Fey followed suit. The Pale Queen offers a new future, a different set of rules. But Tír na nÓg has always stayed apart from politics. I told her, we are not interested in your war. And she told us that we were not a threat, that she had no quarrel with us."

"What about me?" I ask. "Why are you so intent on keeping me here?"

She doesn't answer for a moment, and I assume I'm going to have to start using the knife.

"It is not for the Pale Queen that we wanted to keep you here," she finally relents. "But because . . ."

"What?"

"Because, when your mother came through here, all those years ago, we tried to give her a better life. We have seen what Mab did to her. The life poor Vivienne is left to live. We wanted to make it better."

"You've seen her?" I ask. "She's been through here?" She doesn't answer the question, not directly.

"We failed her. We were unable to give her a pleasant dream, and even now her own dreams are shattered, clouded things. We had hoped that in giving you the same offer, we could right the wrong we did unto her."

"Is. She. Here?" I demand.

"She . . ."

I focus my attention back on the ring. And sure enough, I feel her. Close.

"You are going to take me to her." I hold the dagger up to her, as though that could force her to do anything in her own kingdom.

"I have seen your heart," she says. "I cannot let you harm Vivienne. Not after what she has been through."

"Then weave her a better dream," I say. I begin walking, following the pull in my gut. I expect the woods to change, for new memories or dreams to leach into my consciousness. But they don't. Clearly, she realizes I'm done playing games.

"Why are you doing this?" the faerie asks. She flutters beside me. "Here, you both are safe. She wanted sanctuary. That is what we gave her. Why would you destroy that?"

"The magic binding her is fading, or did you not notice? She's going to die no matter what."

"Not in here," the princess says. I actually stop. Her words strike me like stones. "Tír na nÓg is its own entity. Vivienne could live here forever, lost in her happy daydream. And you . . . Your contract holds no sway here. You don't have to harm her. You don't have to fight. You two could live here. Together. Happily. Forever. No other person, faerie or mortal, could offer so much. You know this."

"I wouldn't have to kill her?"

"You have already seen that the magic binding you has no power here."

Her words hit home stronger than I want to admit. I drop to my knees, overwhelmed by this warring sense of burden and release. This was the way out all along; I don't have to kill my mother. She doesn't have to die. Princess Meadowsweet could create a new life for us, a different dream.

"We could live together," I say. I don't know if it's to myself or to her. "She could be a real mother. And I could be a real daughter."

The faerie hovers by my shoulder. Her words drip soft honey.

"I could make the rest of your life feel like nothing but the dream of a dream. You would never age, not physically, but you could live a thousand lives with her. You could be the daughter you always wanted to be. Could feel the love you've always wanted to feel. You could be safe."

"Did she put you up to this, too?" I whisper. "The Pale Queen? Did she tell you to try and keep me here?"

"She said only that you were no threat to her, and that we could take you in to right the wrongs we'd done by letting Vivienne go free years ago. It is our way to make amends. Let us gift you this. Let us make it right, by giving you the future you so desire."

I know I should say no. Nearly twenty years of training—I should have my dagger to the faerie's throat.

I can't move, though. I can't find the spark.

I could have a home.

"Take me to her," I whisper. "Please."

Nineteen

The princess doesn't play any more games.

She reaches down to take my hand and help me to my feet, which feels strange since she's the size of my palm, but like the faerie bartender Celeste, she's packing some hidden strength and magic. She doesn't let go of my pinkie as she guides me through her kingdom. I have no doubt there's a faster way to my mother; she wants to give me the grand tour.

We pass over hills and through glades, wend our way down cobblestone paths that roll along brooks and ponds that glimmer in the sun like, well, honey. Birds flutter through the air, their song as sweet as flutes. Although the place is green, it is nothing like Oberon's kingdom, which always felt like something from the Midwest. This is a verdant playground, everything green and gold and grey, like the Scottish countryside. Minus the rain.

I don't pay much attention to the scenery, though. Even if a part of me is repeating *this could be my life*, I'm focused on the woman waiting for me at the end of this walk. My mother.

Hope blooms in my chest. It's not a feeling I'm used to. It is as warm and intoxicating as the sunlight in the trees, and just as foreign to my Winter-hardened skin.

We could live here. We could let the rest of the world go to shit and live here in this Eden. Whatever we dreamed, we could create. I wouldn't have to kill again. I wouldn't have to wonder again. I'd know what it felt like to be loved. I'd know what it felt like to have a home. I'd never fall prey to a contract or faerie ploy again.

Finally, the path turns, and we find ourselves at the edge of a low hedge maze, the topiary reaching just to my knees. Viv sits in the middle of the maze, a tiny golden faerie floating around her. Vivienne is laughing, wearing the exact same smile as when I saw her on the trapeze.

And for the first time since I've started this mission, I let myself smile at seeing her happy. Because here, I don't have to end it.

I walk forward, stepping over the hedges and ignoring the maze. My mother doesn't look up at me, not at first. When she does, the faerie flits away, and it's just the two of us in here. She brushes the dust off her knees as she stands.

Her eyes.

Gods, her eyes when she sees me.

Her smile widens, and her eyes fill with tears.

"Claire," she gasps.

I don't expect it.

She runs toward me, and before I know it, her arms are wrapped around me and she's crying and laughing, and I'm doing the same.

I have never been hugged. Not like this. But my body knows how to respond.

"My baby," she cries. "My baby girl."

"Mom." The word comes out as a choke. This time, I don't fight off the tears. I don't have to be cold and hard here. I don't have to be strong.

This is my mother. And she *knows me*.

"How?" I manage. It's all I can say. I'm not used to trying to talk through tears. I'm not used to letting myself cry this hard.

"I don't know," she replies. "But being here . . . I remember. I remember you being taken away. And now I've found you, and that's all that matters."

All that matters. It's all that matters.

"How did you find me?" she asks.

"I just knew. I could follow you anywhere."

"I'm so glad you did. We're here now. We can be a family."

I squeeze her close. It's not a Construct squeezing me back—I can feel her pulse, hear her heart.

This feels good. So good. I could stand here forever, holding her. Being held.

"I love you so much, Claire," she whispers into my hair. A sob racks me, makes me shudder.

The ground shudders, too.

"What was that?" I ask with a sniff.

"What was what?" she asks.

I'm not asking her. I'm asking the princess. I lean back from Mom's embrace and look to the glowing orb of magenta waiting a few yards back.

"What was that?" I ask, a little louder, though I know the sprite heard me.

She flutters back and forth for a second, clearly agitated. Clearly trying to hide it.

"Nothing," she replies. "Just a tremor."

Just a tremor. In a land that doesn't have tremors, or any other natural disasters.

I step back from my mother, sniff hard.

"Claire, what's wrong?" she asks.

"The Pale Queen lied to you," I say, still looking at the faerie.

"Surely she did not," the princess replies.

Things click slowly, the gears of my brain stuck tight by emotion.

"You know she did. She wanted us here to get us out of the way. That's why she offered you safety. But Faerie can't survive without balance between the kingdoms. You can't survive."

"We survived through the chaos at the dawn of time," the princess says, floating closer. "We can do so again."

"You can't lie," I mutter. "But that doesn't make what you say true. You believe her. But she won't keep her word."

The walls creep back up around my heart. No, they don't creep, they rush back. Flesh becomes stone; emotions dry to dust. I glance to my mother, who's watching this all with confusion plastered on her face.

"Claire," she begins.

"She doesn't remember, does she?" I ask. "Not really. This is all just a dream you gave her. The daughter returned. The life yet to be lived. She doesn't know about the circus, or what happened. She doesn't know about being the Oracle."

"We do not speak of such things!" Meadowsweet hisses, and it's not my imagination—the sky actually darkens with her anger.

"Oracle?" Viv asks. Her forehead creases at the word. "What is . . . ?"

Meadowsweet is by my ear in an instant. "You will kill her if you speak of this."

"I thought she was safe here," I say, more a demand than a question. My mother shivers, wraps her arms around herself as if it's suddenly cold. I'm standing right by her, but her eyes skate over me as though she's lost somewhere far, far away. "Or is your magic failing, too?"

"Claire," Viv whispers. "I feel . . ."

I'm pissed. Rage boils through my veins, and it's not just at Meadowsweet for her shortsighted lies; it's not just at the Pale Queen for this entire damned situation. It's at me. Because as I stare at my mother, I can't find the coldness within I had before. All I can think of is how we could have lived the perfect life here. Could have.

"You said this place was safe," I say, gesturing around. "But you can't escape this, either. The Pale Queen told you you'd be spared. But she's not in control of Faerie any more than Mab or Oberon. When Faerie falls, you'll go down with the ship."

"Faerie?" Vivienne asks. "Where is . . . ?"

"Shut up!" I scream. I turn on her, and there are tears in my eyes. I am pissed and hurt, and I am not made to feel the latter, which pisses me off more. "Just shut the fuck up!"

Her eyes go wide. Magic flows over my skin as Meadowsweet tries to calm or enchant me, but I'm ready for it now. The runes on my back burn white-hot. I will not be blinded again. I will not let her try to confuse me with lies of what can never be.

Like the woman in front of me. The mother I can never have. The life I can never live.

Even here, in the land of dreams, I'm denied this. I will never know love. Or home.

Before, I was okay with that. But now I've felt it. Truly *felt* what it meant to have everything I'd ever wanted.

And now, I have to kill it.

"You are the Oracle," I say, grabbing my mother's arms. Her skin is already hot. "You used to work in the Immortal Circus. You were in love with a magician named Kingston. You had great, terrible powers. And you used them to save the world."

Her skin gets hotter as I speak, and at some point I realize I'm not holding her, I'm holding her *up*. A whimper comes from her lips.

"You're killing her!" Meadowsweet screams.

"I know," I whisper. I don't look away from my mother's eyes, which are rolling around wildly. "You must remember, Viv. Mom. You are my mother. You gave me up to the Faerie Queen. Your own daughter. To save the world. And now I have to do that to you. I have to give you up. To save the world."

Maybe it's the pain. Maybe she remembers. But a tear rolls from her eyes and a moan escapes her lips and her shaking gets worse. She crumples to the ground despite my grip.

But I feel it. The power inside her. It grows and glows with golden heat, as if she is a sun, a burst of light burning at the center of her chest. I feel her power, and I feel the spark within me—my own blood grows hot, and as I kneel beside her, I realize my hands glow faintly.

"What are you doing?" Meadowsweet shrieks. "You've ruined everything!"

I know. I know I've ruined everything.

I grab a dagger from my boot. Simple iron. No enchantments. Nothing to numb or cause pain. My mother shakes. The light around her grows, becomes blinding, and I know it hurts her so much that she can't find the strength to scream.

I'm not bound by contracts. I'm not moved by anger, or coldness. I look at my mother on the ground, the woman who loved me more than anything else in her world. The woman I wanted to love more than anything else in mine.

I drag the dagger across my palm. Blood pools and glows in the light. Like honey.

"I love you," I say through my tears.

And I lift my hand to her lips, let my blood pour across her tongue. Blood pumps. Light spills from my veins. Through hers. Through mine. The light. *The light.*

"Tell me," I gasp through the pain. "Tell me where to find her. Tell me how to kill the Pale Queen."

My mother screams. But she is not my mother, not anymore—her flesh is golden, her flesh is light. It spills around me as my flesh burns with hers, and I'm screaming, too. On my finger, the ring goes colder than ice.

"Her name is writ in hell!" she cries out, "In blood and twilight, her name is spelled, and this name shall be her downfall. She must die where her shadow began. Where she ended, she must end again."

The light blinds. Screams through my ears. I see her, my mother, standing before the circus with bloody jeans, Kingston holding her hand. I see her, golden and powerful, light streaming through her fingers as the circus bursts into flame and Kingston holds her close.

I see her, lying in a hospital bed, holding me in her arms.

"Claire! Claire! My baby! My Claire!" Her words strike deeper than daggers.

Then the light dies, and I no longer see her.

The ground before me is empty. Blackened.

The only trace I have left is her blood on my palm, staining the frosted ring red, and the wound within that is burned deeper than flame.

Twenty

"Out. Get out."

The princess is at my side. She doesn't touch me, but her words strike like hammers.

I can't look away from the space before me. Tears roll down my face. They evaporate the moment they touch the ground.

I can't move. I can't force myself to believe that this has happened. I killed my mother. I killed my own mother. I can't even blame a contract. I killed her. In cold blood.

"I said, *get out!*"

I do move then. Before I can think, I am on my feet and Meadowsweet is gripped in my bloody hand.

"You. You did this." My words are bitten off, my teeth gritted so hard my jaw could shatter.

"I did nothing."

"You did. You—you showed me. You lied to me."

"I showed you what could be," she says. Her sweet voice is laced with malice. "It is not my fault that it broke you."

"I'm not broken!" I scream, throwing her to the side. I fall back to my knees, my hands pressed to the scorched earth. Trying to find a trace of her. Praying she will come back. *I'm not broken. I am strong. I am strong.*

"You are weak," whispers the princess. "And you have committed the gravest crime. The world of dreams is closed to you. May you forever walk the earth in a nightmare. May even your death fail to be a release."

I turn around to face her, to tell her to fuck off. But the moment I shift, the world falls away, and Tír na nÓg is replaced by darkness.

Twenty-One

"There you are," Eli says. "That was positively maddening."

I don't move. I'm still crouched on the ground, but this earth is cold. Covered in small bones. I can't stop seeing her. My mother in the hospital bed. Her blood on my hand.

"Claire?" he whispers. "Claire, what's wrong? Are you *crying*?"

I don't respond. I don't tell him to shut up or fuck off. I can't move and I can't speak. He kneels by my side and puts a tentative hand on my shoulder.

"Claire? What happened?"

"I found her," I whisper. It comes out as a sob. Eli's seen me covered in blood. He's seen me having sex. But he's never seen me cry. I feel exposed, but I'm too broken to cover it up.

"Who?"

I say nothing.

"Ah." He pauses, brushes my bloody hand with his. "And I take it things did not go well."

I shake my head.

"Where did you go?" he asks. Not *what happened?* Not *why are you in tears?*

"Tír na nÓg."

"Ah," he repeats. As though that explains everything. Maybe it does. *I killed my own mother without the pull of a contract. I am a monster.*

And for the first time in my life, I don't feel any pride in that.

"I have no doubt they showed you many wonderful things," he says quietly. "But they don't change our reality. They are dreams, Claire. That is how those faeries feed. The world still turns."

"I killed her," I say. I sniff hard. I try shoving down the emotions. Try burying them deep below Roxie and every other betrayal I've faced. I can't. Because I felt my mother's love, and then I killed her.

"You had to." His voice is soft. So soft. Like he actually cares. I want to lean against him and take comfort.

I don't.

"I know," I say.

"What did you discover?"

I take a shaky breath.

"I don't really know."

"Tell me."

It's hard to remember through the tears. Through the light. "Something about her name being written in hell. That I have to kill her where she began and ended."

He sighs. Like me, he realizes it's not at all helpful.

"Was it worth it?" I whisper. I can't even hate myself for being weak around him. I can't be anything else. "Was that worth her life?"

"It will have to be."

He stands. "Come on, we should get you—"

"Claire."

Oberon's voice cuts through the darkness. I look up, wiping the tears from my eyes. I won't ever be weak around him. But when I see him, I realize that's not a problem.

"Claire, please," he says. His voice cracks along with his image. He glows in the darkness, and I know it's a vision, some sort of magic. "Please. I need."

He looks away, and the vision shatters.

"Curious," Eli says. He brushes dust off his pants. "I didn't peg Oberon as one to send a booty call."

"He isn't."

"Let's go. You've done what you were sent to do. I'll take you back to Winter. I think you deserve a bath. And this time, the drinks are on me."

He extends his hand. I look at it for a moment.

My world has just shattered. I killed my mother. I destroyed the one person who could ever truly love me.

"She's going to him next," I whisper.

"Who?"

"The Oracle. I killed her. And now she'll be reincarnated in his service."

Eli doesn't speak for a moment.

"We cannot think of that. Come on. You've done your job. It's time to go home."

He doesn't understand. He doesn't know what this blow to the gut feels like. I can't move. I can't go home. I was a weapon before, but I am broken. No one has use for a broken weapon.

I've betrayed my mother a thousand times over. Is that why Oberon appeared? Did he feel it, her death? Did he want to gloat? Eli said the Wildness obscured magic. That would account for the faulty projection.

"Come on, Claire. Don't make me drag you."

I look up at him. Unflappable Eli. The biggest asshole I've ever known. And now he's trying to take care of me.

He's right, though. I shudder as I try once more to shove my feelings down. He's right: the job is done. The past is dead. It's time to go home and tell Mab.

I take his hand and let him pull me up to standing. It's the second time in a week I've killed someone I cared for. The second time my victory felt like a failure. Not even the promise of a hot bath and two bottles of bourbon makes me feel better. I am numb. Cold. As if everything has been burned out. The ring on my finger is still frosted with iced blood. It's all I have left of my mother. A reminder of my failure. But a reminder of her love. I consider tossing it, but don't. I will remember this. Her. I won't let her death be in vain. Ever.

We trudge through the forest together, Eli's eyes casting everything in a faint-blue haze. Not that I pay much attention. Everywhere I look I see my mother. I am cold. Too cold. Will I ever feel warm again?

Light ripples through the trees.

"Claire. Claire, please." I look over to Oberon's projection. His eyes are wide, frantic.

No way. Oberon looks scared.

"Please help. She's—"

The projection fades.

Despite the chill in my veins, sweat breaks over my skin. Oberon is never afraid.

Then I remember the Pale Queen's promise. A distraction.

My hand grips Eli's arm. "It's her. She's attacking Summer."

He shrugs and continues walking. "Not your circus, not your monkeys. You've done your job. Now you deserve a break."

The ground trembles.

"I can't." My words come out as a gasp. Because I know that if Summer falls, Faerie won't last long. I can't rest. I can't let this slide by. Even after what I've done. My job isn't over yet. "I can't let her overthrow him."

The cold in my veins makes it impossible to move, but I drop to my knees and pull out my chalk and begin scraping a portal into frozen ground.

Frozen.

"Eli, is it colder than before?" I ask as I draw.

"So it seems. In a land without seasons . . . Perhaps your Summer King is already gone."

"He can't be," I say. I press the chalk deeper, digging into the frozen earth. My arm is going numb, the magic that usually filters down my skin seemingly muted.

"That won't work, you know. I told you, magic works differently here."

"And the Wildness responds to need," I say. *This place has a sentience.* Eli said that. I just hope he's right. "Right now, it needs us as much as we need this to work."

He can't be dead. The Summer King can't die.

I sketch faster.

When I grind up the chalk and blow it over the sigils, the dust falls flat. No whirl of magic. No flare of heat. I press my hand to a symbol, will my power into it.

But there is no power.

"Eli, I . . ."

"What is it?"

"My magic. It's gone."

You carry her spark . . . Did I lose it? In giving her my blood, did I lose my power?

I can't even feel frightened by it. I'm already broken. This should not surprise me in the least.

He gives me a look. One that says he fully expects me to explain myself. Soon. But he also seems to catch the gravity of our situation. Rather than interrogate, he kneels at my side and lays his hand on the chalk next to mine.

"Well then," he mutters. "Looks like I'm saving your ass once again."

Twenty-Two

We step through the portal in a silent fugue. I have a dagger in hand, the blade held between numb fingers, and the cane Eli normally walks with has turned into a wicked rapier—proof enough that even he is on edge. *I am broken. I am weak. I can't save anyone.*

The moment we enter the throne room, we're ambushed.

It happens in a heartbeat, so fast that neither of us have time to react. Hands on my wrists, ropes around my ankles, my dagger knocked free, and my legs kicked out from under me. From the grunt I hear, Eli doesn't fare any better. Before I can even take in the room, we are both brought to our knees.

The throne room is ringed with Fey, and in the center, standing before the throne like an angel of death, is the Pale Queen. Her robes of the palest aquamarine glow in the light cast from a high stained glass window, her lace mask obscuring everything but a smile. And at her feet, lying in a pool of sap-like blood that stains her blue hem brown, is Oberon.

"I had hoped," the Pale Queen says, "that you would arrive in time for this."

She doesn't look at us as she speaks, doesn't tilt her masked gaze from Oberon's gasping body. I don't see any wounds or slashes in his suit, but blood flows freely from him, as though his skin is nothing more than cheesecloth. He gasps blood; rivulets trickle down his face, and more mats his curled hair and antlers. Everything the blood touches withers brown.

"Let him go," I say, and am immediately rewarded with a slap across the face. Hard. My jaw nearly dislocates, but I don't feel the pain. I am too far gone to feel anything right now; this is all just a thin dream.

The Pale Queen laughs. "After working so hard to reach him? After all he has done to me? And to you? No, my dear. I don't think I will."

It's then the situation strikes me, like a lance to the heart; I killed my mother to find this woman, and now here I am, minutes later, facing her. My mother died for nothing. I have found the Pale Queen. And even with the Oracle's guidance, I have no idea how to kill her. No magic to send her packing. *Her name is writ in hell. She must die where her shadow began.*

The guards hold my hands behind my back, away from my daggers. But they don't know about the weapons hidden within my flesh. There is one card I'm holding within my wrist. One I have never used, because I don't know how it would play out. *Judgment.*

I don't have any other choice. My thoughts are slow as I summon the card from my skin, the paper brushing against the palm of my hand. I can only blink and see my mother's glowing body. I can only hear her screams.

And I know that this won't work. I have no power to fill the card. My mother decreed the Pale Queen's final moments. There's no way this is where the Pale Queen began and ended. My life isn't that easy.

"Oh, Claire," she says. Her voice cuts through my sluggish thoughts. "I thought we saw eye to eye on this."

She's at my side in a second. The moment she nears, I can smell the snap and tang of Dream; it fills her, infuses her, as though she is made of nothing more than knit magic and an illusion of flesh. Before I can cast the card into the room, she grabs my hand and yanks it before her.

When she sees the card, she laughs.

"My dear. You *are* hurting, aren't you? To think this petty magic could harm me." She plucks the card from my fingers, and it instantly dissolves into ash. Then she notices the ring.

"Where did you get this?" she asks softly. A single finger strokes the ring, making the metal burn. Even in my daze, I feel the pain. I inhale sharply, trying not to scream.

"It was my mother's," I say. *Was. Before I killed her. To find you. To kill you.*

To fail.

She smiles.

"Of course it was. Why would she not take it? She would have seen it as fitting."

"What are you—"

Before I can finish the sentence, the queen snaps off my finger.

I don't hear the pop, not through the pain that jolts down my arm and ricochets through my head. I don't even hear myself scream, not until the pain dies down a minuscule amount and she covers the bleeding nub with her finger. Another burst of pain shoots through me, hot and acrid as the scent of my burning flesh fills the room.

Then she turns, and I am left gasping, my arms limp in their sockets from the stress of the pain. I dangle between my captors like a broken doll. And my finger rests a few feet away on the carpet, charred and ringless.

"I'm afraid I cannot let you keep this"—she holds up the ring—"lest you become more a nuisance than you already are. I gave you the choice, Claire. I offered my protection. But even my patience grows thin."

Oberon chokes something. I can't make it out, but it sounds a lot like *run.*

"Now," the Pale Queen says, turning back to Oberon, my ring now on her finger. "What shall we do about *you*?"

He gasps again, struggles to move. I don't even budge. It's all gone to shit. All of it. What could I possibly do to make it better?

The Pale Queen kneels before him, her robes soaking up his blood in a grisly stain.

"You think your status makes you invincible," she whispers. "That power gives you immortality. But I have seen the truth. There is no immortality. Only death, only the oblivion. And it waits for every creature, even the mightiest of the Fey."

She leans in close, as if she is about to kiss him, her hand on his chest.

"And you, Oberon, mightiest of all, toying with the lives of mortal and Fey alike. You, who have believed yourself to be a god. Let your death be a message to all who oppose me. Even faeries can die. Even the immortal must surrender to the void."

She presses her hand into his chest, his ribs popping beneath her fingers as she squeezes his heart. He doesn't scream, but his bloody gagging fills my ears as his body pales. Like a sweeping drought, his skin hardens and cracks away from her hand, until he is nothing but an empty cask of clay. She stands and dusts her hands on her robes, leaving traces of soot and old blood. When she turns away, looking out to the Fey surrounding her, the brush of her robes dislodges his body, dissolving all that is left of the great King Oberon to ash.

"Let it be known," she calls out to the crowd, and it's only then that I realize that the Fey around us aren't only her minions. There are others lined up in the great hall—dryads and wisps and the like—held hostage by the Pale Queen's army. "And let my message ring to every corner of Faerie: all who oppose me shall die. Too long have we toiled under the rulings of the elite. Too long have mortals and Fey danced for rulers who play god. *We* are the gods now. Join me, and live in freedom. Oppose me, and end up like your precious king."

There's a roar of applause and agreement from her minions. But those Summer Fey who stayed—those who would live and die by their king—stare on in silent horror.

The Queen turns to me then and walks over slowly. When she speaks, I know it is meant for me alone.

"I could kill you, you know. But unlike your mistress, I do not harm those who are innocent. And so far, you are innocent in my eyes. You have not directly opposed me. And you are certainly not a threat. Remain as such, and I will let you live." She kneels before me and whispers, "We are not meant to be livestock for the Fey. We are not meant to be their toys. They need us more than we need them. Remember this when you find yourself with a choice. Do you wish to be the pawn, or the hand moving it?"

"I. Will. Kill. You," I hiss, my teeth clenched so tight I'm afraid my jaw will snap.

She laughs and pats my cheek.

"Good luck with that, sweet child. I have already died a thousand times over."

She nods to her guards as she stands and steps away.

"Let her go."

The guards drop my arms without question. But I can't attack—my limbs won't move. They are lifeless as spaghetti. I need to kill her. Have to kill her. Have to avenge my mother.

"Eli," I mutter. If I release him from his contract, he'll kill everyone in this room in a heartbeat; I don't even care if that includes me. So long as it includes her. "I release—"

"Not so fast, my dear," the queen says, her voice tinted with laughter. "You have fire. You're willing to break the rules. If only you broke them for the right person."

"Thirty seconds, Eli, I release you."

But before Eli can do anything, she's there. And not at me. Her hand is around Eli's neck, her face only inches from his. His skin hisses under her touch, and when she squeezes, small breaks of blue light shatter between her fingertips.

"I do not think that will be necessary," she says. She smiles at him, somehow binding him to his body. He should be free. He should be darting around the room like a demon, devouring the souls of everyone here. But he's bound. Somehow, she trumps even his power. "Unlike you, my dear Claire, this one could be a true threat. I think I will take him with me. He could be of use."

She looks at me, her fingers still clenched on his throat.

"Tell your queen that she has three days to surrender Winter. Or I will destroy everything she owns and loves. Including you." She winks. "I'll let you figure out which category you fall under: Does she own you, or love you? Though I think we both know the answer to that question."

There's a pulse of magic, one that reeks of brimstone and smoke. Then she's gone, pulled from the world in a whirl of ash. And Eli's gone with her.

I look around at the Fey still ringing the room. Some begin to leave. Others stare at the space she occupied, as if uncertain what they've seen. Even her followers stare at Oberon's remains in silent horror.

To speak of revolution is one thing. To see it in bloody action is another.

I try to struggle to my feet but fall over instead. Pain lances through the numbness, and my vision clouds at the edges. I try to turn my head, but all I can see are the ashes of Oberon. All I feel is the ice that drags from the corners of the room, the darkness overhead gathering like the weight in my chest.

It was all for nothing. All of it. Eli is gone. Oberon is dead. My mother is dead. The Oracle couldn't save him, and I couldn't save her. I couldn't save anyone. All I did was damn them.

The Pale Queen was right: I was helping her. Whether I wanted to or not.

Someone kicks me in the back of the head. Hard. My vision swims.

"What do we do with her?" the faerie behind me grunts.

"The queen wants her alive," someone else says. I see boots crunching on dead grass as the speaker picks up my finger. "But clearly not all in one piece."

I hear a crunch that I don't want to believe is the sound of chewed flesh and bone. Nausea floods my stomach and the darkness rings deeper. Just beyond the edge of my vision, someone kicks the ashes of Oberon into a cloud.

"Well then," comes the first voice. "Let's see just how compact we can make her before sending her home."

A sharp pain in my side makes my vision flare red. I gasp again, choke on . . . something. Dimly, I realize it's not Oberon's ash falling around me.

As the world fades to black and white, in the heart of what once was Summer, a heavy snow begins to fall.

Acknowledgments

I'm constantly amazed by how this story world of dark faeries and circus scandals has grown. If you had told me years ago, when I was writing the first draft of *The Immortal Circus* for my grad program, that this would become a full series—and spin-off!—I would have called you crazy.

But here we are, book two (or book five in this world), and the show keeps growing. There are dozens of people to thank. But I'll try to be concise.

First and foremost, my deepest thanks goes to my amazing friend and agent, Laurie McLean of Fuse Literary. She's been my knight in shining armor from the start.

To my family, for letting me follow my dreams, however crazy they seemed at the time.

To the entire team at 47North, for putting full faith in this entire series. I couldn't ask for a better, more innovative crew. A special thanks to Jason Kirk, for helping this story take center stage, and to Nicci Hubert and Rebecca Jaynes, for being such rock star editors.

To Will Taylor, for helping me hammer out faerie politics and intrigue over enchiladas.

To Danielle Dreger and Kristin Halbrook, my Seattle writing family, for keeping me on task.

To the amazing community of circus artists the world over, who have always made me feel at home.

And to you, the readers and Dreamers, for constantly inspiring me and pushing me to breathe new life into this world. This one's for you.

About the Author

Photo © 2014 Kindra Nikole Photography

Originally from small-town Iowa, A. R. Kahler attended an arts boarding school to study writing at the age of sixteen. Since then, he has traveled all over the world, earning a master's degree in creative writing from the University of Glasgow and teaching circus arts in Amsterdam and Madrid. He currently lives in Seattle, Washington. For more information, please visit www.arkahler.com.